THE C
TABLE

Tricia Dordey

TRICIA DURDEY

*Cinnamon*Press
INDEPENDENT INNOVATIVE INTERNATIONAL

Published by Cinnamon Press
Meirion House
Tanygrisiau
Blaenau Ffestiniog
Gwynedd LL41 3SU
www.cinnamonpress.com

ISBN 978-1-909077-76-8
British Library Cataloguing in Publication Data. A CIP record for
this book can be obtained from the British Library.
Designed and typeset in Garamond by Cinnamon Press. Cover
design by Adam Craig © Adam Craig.
Cinnamon Press is represented by Inpress and by the Welsh Books
Council in Wales.
Printed in Poland

Acknowledgements

I am very grateful to my fellow writers, Susan Clegg, Suzanne
McArdle and Laura Wake for their insightful appraisal of
early sections of The Green Table, and to Linda Kempton
and Noel Williams for reading the full manuscript – their
encouragement and criticism were invaluable. Thanks also to
Aidan Shingler for listening to my readings of early drafts.
Special thanks to Celia Rees, the late Jan Mark and my editor
and publisher, Jan Fortune, for believing in this work from
the start – Lumb Bank, Yorkshire, 2005.

THE GREEN TABLE

For Wolfgang Stange and Amici Dance Theatre
In honour of Kurt Jooss 1901-1979

Prologue – 1933

Germany

Herr Brandt threw his newspaper down, took off his glasses, and peered at his daughter, Hedda, so it seemed for a moment as if his exasperation was directed at her.

'What's the matter with people?' he said. 'They'd do better enthralled by a farmyard pig.'

The morning sun caught the edge of his sunken face, his grey temples. How vulnerable he looks, Hedda thought, for all his rage.

'The Little Chancellor, strutting about, puffed up with his grandiose ideas. All this adulation he inspires is not only idiotic, it's extremely dangerous.'

He spoke with such vehemence that Hedda had to smile despite everything. He never voiced Hitler's name. It was always the Little Chancellor, or the LC, spat out like a bad taste.

'He'll be our downfall. But nobody listens to an old man. If only we lived a hundred years or more, we might actually learn something. That would be progress.' He settled back in his chair and sighed. 'So what's the news with the dance company?'

'It's not good. Kurt Jooss called me into the office after rehearsal. You know he was asked to dismiss Fritz Cohen, our composer, I told you that, and he refused, of course. Well the Bigwigs haven't let it go. They've now demanded that our Jewish dancers are dropped too.'

'I'm sorry, very sorry. How did Herr Jooss seem?'

'He'd rather disband the whole company than dismiss anyone. He's very concerned.'

'I'm sure he is. There will be repercussions.'

'I know Papa. The costumes and sets are packed for the tour already, in case we have to leave in a hurry.'

For a moment mischief brightened Herr Brandt's eyes.

'So inspired of Jooss to imitate the Little Chancellor and his cronies – very clever choreography indeed. Of course the LC and Co can't have liked it greatly, prestigious prizes or not. Nobody likes being laughed at.' He chuckled. 'But it's a serious matter, very serious. I'm concerned for you.'

'I'll be all right. They won't be interested in me.'

'Don't be naïve, Hedda. Leave naivety to your sister.'

He looked at her sharply, then eased himself out of his chair. He moved across the room gripping the furniture to steady himself.

'Well we can still have coffee and a slice of Frau Muller's cherry cake to cheer the morning. You must be hungry after rehearsal.'

'I'll make coffee.'

'No. You sit there. You look worn out, my girl.'

From the kitchen she heard him opening cupboards, the rattle of the cutlery drawer, sounds she had known all her life. Am I naïve, she wondered? Papa has always seemed so courageous to me, but if he considers me naïve, I'm sure he is too – certainly where his own actions are concerned.

As Herr Brandt shuffled back with a tray of coffee and cake, he asked 'Have you told your sister all this?'

'No. She's so touchy these days. You know that. She might suggest Kurt should have obeyed orders, and I'll fly into a rage and it will end with a quarrel.'

'Tell her. Might bring the foolish girl to her senses. She's as besotted with the LC as the rest of the country. How can I have bred such a girl?' An expression of mock despair crossed his face. 'What will we all do, Hedda? I'm an old man. I didn't survive the Great War to see my country rush headlong towards another disaster.'

'You're not that old yet.'

'I feel old. My bones ache with outrage.'

She laughed.

'Well mine ache with dancing, every day and night.'

She poured the coffee, passed him a slice of cake.

'Delicious cake, tell Frau Muller. I didn't realise I was so hungry.' She had rushed for the tram straight after Kurt had told her the news. There had been no time to stop at the coffee shop by the studio.

They were quiet as they ate. Out in the garden she heard the soft calling of a wood pigeon in the apple tree.

'You must be careful too, Papa,' she said, thinking how he would be unable to keep his mouth shut.

He appeared not to have heard.

'You're like me,' he said. He leant back in his chair. His hand holding the plate relaxed, so crumbs of cake fell into his lap. 'That child is so proud and angry, your mother used to say, not like a little girl should be. I'd always take your side. It's a good anger, a righteous anger, I'd tell her. Don't ever lose your anger.' Absently, he brushed the crumbs to the floor. 'Do you know how loved you are, Hedda?' he said after a moment.

She was jolted by his words. Her eyes filled with tears.

'Why are you saying these things? I'm not going away.'

'Don't ever forget.'

She turned to look through the window at the golden-leaved poplars.

'It's a beautiful day,' she said.

Frau Muller was polishing the dining room table the next day when Hedda let herself into her father's house.

'You've just missed him,' she said. 'He was off early to see an old friend in the country. He said he'd be staying there for dinner. No need for me to cook tonight, he said.'

'Thank you. I'll just use the telephone.'

Hedda left the room to avoid further conversation with the old lady. Perhaps it would be less painful not to see her father, not to have to say goodbye face to face. She sat down at his desk and took a sheet of paper.

My dearest Papa, It's all happened sooner than any of us thought. Yesterday evening Kurt received a message by telephone from a friend who has inside information. His friend said it was

9

imperative we leave the country immediately. Kurt told us this morning after class. They've ordered his arrest. We leave tonight for Holland. I'll write as soon as I can.
Look after yourself.
Your Hedda.

She read it back. It sounded so perfunctory. She rubbed her eyes, realised she'd been holding her breath. He would understand she couldn't write what she really felt. She put the note in an envelope, and telephoned her sister.

'Can you meet me in town there's something I need to tell you? Today… as soon as you can…I'm at Papa's. He's fine. He's gone out …yes it is urgent.'

Hedda could hear a tone of excitement in Gitta's voice. Despite complaining it was short notice, and how busy she was, Gitta couldn't hide her curiosity.

They met in a café by the rehearsal rooms. Gitta was already waiting. Poised, and perfectly dressed in a cream linen dress, she turned the pages of a book. Her coat was draped over the back of the chair. She looked Hedda up and down as she approached, so Hedda was immediately aware how untidy and worn she must look, still wearing her work dress under her jersey.

'I came to say goodbye, Gitta, at least for the time being,' she said, as she positioned herself so she could see everyone who came through the door. Briefly she told Gitta the situation.

'But what are you saying? It can't be so bad that you must run off without even waiting for Pa to come back from a day in the country?' Gitta's hands clasped the coffee cup, but she didn't drink. The coffee grew cold. 'So I'm left to look after him alone? Sometimes I don't understand you.'

Hedda recognised her petulant expression – a glimmer of the child in the adult face. Gitta had no idea how shocked and frightened Hedda felt.

'No you don't understand, do you?'

'And why can't you wait until after Mari's birthday? She expects you to come for tea. You said you would. At least wait until then, if you must go.'

'I haven't forgotten. Thankfully I bought her present early.' She took Mari's small parcel from her bag. It was very pretty – a glass bead necklace for her little niece. She'd wrapped it in pink silk and tied it with a green bow. 'Tell her I had to go away, but I'll come back just as soon as I can.'

'Where are you going anyway?' Gitta interrupted.

'The Netherlands – to begin with.' She glanced round the café.

'Don't be so melodramatic, Hedda. There's nobody listening.'

'Ssh. Please speak quietly. Imagine if you were in Kurt's situation. You're given orders, and you refuse to obey. Kurt made a personal visit to the Arts Bureau to defend the integrity of the company. I'm afraid it only made things worse. They've drawn up a list of others, as well as Jews, who must be dismissed – the wording was homosexuals and other degenerates.'

'But if Jooss has refused, then they can't do anything, can they? Why would they anyway? You're not that important.' Gitta took a mirror out of her handbag, and dabbed at her face with her handkerchief. 'You can't be leaving just because you don't like being told what to do?'

'We're all in great danger,' Hedda answered. 'They're hardly likely to ignore Kurt now, especially with his high profile.'

'I don't believe it's as bad as this. You exaggerate.'

'And you're just locked in your cosy little world of husband and pretty house…'

'You're so angry. Why are you always so hard on me?'

'I'm sorry. I'm sorry. I don't mean to quarrel, especially now.' She reached to touch her sister's arm. 'But don't you see what's coming, even though awful things have happened to so many people already? Or do you just choose to ignore it?'

Gitta put away her mirror, and reached round for her coat.

'You always quarrel with me. I always think it will be nice to see you, then you criticise me for everything – the way I live, my husband. Sometimes I think you're jealous.'

'Gitta, I just can't believe that you don't feel the tension. You know how bad it's been recently for Papa's Jewish friends. There is no time for long good-byes. Kurt is in very grave danger. We all are. There's no question of him going alone.'

Gitta's cheeks flushed. She wouldn't look at Hedda.

'But you are going though Papa has been unwell, and without saying good-bye to him. You'll break his heart.'

'He'll understand. I saw him yesterday. We talked then. Am I to stay and get myself arrested? I'd be no use to anyone then. That's how serious it is. Gitta say goodbye to me. Wish me a safe journey.'

Gitta turned away.

'I must get home. I'll be late for lunch as it is.' She stood up. 'You're all running away. How cowardly.'

The last Hedda saw of her was her gloved hand on the glass door, the fall of her blue cashmere coat as she stepped out into the street; her elegant, beautiful sister. In her haste, she'd left behind the birthday parcel for her little girl.

Hedda sat at the café table, looking at Mari's gift. She had no strength to follow Gitta, her limbs felt heavy and weak. She couldn't bear Mari to think she didn't care. She'd have to run to the post office with the parcel before going home. She must write a letter to her friend, Monicke, who shared her apartment. And there was the packing. What should she pack, what does anyone take when they don't know when, or if, they'll return? I wish it hadn't been like that with Gitta, she thought, but I'm glad I didn't tell her too much. She's so influenced by Ernst and I don't like him at all. I never have. She can't be trusted to keep her mouth shut. How can she be so blind? Or does she believe herself, and her little family, immune?

There was no time to lose. She couldn't sit all day staring at the grain of the table, listing things to do. She sprang up and strode to the door, pulling on her coat as she went. Only later she realised she'd forgotten to pay for their coffees.

In her small suitcase, on top of her nightwear, underclothes, and dancewear, Hedda folded her best winter dress, a warm jersey and her notebook. She was indecisive and confused. Surely she would be home again soon? It wouldn't matter that she took so little with her.

She wished Monicke would return early from visiting her mother. Monicke would be talkative and reassuring. She'd make her a mug of hot chocolate, and sit on the bed watching her pack, and making practical suggestions.

She looked around the room, letter to Monicke on the mantelpiece, next to an envelope with rent for the landlord. Her eyes settled on a porcelain vase her mother had given her the year before she died. She loved its rounded shape, the pale blue-green glaze. She looked more closely and saw where the light fell on its smooth surface, a miniature image of the world outside; the blaze of setting sky behind dying leaves, the church spire, the brilliant blur of a tram passing. She moved slightly and there was the tiny reflected interior of her room – the long window, the table with autumn crocuses, the shelf overfilled with art books.

She picked up the vase, held it to her forehead feeling its coolness, thinking to take it wrapped in her warm jersey. But that was absurd.

The rain started as Hedda left home. By the time she reached the tram stop it was falling heavily – unexpected after such a beautiful day. She found a window seat, and watched the familiar streets fly past, trying to record the cafés, shop-fronts and gardens in her memory, in case she was away too long.

The opening music of The Green Table sang in her head, the percussive chords before the lights went up, and the frivolous tango began. She went back to the night of the competition in Paris, waiting off-stage with the rest of the company, her face tight under the mask, her white-gloved hands, the stage pistols ready. It had felt intoxicating, despite their nerves. How jubilant they'd been when they heard Kurt had won. That was only May, but in so short a time everything had changed. It seemed long ago.

She saw two of the other dancers at the station. They were buying cigarettes at the kiosk under the arch. Dietrich looked at her, nodded, without smiling. She wanted to say something, then didn't, and he passed by. They'd agreed to travel singly or in pairs, to avoid drawing attention. It was safer that way until they crossed the border. Darkness had fallen, the rain a fine mist under the streetlight. She stopped, checked her documents again, thought she'd lost her ticket, but found it in the pocket of her coat.

She sat in the corner of the carriage. It was damp, with the smell of wet wool, and burning coal. She lowered her head and tried to shut out the night, to feel herself in her bed at home, warm, drifting into sleep. The hiss of steam startled her and she opened her eyes to see the man opposite take a meat pie from his knapsack and tuck into it regardless of everyone around him. She watched in fascination. He ate like a pig. She felt sickened. He had the bulbous face of a German peasant.

Her father would be home from his day out. He'd pour himself a brandy and go into his study, as he always did. He'd find her note. Oh Papa.

She must have moaned aloud. The man with the pie stared at her with curiosity. She averted her eyes; saw her

reflection in the window of the carriage, pale and tense —
for a moment the face of a stranger.

She looked at her watch. In a few hours they would
arrive — Amsterdam, and the early September morning, a
place of safety. But she couldn't see beyond the night. She
should try to sleep. Damp rose from the floor of the train
into her boots. She felt so cold.

Amsterdam – Katje

If she nodded her head and blinked as fast as she could Katje found she could make the choir jump up and down. They looked so funny with their mouths opening and closing, jumping along with the music. Werner prodded her, and she turned round and made angry eyes at him. He brought his hand to his mouth, his giggles bubbling between his fingers.

'What?'

'Why are you nodding?'

'Because I want to.'

How serious they all were – all of them – even Werner when he practised the piano, sitting straight-backed in the cold parlour, playing the same little tune over and over, as she stepped round the edges of the carpet making her dances – Werner trotting out to his lessons with his music tucked under his arm, his face solemn with concentration.

Slow down, you talk so fast. Gabbling Katje. When they knelt and said prayers, their voices a low drone, she wanted to laugh loudly, like Aunt Minna.

Katje's mother didn't approve of Minna, who was not a real aunt but an old family friend from America. Minna spoke American English – so fashionable, so loud.

Aunt Minna took her on the tram to the Dance Club. Minna's gentleman friend picked her up and whirled her round and round until she was dizzy and the room spun. His whiskers scratched her cheeks, and he smelt of cigar smoke and sour spit. When he stopped, she could see his shiny pink gums and the gold pieces in his teeth.

'My, you're a heavy girl,' he said.

They talked on and on until their voices became serious, and their smiles disappeared. 'The Dutch will preserve their neutrality,' someone said, and then they were quiet for a moment.

Neutrality. What did it mean? Katje danced along the edge of the ballroom floor, wobbling as she walked, and falling over. 'Neu-tral-ity,' she sang. Everyone laughed, so she did it again.

'You're a little clown,' Minna said.

One night Aunt Minna took her to see a ballet. 'A treat for my girl who is always dancing.' The theatre was ivory and gold, with red velvet seats. Katje kept very still then, in the scratchy seat, in her best dress, Minna's mint-scented fur coat against her face, and the sniffs and sighs of the audience all around her. She watched the dancers – the men with their white gloves, masked faces, and tight black suits. They bowed from the hip, heads nodding, and their thin legs pranced with pointed toes. They waved their arms wildly as if they were shouting 'Listen to me. No, listen to me. You will listen!'

'You're very quiet, my little one,' Minna said to her, when it was over.

The moon shone behind the trees in the square. They waited by the stage door in the damp cold as the dancers and musicians came out chattering, arm in arm, in their long drab coats. One of the dancers, a small lady with wavy black hair, smiled at her and asked if she'd enjoyed the dancing. Minna asked her to write in the programme.

Katje played in the bedroom later that night. Her hairbrush was a pistol; her bed was the Green Table. She pranced around on the balls of her feet, jumped up and bounced on the mattress, and thudded back down to the floor again, waving her arms and shaking her fists like the Gentlemen in Black. La-la la la la, she sang. Then she drew the hairbrush from the belt of her dressing gown. Bang bang – she shot a bullet into the ceiling.

She imagined Death, wearing long black boots and the face of a skeleton, bursting through the door in a cloud of smoke, and she threw herself face down on her bed.

Amsterdam – Hedda

A small crowd had gathered in the square, waiting in the cold to greet the dancers as they left the theatre. They applauded, smiling, when they saw Kurt Jooss.

'I think they love us,' one of the dancers said. 'It's like Paris all over again.'

Chattering and laughing, they drifted past the fountains, towards the bar of the American Hotel. Hedda, trailing behind, was stopped by a tall woman in a fox-fur coat, holding the hand of a little girl. They wanted her to sign the programme. The woman spoke English. As Hedda wrote her name, the girl looked up at her with a rapt expression. She had blue eyes, a very Dutch face, Hedda thought, like a Vermeer painting. She bent to speak to her.

'Did you enjoy the dancing?' she asked, in hesitant English, hoping the child would understand.

The child nodded vigorously, and hopped from one foot to the other in her excitement.

'Where's your next show?' the woman asked.

'We go to France, and Belgium, and then to America.'

'Oh, but I'm from America. You must be sure to have a great time. They'll absolutely adore you there.'

'Thank you.' Hedda shook the hands of the American lady and the little girl, and wished them goodnight. As she neared the hotel, she glanced back. They were standing at the tram stop. The child, seeing her, jumped up and waved. Then a tram drew up and she lost sight of them. Suddenly light-hearted, she ran up the steps, into the yellow-green glassy interior of the American Hotel.

She left the bar late, tired and giddy with drink, to walk back to her lodgings. Kurt, staying in the same district, said he would go with her. She was glad, feeling the need of his company. They'd had no chance to talk recently.

'I like this city,' she said, as they turned away from the brightness of the square.

'Me too. It has a distinctive smell. Have you noticed?'

'Water and decaying leaves, or is it the sea? If I could paint I'd be happy here. Flat sky and land, and all this water, and the light that changes all the time. I'd walk with my head up, looking at the clouds between the gables.'

'You have such a way of seeing things,' he said. 'Like an artist, even if you don't paint.'

They walked slowly, looking down into the dark water lapping against the lock gates on Singelgracht.

'And they loved us, didn't they?' she said, but he had stopped to look back at the clock tower of the American Hotel, and more distant still – beyond the fountains – the glittering of chandeliers through the windows of the theatre. He seemed distracted. 'You must be worried all the time, Kurt?' She was talking too much – the performance, too much wine after days of anxiety, the release of tension. She wasn't considering him, his responsibilities.

'Let's keep walking. It's getting cold.' They crossed the canal and the tramline, and walked in the direction of the park gates. 'We can cut across the park.'

'We left Germany just in time,' he said, as they turned into the park. 'I heard the Gestapo came for me the next day.'

'Oh no – a terrible thought – if you'd delayed.' She wanted to take his arm, as an old friend, but felt awkward. She kept her hands in her pockets.

'Have you thought what you'll do, after the American tour I mean? You'll never be able to go back, I suppose.' But that seemed too final, too awful. Things had to change for the better one day, surely?

'I have friends in England, in Devon. They live on a large estate, with gardens and outbuildings. They've offered me a place I can live and teach, where the whole company can have a home. They're so incredibly kind. I haven't told anyone else, Hedda. Please don't say anything yet.'

England – so far away. She had often thought she wanted to leave Germany, until now, the reality, the thought of her father – they had always been close, and he would miss her terribly. He'd sent a telegram. *LC in ascendance. Bleak. Understand no return. Am with you always. Love.* Did he mean that he understood, or that she must understand? She missed their long discussions, and arguments, his passion. She missed the untidy warmth of his house.

'I should go home,' she said. 'Was I a coward to leave?' She hadn't intended to voice her thoughts.

He stopped abruptly.

'Not unless we're all cowards,' he said. 'I don't think there'll be any going back to Germany. Not for a long time. Not as things are.'

'I didn't mean...oh I don't know what I think.'

They walked on slowly.

'Listen Hedda, if you go back, even if they leave you alone, you'll never work as a dancer again, nor teach or choreograph. Not in Germany.' He offered her his arm.

'What other work would I do? Maybe there's something.'

'You'll always dance,' he said. 'It's in you so deeply. You'd be unhappy with anything else.'

'You're right.'

The park was quiet, the city traffic distant. The sound of their boots striking the path was rhythmic. Their breath too – a slower rhythm, enduring, relentless.

'For me dancing is essentially moral,' he said after a while. 'It would be unworkable to stay in Germany under Nazi rule, even if this hadn't happened.'

'Dancing is essentially moral,' she repeated quietly, seeing no need to ask him to explain.

They came to the other side of the park. A gust of wind shook the dry twigs of the shrubbery. Hedda shivered. The lighted windows beyond the gates looked warm and welcoming as they went through onto Van Eeghenlaan, and turned towards Jacob Obrechtstraat.

They slowed down, having almost reached Hedda's lodgings. A tram rattled past the Concert Hall, then the sound of someone walking fast, a woman's footsteps, more urgent than their own. How long will the other choreographers last in Germany – Laban, Wigman – Hedda wondered? How long before they too displease the Little Chancellor?

'You're a very great choreographer,' she said. 'I'm sure you know that. People will talk about you in years to come. They'll write books about your work. I've loved working with you, every hour of it.'

'Thank you. You sound as if you think it's over,' he added after a moment.

'I don't know,' she replied. 'Nothing seems clear. My future – I don't know…'

'We've become exiles, Hedda. Overnight.'

They embraced and parted at the corner of her street. She watched him walk away, his easy grace – until his figure blurred into the darkness. I admire him so much, she thought. He's made me the dancer I am. Life in another dance company, without him, was unimaginable.

She unlocked the door. A lamp had been left on in the hall, but everyone must be asleep, there was no sound. She crept up to her room.

Before making her way along the landing to the bathroom, she undressed, switched off the bedroom light, and looked out from her balcony at the quiet tree-lined street, so far from home. She longed for the warmth of another body to lie beside her.

Part One
1939 Amsterdam

The Dunes

'Werner, come out! It's a wonderful night.' Katje whispered. 'Are you awake?' She opened her brother's bedroom door.

Werner sat cross-legged on the bed in his nightshirt, bent over his book in the lamplight.

'There'll never be another night like this.'

'I'm reading.'

'You've all the time in the world to read.' She leapt into the room and onto his bed. 'I just can't sleep. I've been trying for such a long time. What are you reading?' She took the book from him. 'Poetry.' She threw it down, stood on the bed and bounced from foot to foot as she leaned out of the open window. 'The moon has made a sparkling path across the sea and the pine trees are majestic. There – that's poetry for you.'

'What are you doing?'

'What do you think? Pa will have locked the door and I don't want him hearing me getting out that way.' She climbed onto the sill.

She heard Werner laughing as she jumped from the window and landed in the bed of sea grass and hollyhocks. She staggered to her feet and brushed the sand from her knees, then set off at a canter out through the wicket gate and across the beach. Behind her the wooden houses squatted amongst the trees in the lee of the wind. The lights were out. Nobody but Werner knew she wasn't asleep in her room.

Under her feet she felt the hard ribs of sand where the tide had receded, and there, far away, the line of darkness where sky met sea. Gazing up, she saw thousands of stars, and in a moment she knew everything – terror and happiness and awe, the very meaning of life itself – though she had no words to say. She started to dance, a gawky, twirling, staggering step, forward and back, splashing, knees high, into the waves and back, over and over.

She didn't see Werner until she was dizzy with glee, her pyjamas splattered with salt water. He was standing wrapped in the blanket from his bed, watching her. She ran to greet him.

'Did you jump from the window too?'

'I went very quietly through the door.'

'So did you see my dance? My wondrous dance. You know, I think anything could happen tonight, as if the whole world is about to change. Even my skin's tingling with anticipation.'

'You looked funny. I'm glad nobody else saw you. Don't hang onto me. You're wet.'

He pushed her away but she kept on jabbing him and laughing until the blanket unravelled and slipped off his shoulders.

'It's a warm night. You're like a skinny old man.' She shook it out and wrapped it around the two of them.

They walked back up the beach and stopped short of the house, turning back to the shelter of the dunes, listening to the distant boom of the sea.

'I love that sound. It's the sound of summer. I hope life does change, but whenever I've thought so before, everything ends up going on in the same dreary old way. Do you know what I mean?'

Werner shrugged.

'Remember Aunt Minna?'

'Oh yes. Mother never approved.'

'I wonder why they were ever friends in the first place. What happened to her?'

'She went back to America I suppose. They fell out anyway before that. Don't you remember Mother and Father talking about her?'

'I liked her. Everything was fun when she was around. She took me to the Stadsschouwberg once to see the strangest ballet. There was Death, wearing a skeleton costume, and funny men in suits.'

26

'It was after that I think that they stopped seeing her. They got angry about something. I can't really remember.'

Werner disentangled himself from the blanket and trod the slithery sand to the top of the dune, and Katje followed grumbling about their parents, as she so often did, their father's strictness and their mother's old-fashioned ways. Sometimes Werner would join in, but tonight he seemed distracted. After a while they lay down in a hollow in the sand dunes. Covered in the blanket, staring up at the sky, they fell silent.

Katje twisted round to look at her brother.

'What are you thinking?' she asked at last.

'About music.'

'You're always thinking about music. What in particular?'

But he was lost to her. She watched his eyelashes flickering, the deep shadows over his fine-boned face. It was a strange face, so different from her own – delicate and intense. He wasn't aware of her scrutiny. She could tickle his face with the long sea grass and he wouldn't do more than brush his hand over his cheek as if a fly crawled over him. He's mysterious to me even though he's been beside me all my life. I suppose I would die for my brother.

She flung herself onto her back and thought about what it would feel like to die for love. But it would be impossible to know, of course. If you were dead you'd stop feeling.

Herr Weiss

One spring morning, Hedda Brandt arrived at her dancing school on the Amstel at the same time as a man who was walking from the opposite direction. They converged at the stone steps leading to the front door. He wished her good morning, and stepped back to let her go ahead of him.

'You must be Fraulein Brandt,' he said. 'Erik Weiss, piano teacher. I rent a room in the basement. I moved in last week.'

'You're German too,' Hedda said. 'It's always nice to meet someone from home.'

He was a tall, striking-looking man in his early-thirties, heavy featured, and slightly balding, with an upright bearing. He wore cologne with a sharp clean fragrance.

'I'll be teaching on Monday and Wednesday. Pleased to meet you.'

His hand was dry and cool.

The following Monday evening, weary before cycling home, Hedda paused in the hall. Whoever was playing sounded very accomplished, she thought. Herr Weiss must be an excellent teacher.

'I'm looking for an accompanist for my Friday and Saturday classes,' she said, next time they met. 'My last one left a couple of months ago and my dancers are getting rather bored of me banging a drum. I thought you might know of someone suitable, perhaps one of your students.'

He replied by letter at the end of the week. He would be happy to be considered for the post himself.

For the first month Hedda scarcely exchanged a word with Erik Weiss. He always arrived and left promptly. He was remote with the children, and had an air of arrogance, but she couldn't fault his playing. He was by far the best accompanist she'd ever employed.

'Could you stay on for another hour next Friday?' she asked. 'I need to work through a piece for a recital. I will pay you, of course.'

'Willingly,' he said, with a perfunctory smile.

'A Chopin Mazurka – here's the score if you want to look through it.'

'That won't be necessary,' he replied.

After classes the following week, she made him coffee to drink whilst she stretched at the barre.

'Now I need to mark the dance for space and timing,' she said. 'Could we just try with you playing up to tempo?'

He played, and she walked through the piece.

'Now dance,' he said, when she'd finished. 'That was just playing at it.'

'I was only marking,' she said, laughing, though surprised by his impertinence. 'I'll gladly dance.'

She expected him to leave as soon as she'd finished rehearsal, but he asked if she'd mind if he stayed longer, no fee required. 'Let's try to improvise together,' he said.

'I'd love that,' she answered.

He started to play. She stood listening, then began to walk round the studio, letting her hands follow the shifting moods and rhythms of his music, until her whole body was caught up in it and swept along. At times he let the music die away, and watched her as she moved in the brief silence, then he'd start to play again, just as she slowed to stillness. After a while it became unclear who was leading, and she felt heady and intoxicated, pushing her body harder than she had in months, flinging herself into falls, and extensions, and defying gravity as she leapt.

He stopped abruptly. Exhausted and surprised by the sudden conclusion to his playing, she slumped against the barre to get her breath.

'It's been a long time since I've worked like that with someone,' she said. 'It feels so good.'

He closed the lid of the piano and crossed the studio to stand beside her. His close proximity discomfited her. She turned to look out over the river in the twilight – the lights from the houseboats glowing through the great elm trees.

'Come for a drink with me,' he said.

'Oh but I'm not dressed properly,' she said, flustered.

'I'll wait while you change.'

She saw no reason to refuse. It would be interesting to get to know him.

Hedda left her bicycle at the studio – Herr Weiss never cycled anywhere. He thought cycling was vulgar, he told her. They walked, with little conversation, to Café de Zwart on the Spui. It was a warm evening and people sat out under the awning.

'I come here after my rehearsals in the English church – the Begijnhof. You must know it?'

'Certainly. I think I've walked, or cycled, every street of this city.'

He ordered a bottle of Bordeaux.

'I never drink beer. Are you happy with wine?'

She wondered if his brusqueness betrayed insecurity. Or was it a supreme sense of superiority?

They sat at a round table in the corner where the window looked out onto the square. The candlelight gave warmth to his features. He drank his first glass quickly, and poured another. She was more cautious, aware how the first sips of wine went to her head. She waited to see if he would make conversation. Pre-occupied, he tapped a rhythm on the edge of the table.

'It's good to meet a fellow German, to speak my own language again,' she said, with some sense of irony, since he'd scarcely spoken. 'Do you miss Germany?'

'Not remotely. I've been back from time to time, concerts and such like, but I've lived here all my adult life. I arrived when I was fifteen.'

'Ah, Germany was very different then, when we were young.'

His eye sockets were deep and dark ringed. He took another drink, and for the first time since they'd sat down gave her his attention.

'You are going to ask why I'm here, fellow Germans always do. I'll tell you as briefly as I can.'

How patronising he is, and clumsy in his manner to the point of rudeness, she thought. Instead of feeling annoyed, she was amused by her desire to put him at his ease.

He spoke in a precise, affected way. 'I was brought up in Cologne. I was a choirboy, then a soloist. I took piano and organ lessons from the organist. Music was my life. Music will always be my life.' As he spoke he pressed his fingertips together, slowly flexing and extending his hands.

'Do you still sing?'

'Never since my voice broke. I had the most perfect voice, angelic, as only boys' voices can be. I was much praised. It changed – overnight, it seemed. Oddly I hadn't anticipated how brutal that would be.'

'But surely young men can develop into fine singers if they're taught properly?'

He closed his eyes briefly, as if irritated or pained by her comment, before continuing to narrate the events of his life.

'I adored my mother. She died of a miscarriage when I was fourteen. I found her lying in her own blood. I still dream of it. My father was remote. He drank too much. We didn't like each other.' His hands trembled. He put them down flat on the table. 'I came to The Hague to live with my aunt. I've never seen my father since.' He drained his glass.

Hedda didn't know how to respond – shocked at the thought of his mother, sympathetic words seemed inappropriate. He got up abruptly.

'Excuse me a moment.'

31

He spoke briefly to the barman, and went out. How odd he is, Hedda thought, rattling off his life story like that. What does he want? Looking out of the window, she saw him in the square pacing around, hands behind his back.

When he returned his manner was quite changed.

'I needed a breath of air. You made me talk of the past, Miss Brandt. You listen too well. Now you must tell me why you are living away from Germany when you miss it so much.' He spoke with a touch of sarcasm.

'I didn't say I missed Germany.'

'Not in so many words, but I can see you do.'

She looked at him in surprise. She supposed there was no need to be guarded with a fellow German. She told him briefly why she had left Germany.

'So I went to England with Jooss and the company. But I was unhappy there – for various reasons it didn't work out. I returned to the Netherlands. I feel closer to home here. Once I'd established my work in Amsterdam, I planned to go back to see my father. I was prepared to take the risk. Then he was arrested.'

She stopped. He was inspecting his fingernails, pushing back the cuticle of his forefinger.

'A political prisoner?' he asked, bringing his attention back to her.

'Yes. He died in prison.'

'Then we both have our sorrows, Miss Brandt. I'm sorry.'

'Don't call me Miss Brandt. Not in that way,' she said, irritated by his affectation.

'Hedda Brandt,' he said more gently. 'If I may?' He took her hand and kissed it with theatrical exaggeration. 'Why the Norwegian name?'

'My father's choice. He said it was prettier than Hedwig. He loved Scandinavia too.'

'Hedda – the warrior. We should have another bottle of wine.'

'Oh no. I must go home. I'm very hungry.'

'Then you must eat. I'll order something for you.' His smile made him boyish and attractive. 'Please stay. I'm enjoying this so much.'

Enjoying – he hadn't appeared to enjoy anything so far.

'I'll stay just a while longer, but I won't eat now. I must get home soon.'

'I relish watching you teach,' he said. 'You are rather marvellous, you know – with those mothers too. How ghastly they are, some of them. Who is this?'

Drink had transformed him. His face had changed, as if a layer of hardness had peeled away leaving him less defined, his features more mobile. Cheeks flushed, he mimed with such accuracy one of the mothers ushering her shy daughter into the studio, that Hedda had to laugh.

'She's the Nanny Goat. She bleats.'

'I do see what you mean.'

'Oh I have names for them all – Suet Pudding, Carte Blanche, the Bad Fairy…'

'Please stop. I can see it all too clearly. I won't be able to face them tomorrow.'

He didn't stop. He made her laugh with his finely observed caricatures, until her face ached.

'Oh I see you in an entirely new light now,' she said. 'And for me?' she asked. 'Do you have a name for me?'

'Of course I do,' he said, looking her full in the eyes. 'But don't worry, you would be flattered.'

But he would not tell her.

It was a clear starlit night, and much later than Hedda had intended, when they left the bar. He said he would walk her home, but reluctant to let him know where she lived, she let him walk with her only as far as Westerplein. She felt light-headed from laughter, and drink on an empty stomach. He'd forgotten all about ordering a meal, and she hadn't reminded him. It would have been awkward eating alone, as he appeared to have no interest in food. Two Germans, spending an evening together and we said nothing about Hitler and the state of Germany, or discussed how it must be back home. It struck her as odd now she thought about it. Instead, once the first awkwardness was over, he'd been very entertaining. She glanced at him as he walked beside her. He was remote again. What a strange man he is. Do I like him? It was delightful working with him – how I've missed dancing with a good accompanist – that's the attraction, and the fact he's German. It was good to speak German again.

'I suppose I should kiss you goodnight,' he said, when they reached the square.

'Please don't feel obliged,' she responded. She laughed, taken by surprise.

He took her hand and kissed it lightly. Then he drew away, looking at her as if he might ask a question. 'Hedda Brandt?' His tone was gentle and amused.

He kissed her again, on the mouth, and she felt a flare of desire, so unexpected that she pulled back. It must have seemed like a rejection. He walked away without turning back to wave.

Brother and Sister

'I'm sick of hearing that same piece of music. What is it?' Katje said, peering round the door into the dining room where Werner practised the piano.

Werner shrugged. He didn't want to stop and tell her. He practised his scales and arpeggios every morning before school, and in the evenings he worked for two hours on his pieces. At the weekend he could work far longer. He never let anything get in the way of his practice.

'You're just trying far too hard. Can't Herr Weiss just let you do it badly once in a while? Anyway I'm fed up with hearing it. So fed up I could scream and yell.'

'You don't understand,' he said. 'If I don't work I won't get any better.' His eyes stung with tiredness.

As a child he'd loved listening to his mother playing the piano, and she'd taught him his first tunes. Later the piano was associated with the sweetness of his first teacher, her kindness and pleasure in his ability. Now he was older, he knew he was fortunate to be taken on by Herr Weiss, who never wasted time with the mediocre. It was very important not to let him down. Music was Werner's whole world, as it was for Herr Weiss too. They were both consumed by the struggle for perfection.

'I do. I understand very well, and it's not a matter of life or death,' Katje said, sitting down beside him, pushing him to the end of the piano stool, and running her hands up and down the c major scale. 'Everything is all right,' she sang, thumping out chords to accompany her cheerful voice. 'Werner is the best pianist in the whole of Amsterdam. So there, Herr Weiss.'

'Please go away,' he said, smiling despite himself. It was always hard to be anything but heartened by her.

Katje was so pre-occupied the day Hitler invaded Poland, that despite all the talk on the radio, she scarcely gave it a second thought. After all there was nothing to worry about – hadn't Queen Wilhelmina declared the Netherlands' neutrality only weeks ago?

Itching with restlessness after a day at school, she waved goodbye to her friends, and cycled out towards the docks. I want to go far away, she thought, as the autumn wind rushed against her cheeks. The stink of fish and seawater held a glamour that spoke of faraway lands – but she had only a few cents in her purse, and she was pragmatic enough to know that freedom required greater means.

She turned back towards the city, past the houseboats, into the narrow streets of the old Jewish quarter, then across the swing bridge to the south bank of the Amstel where Werner came for piano lessons. She stopped under the trees. Still astride her bicycle, she rested against the handlebars, and listened to the cries of the gulls.

She was aware of the rhythmic beat of a drum and a woman shouting. The sound was coming from the top floor of the building behind her, where Herr Weiss taught Werner. The window was open, and she saw the neat heads of girls bobbing in and out of sight.

'Stop, start again, that is all wrong. Now, like this, lead from the head, let the body follow…good, now again. Turn turn step leap – step step fall…' It was a German accent.

She left her bicycle against the tree and ran up the stone steps to read, *Hedda Brandt Dance Studio*, on the brass plaque. She brushed her fingertips over the name. Then she pushed the door. It opened and she walked into a narrow marbled hall and stood gazing around for a moment. Now she had left the street it seemed obvious she must climb the stairs that spiralled to the third floor and that voice.

She entered an anteroom strewn with clothes, coats and outdoor shoes. It smelt of socks. The door to another room was ajar, and through the gap she saw girls running across the floor, their arms reaching forward and up as they

36

ran. She pushed the door wider. A dark-haired, finely built woman with a severe face came towards her.

'What is it you want? I'm teaching now.'

'Is it dancing class?'

'Of course it is.'

'I want you to teach me to dance.'

As soon as she'd spoken Katje knew beyond any doubt that she had to join the class.

'What's your name?'

'Katarina de Jong.'

'Then, Katarina, if you are serious you may come to speak with me on Saturday, say eleven o clock. I will want to see you dance, so you must be prepared to join in my class. Now you must go.'

The door was closed.

Now my life has changed, forever, Katje said to herself, as she ran down the stairs and out into the street.

Werner never gave much thought to the other activities that went on in Herr Weiss' new premises, although he sometimes saw the girls arriving for class, carrying cases, their hair tied up. Herr Weiss taught from a dark room at the back of the building. It was quiet, and the lace blind obscured the view of the opposite windows.

Werner sat in nervous anticipation at Herr Weiss' piano. Sometimes his hands were possessed of a fine intelligence and seemed to play by themselves. Today he stumbled as soon as he started.

'I'm sorry.'

'Start again.'

His fingers felt thick and inarticulate.

'I have practised,' he said.

Weiss sighed.

'It doesn't show. This is an elementary mistake.'

Tears sprung to Werner's eyes. He bit his lip.

'Try once more.' Weiss got up and paced. 'Go on.'

It was said in the tone of a command. Werner began, slipped up again and stopped, took a deep breath and closed his eyes. Failure roared like a river in his ears. It was hopeless. Herr Weiss put his hand on his shoulder.

'Don't cry about it.'

'Let me try once more.'

He'd played so badly there was nothing to lose. The tension snapped. As soon as he started he knew he would do it this time.

'At last. That's better,' Weiss said. 'You must strive to be flawless in your technique. There are many young people out there who are good. You must be better than all of them. Strive for perfection. That is all I'm interested in, and so you must be too.' His fingers brushed the back of Werner's neck.

On his way home, Werner walked with Herr Weiss as far as the Spui. Weiss was going to the church in the Begijnhof to practise the organ. They said good evening, and Werner watched him walk away. After a moment he followed him through the short vaulted passageway from the street, down the steps into the peaceful square, just in time to see the door of the little church close. He wished he felt confident enough to go in and listen. It would be a whole long week before they met again.

He stood under the window by the maple tree, facing the statue of Christ. Looking through the tracery of the window he could see the silvery gleam of the organ pipes and the line of gabled roofs reflected in the glass.

The first notes of the organ sounded. How majestic the sound was. It reverberated through the wall, into his body, and in his mind he saw immense cathedrals with cavernous interiors, and imagined the beating wings of angels in the darkness.

Werner thought about Herr Weiss all the time. He thought of him in the day, during school, and when he

38

woke in the darkness of night. He told himself it was because Weiss was his only way into a world of music and without music his life was worth nothing. The skin on his neck still felt the touch of Weiss' fingers. Was it possible that Weiss cared about him?

As he crossed the last bridge before reaching Leliegracht and home, he heard Katje's footsteps trotting behind him.

'Oh Lord. We're both going to be late for dinner,' she said as she reached him. 'We'll be in terrible trouble.' They heard the clock strike the quarter before six. 'The thing is I've had an adventure, oh yes and I think I saw your Herr Weiss.'

'How? Where?'

'You don't need to look so shocked. It must have been just before your lesson. He plays the piano for a dancing teacher. She has a school on the third floor in the place where he teaches. Anyway, I want to have lessons with her. I'm going to ask Pa if I can. I left my bicycle near home, and I've been walking around thinking ever since. I didn't want to go home, but I quite forgot the time. And you also forgot!' She took his arm. 'Never mind. I'll distract them talking about my dancing lessons, and they'll be so amazed at the idea of me dancing they'll forget all about our lateness.'

Werner knew their father would assume a disapproving silence and that without Katje he would be treated more severely. Katje always won him round, and defended Werner from his disapproval when she could. These days he was certain he didn't belong with his parents, that he was in an intolerable place where he couldn't possibly grow into the person he needed to be. The furnishings in the hot rooms of the family house stifled him; the clean-shaven smell of his father was insufferable.

Werner entered the dining room first and took his place at the table. Katje followed. Both parents sat waiting.

'I'm sorry to be late,' he said, looking down at the white cloth.

'Oh we're both so sorry,' Katje said. 'It was my fault really. I bumped into Werner after his lesson and started to tell him all about my day, and before we knew it time had flown away.'

'Be quiet and sit down,' their father said. 'We will pray.'

Katje clasped her hands and bowed her head. Werner, his eyes half open, saw her turn to him and grin.

'Lord, we give you thanks for our food, and for your good grace and eternal love. Amen,' they chanted.

'Werner, it's up to you to be punctual,' their father said as he unfolded his table napkin and spread it over his knees.

'I'm sorry. Herr Weiss ran over with his lesson.'

'You have a watch.'

'Yes. I'm sorry.'

Werner pressed his palms into his thighs. Katje poked his shins with her foot.

'I want to dance,' she announced. 'I want to have dancing lessons. Would that be all right?'

He saw the startled look on their mother's face.

'Perhaps dancing is not so suitable for you Katarina, now you're no longer a little girl. What do you say, Papa?' She looked across the table to where their father crumbled his bread between his fingers, and then she ladled the pea soup from the tureen into their bowls. 'Perhaps you would like to study music instead?'

'No. I want to dance. I need a proper teacher, someone who knows what she's doing. I found her too. She's a German lady, her name's Hedda Brandt. May I start classes with her? Please.'

'Perhaps piano lessons would be a more sensible idea?' their mother said again. 'Like Werner.'

'But I am not like Werner. I can't imagine practising the piano all day and night.'

She and Werner caught each other's eye.

'I want to dance more than I've ever wanted anything.'

'For goodness sake stop being so dramatic.'

Katje put down her soupspoon and stared at the white cloth where a drop of soup had stained it green.

'Eat up your meal.'

'I can't. I don't feel like it. I won't eat again until you listen to me.' She pushed back her chair and sat upright, with her lips pursed.

'Katarina do as you're told and get on with your meal,' her father said.

She blinked. Her eyes had filled with tears. She picked up her spoon and dangled it limply in her hand, then swung it backwards and forwards until it fell onto the table. Her mother sighed. Werner felt sorry for Katje. After all they were angry because of him. An uncomfortable silence followed.

Their father finished his soup and wiped his mouth with his napkin.

'Who is this Hedda Brandt?' he asked.

'She's a dancer. She has a school on the Amstel, near Rembrandtsplein. It's the same building where Werner goes for lessons. I'm going to see her on Saturday morning.'

'So you have already taken it into your own hands?'

'No no, it's not like that. She told me to come back. I disturbed her lesson you see, so she couldn't talk then. I'm sure I can save my pocket money.'

'That won't be necessary,' her father said. Then he turned to his wife. 'Perhaps you should interview the woman and discuss dancing lessons with her before we make a decision. It can't really do any harm.'

Werner saw Katje breathe out slowly.

'Thank you, Papa,' she said.

The meat followed and they ate in silence. The sound of their chewing and swallowing made Werner want to leap up from the table and run outside and shout.

41

Notebook

Hedda's blue notebook, which served as a journal as well as sketchbook (unlined paper, blank card cover on which she wrote the season and year), was small enough to carry in her handbag. She also carried two soft-lead pencils, with sharpened points – ideal for drawing as well as writing. Choreographic notes were later transferred to larger workbooks kept in her office in the studio.

She was returning home on the train with Erik Weiss, from a performance in Leiden. Opposite her Erik sat with his eyes closed, his hands folded over his music case. She opened her journal to read the last entry, only a week ago.

August 19th 1939 first performance with Erik Weiss in Utrecht, our new work, Shape Shift, very well received.

Underneath was a line drawing of Erik at the piano. She had captured exactly the imperious poise of his head.

Also danced Mazurka, Partisan Girl, Morning Song, with Erik accompanying. He's far the best accompanist I've ever had. He was loquacious on journey home. Talked of making a full-length ballet with me. He has grand plans. He's taken to bringing bottles of wine into my office, storing them in the cupboard, refreshment after the long day, he says. As he's better company after a drink, I don't mind. There's a great future for our work together, he keeps telling me. I hope he's right.

This evening she doubted it. She looked at his large head, resting against the back of the seat; his flushed face, mouth tight with annoyance. In a moment, with one angry exchange, his mood had changed from boyish exuberance to coldness. She'd berated him for playing the Chopin at a much quicker tempo than they'd ever rehearsed, forcing her to push herself to the limit, blurring the steps, stopping short her turns and balances.

'But it worked so much better at that tempo,' he'd said, smiling. 'You were splendid. Fiery.'

'That's not the point. You took liberties that weren't yours to take.'

'The audience loved it, what are you complaining about?'

'It's a matter of respect and trust. What do you think rehearsals are for? Some kind of pointless exercise you can ignore at a whim?'

'Are you questioning my professionalism?'

'In this instance, I am, yes.'

He'd turned to look into the darkness through the train window, wouldn't discuss it further. His sulkiness was exasperating.

She wrote the date on the top of a clean page.

Train Leiden to Amsterdam. Wish this journey over. Exhausted. Current news: Concern re Germany, potential invasion – Europe? Great Britain naïve – Chamberlain is a gentleman and doesn't seem to have the measure of AH, who is no gentleman. Netherlands, even more naïve, maintains a stance of neutrality. Tried to discuss with Erik. He's not naïve, just impossible.

She had no heart to write about the performance. Her anger died away to weary dispiritedness. She let her hands fall onto the open page and glanced round the compartment. It was a late train and there were few passengers other than an old man reading a newspaper, two seats away, and a young couple, arms round each other in the corner. She picked up her pencil again and drew a little sketch of the woman's foot and ankle glimpsed under the seat, then moved to Erik's hands, his loosely clasped fingers, the buttons of his cuffs, and the edge of his music case, resting on his knees.

Maybe he'd wanted the best for her? Had she been too hard on him? Her loneliness was acute and painful.

Glancing up, she saw he was watching her. She met his eyes. He didn't look away as she'd anticipated, but instead held her gaze so long it was unsettling. Had she misunderstood? Was there intimacy, even love in his expression?

'Forgive me,' he said.

She nodded. She was shaking. It must be exhaustion and hunger. She looked down at her notebook. In confusion she wrote.

Erik is right – the Mazurka works better with a faster tempo. Something new was created by the fact I was so unprepared, the dance was no longer predictable. The audience saw that. I've rarely received such enthusiastic applause before.

Does Erik just want the best for us both, and our work? Or is he manipulating me? I would so like to be able to trust him, wholeheartedly.

The Interview

Hedda sat in the window of her office with her coffee. Erik had left abruptly, for a breath of fresh air, he said, after Hedda had made a comment about him pouring a glass of wine so early in the day. It was tiresome the way he was so easily offended. She heard the church clock strike eleven, and there was Katarina de Jong running towards the studio, her unbuttoned coat flying out around her. She careered into Erik. He caught hold of her shoulders, steadied her, and they exchanged a word, then Erik walked on briskly.

She'd forgotten she'd told the child to come back, and now she heard her footsteps clattering up the stairs.

'So you came back, Katarina,' Hedda said, opening the door. 'And so eager you ran all the way up the stairs.'

'I was worried I'd be late, and then I crashed into Herr Weiss. He's my brother's piano teacher. So embarrassing.'

'And my accompanist,' Hedda said. 'Come and sit in my office. Would you like a glass of water?'

'Thank you, but I'm all right.'

Katje sat tall, on the edge of the chair, her hands clutching her school satchel, Erik's unfinished glass of wine beside her. Hedda wished she'd had the presence of mind to remove it before letting the girl in. Katarina must be about thirteen, strong-boned, open-faced with a big smile, porcelain-smooth skin, and fine blonde hair in a ponytail.

'So you want to dance?'

'With all my heart.'

'Have you ever had any ballet lessons, or any kind of dancing?'

'No. Except my Aunt Minna used to dance with me, when I was very little. I suppose that's too long ago to count.'

'How do you know you want to dance, Katarina?'

'It's a strong feeling,' the girl answered, touching her heart. 'It was only this summer when we were on holiday, one night on the beach, and I danced. It felt brilliant, but I still didn't know what I really wanted. I was like a chicken waiting to lay an egg. Then on my way home from school that day, when was it? Only last Wednesday. I heard the drum, then the piano music and your voice, and I just knew.'

'Just like that?'

'Yes. The egg hatched. I knew straight away that you were the person.'

Hedda laughed.

'And is that all?'

'Yes. I've told you everything.'

'Are your parents happy about it?'

Her face clouded.

'I don't know. They're not sure. My mother wants to interview you.'

'Ah, I see.'

Katarina flushed.

'Oh please, don't send me away,' she burst out. 'I'll make sure they let me. I'm determined.'

'People don't normally walk in from the street in the middle of my class and demand that I teach them,' Hedda teased. Seeing Katje's distraught expression, she continued more kindly. 'Of course I won't send you away. You can try the next class, and then we'll decide what to do. Run along and get changed, if you've got anything to change into.'

'Oh I have, in my bag. Not proper things, but better than what I'm wearing now. Thank you so much, Miss Brandt.' She wrung her hands together like an opera singer. 'I'll make sure you never regret it.'

She was on her way out when she stopped in front of the photograph on the wall by the door.

'Oh – I once saw those men with the white gloves in a ballet. It was when I was little, with Aunt Minna.' She turned her excited eyes to Hedda.

'It's called The Green Table, by a choreographer called Kurt Jooss. I danced in his company.'

'I must have seen you dance then.'

'It was 1933 when we performed in Amsterdam. We'd just escaped from Germany.'

'Escaped?'

'When Hitler came to power – but that's another story.'

Katje stared at the photograph, lips parted, mesmerised.

'1933, I was eight then. Miss Brandt, what part did you dance in The Green Table?'

'We all danced the Gentlemen in Black, but I had my own part too.

'What was it?'

'The Partisan Girl.'

'Then I've found you at last.'

Hedda laughed.

'Well I suppose you have. Now off you go and get changed.'

Katje had brought Werner's shirt to wear over her thick tights. She was aware of her bigness and eccentric dress as she stood in the corner of the studio. Eight girls in neat blue tunics lay on the floor stretching their legs. Herr Weiss, Werner's piano teacher, brushed past her, crossed the studio and sat at the piano.

'This is Katarina de Jong,' said Hedda Brandt. 'She's joining you for today. Elise can you make room for her beside you. Katarina, you can follow Elise, she knows what she's doing.'

A girl with a pale thin face and dark curly hair smiled, and shuffled away from the wall so there was room beside her.

'Maria, sit up… stronger, lift out of your hips. Jani, take the tension from your shoulders.' Hedda Brandt sat cross-legged on the floor, and they began.

It was not like dancing around the bedroom, or splashing in the sea, or ice-skating, or any of those things Katje did so naturally and vigorously. She rolled too late, turned the wrong way, but she would not stop or give up. She found it easier to imagine she was a bird with broken wings, or a fish left flapping on the beach by the low tide.

'I'm so sorry.' She bumped into Elise.

'It's all right.' Elise giggled.

'Now we will stand,' Hedda said. 'Jani, could you fetch the chair for Elise?'

She saw then that Elise had something wrong with her left leg. It was weak and sometimes dragged, and there were crutches placed beside the piano. She pulled herself onto the chair and danced with her arms and her whole body, then stood up and took a few steps, balancing on her strong leg. Anything then seemed possible, and Katje launched herself across the room with renewed energy.

'Elise, that is lovely, that is what I want to see,' Hedda said. 'Katarina will you concentrate or leave the studio. Turn, not like that, slower, fix your eyes on one place. Now bring your focus back to that space. You are wrong, all wrong! Try it again until you get it right.'

'I am trying,' Katje said. 'So hard that I'm shaking with the effort.' She pointed to her legs. 'Look.'

She saw Miss Brandt smile as she turned away.

When the class was dismissed she hovered for a moment, but Miss Brandt was too busy speaking to Herr Weiss to notice her. So that was it. She had missed her opportunity by being so clumsy. She thought she might cry, but she mustn't give up. She would ask to be seen again in a few weeks. Until then she would practise everything she could remember.

In the changing-room Elise was pulling her tunic over her head and reaching for her street clothes. Her wooden crutches lay against the chair beside her. Katje pretended not to notice them. She had been taught not to look at such things.

'Don't worry, Miss Brandt is very kind even though she seems stern,' Elise said. 'She just cares so much. It's the spirit of dance she wants, the right energy, not only accurate steps.' She smiled at Katje. 'You had lots of spirit.'

The studio door opened and Miss Brandt called her into the office.

'Good luck,' Elise whispered.

'Sit down,' Hedda said, and closed the door.

Katje sat on the chair by the window. It seemed too intimidating to sit behind the desk. A red scarf was draped over the back of the chair. The room smelt of coffee and decayed flowers. There was an open tin of biscuits and half a bottle of wine on the shelf beside her. She looked directly at Miss Brandt and smiled.

'So how do you feel after your first class?'

'I'm happy and sad.'

'At the same time?' Hedda, one elbow on the desk, rested her chin in her palm.

'I'm happy from dancing and sad because I was terrible. I want so much to join your school you see.'

'Ah that is a good place to be, a good place to learn from. There's no reason to be sad. Have I turned you away?'

Baffled, Katje looked into her amused eyes.

'You did well enough Katarina. Of course it's hard. It's always hard. You will find an indication of my fees in the letter I give you. Your mother can arrange a meeting with me if she wishes. Next Saturday afternoon would be a convenient time, when classes and rehearsals have finished.' She took an envelope from a drawer in her desk. 'If your parents are in agreement, you can stay in this class, although

49

it will be difficult at first. The other classes are for children and you'll be out of place, so I'm making an exception. I ask you in return to work very hard. That is the only way. I don't care if you never dance another step after you have left my studio, but while you are here I demand everything. Otherwise you go. My school is busy and I don't need more students. Do you understand?'

Katje nodded.

'With all my heart, I understand. I'll always work as hard as I can.'

The brilliant autumn sunshine fell between the trumpets of white lilies on Miss Brandt's desk. Katje knew her mother didn't like lilies. She always said they were too heady and overpowering. Her mother sat upright in her dark, buttoned up coat and hat, her hands folded on her lap. She had put her gloves on the desk beside her. Miss Brandt also sat with her straight dancer's back. She was wearing a blue shawl embroidered with pink roses, over her teaching tunic. She made elegant arm gestures as she talked about her ballet training, and dancing in Kurt Jooss' company in Essen. Katje knew her mother was not impressed by a dancer's life. She was probably wondering why Hedda Brandt was unmarried, and why she'd settled in Holland.

'We have never been keen for our daughter to dance,' Mrs de Jong said. 'It seems altogether too showy. Inappropriate for a big girl.'

Katje squirmed with embarrassment, but Miss Brandt paused, looking down at her slim hands and stretching them on the desk. Then she looked directly at Mrs de Jong and spoke in a quiet authoritative voice.

'Katarina is rather tall. Dancing will be good for her deportment. There's a tendency for taller girls to become stooped. It's a shame.' She smiled. 'But I understand entirely that dancing is not for everyone, that it's perhaps against your principles, and I would not presume to argue otherwise. I'm sure you will agree though, that young people can learn so much about discipline through a dancer's training. It can prepare them well for adult life.' She stood up. 'Now I'm afraid you must excuse me, I have a rehearsal in half an hour. I hope, Mrs de Jong, that you will not regret your decision, whatever it is.'

She ushered them to the door.

They walked away from the studio in silence, and were about to turn the corner, when Mrs de Jong remembered she had left her gloves on the desk. Katje agreed to run back for them.

She galloped up the stairs. Miss Brandt was still sitting at her desk. She looked up.

'Ah yes, your mother's gloves.' She pushed them towards Katje and resumed writing.

Katje took the gloves but didn't leave. Miss Brandt glanced up, sighed, and put down her pencil.

'I see you're a very determined young woman. Let me give you a word of advice. If you really want this, you must take care how you ask. You must ask with generosity.'

Katje looked at her blankly.

'I see I haven't expressed myself well. How shall I say it? Try not to argue too much if your parents are against you coming to me. Don't push too hard. It doesn't always work. It makes your opponent stronger – in this case your mother. Always try to see the other person's point of view. Be generous, but above all quietly persistent. It takes a kind of mental energy, similar to physical energy. Like dancing you get better at it with practice.' She smiled. 'I can't do any more for you Katárina, but I do hope we'll see each other again.'

Discord

Hedda, wrapped in a red scarf, sat on the floor of her office. Erik was on his chair by the window. They'd just finished rehearsing and she was looking through the shelves for a music score, and nibbling pieces of chocolate with her strong black coffee.

'I like to work with you,' he said, surprising her. He had rarely spoken to her with such genuine warmth.

She looked up at him and smiled.

'We're a good partnership,' she said. She turned back to the bookshelf so he wouldn't see how moved she was. 'I wish you could have met my father. He'd have been proud of our work together.'

'Did he play the piano?'

'No. He was an academic really, a linguist – not an artist, though he loved to watch the company. He was brave, the most courageous person I've ever known. We were always close. It was always Papa and me, and Gitta and Mama, after my little sister, Hanna, died. Not that we weren't all close as a family.'

'How fortunate you were,' he said.

He sounded wistful. She felt the familiar ache of sympathy for him.

'Papa used to do what you do, create names for people – though he wasn't so good a mimic as you, not as funny. I always remember how he called Hitler the Little Chancellor.'

'Little. That was hardly accurate.'

'Well of course it was meant in irony,' she replied. 'Hitler's a tyrant, but isn't there something so small and utterly insignificant about him too – as if there's really no person at all behind that ranting façade, just a terrible absence, is it absence of compassion, of soul, do you think? I'm certain he'll invade the Netherlands before long. How will it all end? Will we ever be able to go home? Not until the whole of Europe has been pulled apart. I can't see anything but disaster ahead.' She stopped, aware that she'd been carried away, and Erik hadn't said a word. She looked up from the sheets of music and caught him staring at her with a little smile of disdain. He adjusted his face too late.

'What's the matter Erik?'

'I'm interested only in music, not in Your Politics,' he said.

'It's not My Politics, as you put it. It's far bigger and more important than that.'

He gave a short laugh and stood up.

'I'm a musician. You are a dancer. Don't corrupt yourself, Hedda Brandt, don't waste your energy.'

He put on his coat.

'Are you leaving already?'

'I've got another rehearsal.' He went to the studio to pick up his music, and then left.

'Good-bye,' she called, but he didn't answer. She heard the street door bang closed. She shook her head. He was the most exasperating man. She went to change into her outdoor clothes. Her hands were shaking. He'd unsettled her more than she wanted to admit.

Kai

It was a cold, still afternoon. Hedda cycled through the park gates and down the main avenue towards Vondelstraat. A chill haze hung over the water. She heard the sharp calling of the coots, their white heads amongst the reeds. There was a splash as a dog gave chase.

In her basket she carried a bunch of deep red dahlias wrapped in green tissue paper. The Hoffmans were always so good to her since Elise had become her student. She supposed it was gratitude that made them so welcoming. She felt at home with them all.

She slowed down as she passed the Tea House. A young man was walking from the opposite direction. She noticed him because he moved with such easy grace that she wondered if he was a dancer, and that perhaps she'd met him before. He glanced at her and smiled as they passed. She got off her bicycle at the gates and wheeled it alongside the laurel hedge, chaining it to the railings of the garden. She ran up the steps to the entrance under the sweep of wisteria at the side of the building.

Dr Hoffman opened the door. Seeing her, his face lit up.

'Hedda, I hoped you'd call by. I need an excuse for a break.' He led her along the hall to his study. 'The girls are still out with Julia.'

She handed him the bunch of flowers.

'Thank you. Make yourself at home. I'll bring some coffee.'

Hedda settled on the sofa amongst the toppling piles of books and anticipated the pleasure of an hour chatting with Marten Hoffman. His company was always so reassuring. It reminded her of being with her father.

She looked out at the garden. A breeze had started up and a shower of pale golden leaves scattered over the lawn. Elise's cat sprang up, kneaded Hedda's thighs, circled round and curled in her lap. She leant back against the cushion, feeling the cat's purr rumbling under her hand. She could drift into sleep.

'You look very tired, Hedda. You've been working too hard,' Marten said, as he returned with coffee.

'I suppose I am.'

'You should take a holiday.'

She laughed.

'And you. Do you ever take a holiday?'

'You know I do, Julia insists.' He glanced at her and smiled as he put the tray down on the desk. 'Marianne made these biscuits. They're rather good. You must sample them.'

'You know I need no encouragement to eat.'

'Don't move. You look so comfortable.'

He put her coffee and the plate of biscuits on a table beside her.

They talked about Elise, and Hedda told him how fine and expressive her dancing was becoming, and how much stronger her leg since she'd been following her radical exercise regime.

'And your classes,' he said. 'Don't ever forget how much you help her too. I have great hopes that she'll be as strong as she ever was, in time.'

'I so admire the way she never gives up, even when it's clearly so difficult.'

'Yes. She's extraordinary.' He stirred sugar into his coffee, took a sip. 'How are you?' he asked.

In Marten's quiet presence, she found herself talking about Erik, and the recent performances.

'You're fond of this man.' It was more a statement than a question.

'Yes, I suppose I am,' she answered. 'I love working with him, that is when he's not in one of his distant moods. Perhaps it's that we're both German, that despite everything I miss Germany. I don't know.'

'Are you troubled that certain differences between you make a closer friendship impossible? You need to know what he thinks and feels. It's important, as you know.'

'I could never dismiss him over ideology,' she said. 'He's my friend.'

'Is he?'

'Yes, even though he's so unreliable and difficult at times.'

She looked down at the cat, stroked his ears flat against his head. She realised, of course, that it was more than that. It was about her father, and Kurt Jooss, and those deep alliances of love and trust.

'I haven't been close to anyone for a long time,' she said. 'I know our main connection is work, but often it becomes more.' She glanced at Marten. He was looking at her with amiable concern.

'Perhaps you're alone too much. It can confuse things.'

'To be alone is my choice,' she said, more sharply than she intended.

'Why?'

It was the kind of conversation she might have had with her girlfriends, not with the father of one of her students. She hesitated before answering.

'I always thought I'd go back to Germany,' she said. 'No, that's not entirely true. It is my choice though, to be alone.' She liked his directness, despite being taken off-guard, and she felt she owed him her honesty. 'I lived in England for a year after we left Germany. It was a beautiful place, Devon, but such a difficult time, all of us in the company thrown together, struggling with the language and feeling alienated, so far from home. And I loved someone, very much, too much. There was no future in it. I had to leave in the end, and I came here. But I never want to feel like that again, so unhappy, so weak.'

'Were you weak? Or is fragile a better word?'

'Maybe.' Since living in Holland she'd never told anyone how she'd felt about Kurt, though he was often in her mind.

'Five years is too long to waste recovering from a broken heart,' he said.

'Oh I have recovered.' She looked across at him and smiled. 'That's why I value my independence so much.'

'You're not made to be solitary.'

Once more he'd disconcerted her. She didn't say anything.

They heard the front door open. The cat sprang off her lap.

'That must be Kai,' Marten said. 'You've never met my stepson, have you?'

'No. Elise has told me about him.' She was relieved at the interruption.

Marten opened the door.

'Kai, come and meet Hedda Brandt,' he called.

She heard swift light footsteps, and Kai came in with a violin case under his arm. He put it down on the bookcase and took her hand.

'I saw you earlier,' she said, recognising the young man she'd thought was a dancer. 'On my way here.'

He smiled.

'Oh yes, I thought we must know each other, the way you looked at me.'

'We don't though, do we?'

'No, I don't think so.' They considered each other with amusement. 'I was worried I'd been rude. Hello Hedda, at last we meet. Elise's told me a lot about you.'

'And me about you.'

Kai picked up the violin again and sat on the arm of the sofa.

'I've just got this fiddle from being mended. It's like having an old friend back.' He took it out of its case, and ran his fingers lightly over the strings.

57

He must be about twenty-five, Hedda thought. Elise had told her his father was Spanish, which would explain why he looked more Spanish gypsy than Dutch, with his brown eyes and dark untidy curls. He'd taken off his overcoat and was wearing an old green jumper, too big for him. Yes he does look like a dancer, she thought, such a straight spine, and that alert way of moving. It's unusual to see in someone who isn't trained.

As if he'd read her thought, he looked up from his violin. He smiled.

'You will stay for dinner, Hedda?' he asked. 'My mother and sisters will be back soon, and they'll want to see you. I'm going to cook.'

Hedda glanced at Marten. He nodded.

'You must stay. I was going to suggest it.'

'I'd love to,' she answered.

'Good. That's settled then.'

Werner

The stairs were dusty and narrow and Werner's back ached with carrying one dispatch of heavy boxes up to the first floor of his father's office, and then more boxes down. It all seemed pointless. Down in the basement his father discussed plans with his partner, Mr Wijnbergen, for the extension of his stationery business.

Werner would help with the donkeywork. Werner needed something to strengthen him – to make a man of him. He'd heard his father say just that at the breakfast table when he went out to fetch an extra jug of milk, and Katje, as ever coming to his defence, said that father was quite wrong – that it was good to be different and stand out from the crowd. It was hopeless – he knew his father despised him. He had paused outside the door and heard him say he'd stop paying for piano lessons if Werner carried on with this obsession for music to the exclusion of everything else. And Katje had insisted that must never happen. Werner would die without his music, she told them, and if they stopped his lessons she would refuse to eat.

Sweat beaded his forehead and the muscles in his back burned. He braced his knee against the wall, resting the boxes on his bent leg for a moment's relief. An image of Herr Weiss rose up in his mind again – watching him with a strange light in his eyes. Herr Weiss had the most extraordinary eyes Werner had ever seen. They changed from blue to grey green – and the way he looked at Werner, as if he cared, as if he was really interested in him. Herr Weiss had beautiful eyes.

'In this world only the best survive, Werner. You must become the best. Don't let me down.'

'I'll never let you down sir,' Werner had replied. And Herr Weiss had touched his cheek just briefly with his fingertips. He had the strangest notion that Herr Weiss was going to kiss him on the mouth, and his heart seemed to soar up with terror and joy that left him weak and shaken. He closed his eyes. When he opened them, Weiss was still looking at him, with a little smile.

'I love Herr Weiss,' he whispered. He'd never admitted it before, insisting to himself that it was music he loved more than anything. Now, standing on the turn in the stairs, he let the boxes fall. He was immobilised by nausea and panic. Once something is realised it can never be forgotten. I love him so deeply, so passionately. I want to be the best pianist he's ever taught. The best in the country. For him.

He'd read that love between men was a perversion of nature. Older boys at school were brutal if they suspected anyone of being like this. So far they'd not suspected him. What if he grew into such a man? A life of loneliness and torment, shunned by everyone. He held his breath for a moment, pressed his hand to his genitals.

'Werner buck up!' His father stood on the stairs below him. 'We haven't all day to get this job done.'

Down in the basement they watched him stumble into the room and put the boxes down in the corner, his father, Mr Wijnbergen, and the quiet young woman – the secretary whose name nobody had thought to tell him.

The Hoffmans

In December the canals froze and the trees, rimed with frost, stood like paper cut-outs against a grey sky. Sitting on a step above Prinsengracht, her ungloved fingers clumsy with cold, Katje fastened skates over her boots and slipped down onto the ice. Dark-coated figures sped by, singly and in long lines. How graceful everyone looked. Once they were at home on the ice, even the clumsiest man became swift and agile as a dancer. Elated, she tottered to her feet, found her balance, spread her arms out and set off.

She had counted the days and the hours until this afternoon – her first visit to Elise's house. The girls at school had been unfriendly since she'd started lessons with Miss Brandt. Not that she cared much. They didn't understand. They never would. She knew she was different. Like Elise, she didn't fit in, and that was fine by her, as long as there were other misfits around.

'I'm flying like a wild goose to Elise's,' she cried, as the cold air stung her cheeks, 'to my new country, my new friends.' She turned under the bridge and down Leidsegracht under branches and past the houseboats. Leaving the canal to cross the tramlines into the park, her legs felt slow and heavy without the skid of metal on ice.

She trotted over the hump-backed bridge, through clumps of bamboo. Cold mist hung over the water, and now the sun was setting there was a pink glow through the dark tracery of trees. She paused to touch the pineapples and lions on the gateposts as she turned into Vondelstraat. To her right was the church with its tall slate turrets, and to the left, no more than ten steps away, was Elise's house.

The apartment was one side of a square ornate redbrick building facing the park, with white stone porch, balcony and lintels. It was surrounded on three sides by a small garden, shady with shrubs. Up seven stone steps, she pulled the bell, and heard someone running along the hall. A little girl with long brown plaits peered round the door at her.

'Katarina's here,' the girl sang out. She skipped off down the tiled hall, and Katje followed her, past the fir tree that lay on its side waiting to be decorated on Christmas Eve, to the kitchen where Elise leant against the doorframe.

'Hi Katje. That was Marianne. Come on in.'

Katje put her skates down in the hall and followed Elise into the kitchen. The house smelt so different from her own – what was it? A mixture of coffee, baked food, and newspaper print, she decided.

Elise's mother, Julia, was mixing dough at a long wooden table. She looked up and smiled.

'Hello Katje. You can put your coat and hat on the peg on the door.' She floured the board and rolled the dough into a ball. 'Elise, will you make us all a drink?'

Katje perched on the arm of the settle as Elise lined up the cups, boiled the milk and mixed in the chocolate. She looked around the untidy kitchen. It was a big room that seemed much lived in. Glass doors opened onto a veranda. The branches of a huge horse chestnut tree spread over the railings, and beyond was the park. Marianne was balancing up-ended dominos in a long line across the table.

Dr Hoffman came in.

'Pa, this is Katje, my friend from dancing.'

Dr Marten Hoffman, a slight, balding man, was wearing a grey cardigan with ragged edges. He held out his hand.

'Pleased to meet you Katarina.'

'Papa, watch.' Marianne touched the first domino and they clattered in succession. He smiled distractedly.

'Have you seen my diary?' he said.

'It's on the table in the hall,' Elise said. 'Pa is always losing things. He needs someone just to run around after him and tidy things away, and Mama's quite hopeless, so it's always me managing everyone.'

At that moment the outside door opened and a voice called out, 'I'm home.'

Marianne leapt up.

'It's Kai!'

A young man came into the kitchen. Marianne flung herself into his arms.

'Steady, you'll knock me flying,' he said as he lifted Marianne and spun her round. He bent to kiss Julia and turned to greet Marten.

'We never expected you so soon, what a lovely surprise, darling.' Julia brushed her floury hands on her apron and reached up to him.

'Kai, this is Katarina,' Elise said. 'Kai is our brilliant brother I told you about.'

Kai hung his coat over the back of the chair and flopped down. Marianne sat opposite, gazing at him, her arms wrapped round her knees.

'Hey Katarina. Don't listen to my sisters. You'll get the wrong idea. They welcome me home and the next thing we'll all be quarrelling again.'

'Ignore him. We never quarrel – not much anyway.'

'Was the concert good?' Julia asked.

'It was awful. The pianist went missing. We were told he'd left suddenly for America. They had to find someone else at the last moment.'

'Why, did he do that?' Elise asked.

'Afraid of what will happen when Germany attacks I suppose. He wanted to get out before it's too late, an opportunity came up – that's the rumour. It was pretty tough performing after one rehearsal with someone new. We just about got away with it.'

'It's like Hedda's story, only then it was the whole ballet company disappearing,' Elise said.

'Yes,' there was tension in Kai's voice. 'Hedda told me about it.' He stretched his arms over his head. 'Oh it's good to be back. A whole week off. I need it.'

'What I don't understand is why anyone would arrest a choreographer and a company of dancers?' Katje said. 'I wanted to ask Miss Brandt because she never told me the whole story.' Her voice seemed to ring in the silence that followed. 'Have I said something really stupid?'

'The company composer was Jewish,' Kai said, shortly. 'Like many of the best.' He got up. 'I'm going to unpack.'

Katje blushed, and bent to stroke the cat that had just wandered in.

'That's Mitze. She's the friendly one,' Elise said. 'Do you want to see my bedroom?'

'Oh yes.'

'Come on then.'

She followed Elise's slow progress to the first floor, along the landing to steep stairs leading to the top floor.

'One of Kai's best friends is Jewish,' Elise said. 'Kai worries about what will happen to him if Germany invades.'

'But won't we stay neutral? That's what my parents always say.'

'Not what mine think.'

'It's funny that we both have brothers who are musicians,' Katje said, after a moment, not knowing what else to say.

Elise moved painfully slowly as they neared the top. Katje had never liked to ask what was wrong with her. For all her usual directness, she'd been taught to pretend everything was normal. Why did Elise have a room so high up when it was hard for her to climb the stairs? Elise paused to rest.

'You go ahead. The light switch is to the left of the door.'

Katje slipped past her and up into the long room. She looked around – the bed with its green and red cover in the corner, a little desk and bookcase, and the white walls covered in photographs of ballet dancers. From the gable window she could see the roof of the Concert Hall in the distance, beyond the dark line of trees in the park. Elise appeared, crossed the room and eased herself onto the bed. She reached for a box of matches on the desk and lit three candles. Below them Kai had started to practise his violin.

'That's the only thing that's like home,' Katje said. 'The sound of someone practising the same bit of music over and over. Only here it's the violin instead of the piano.'

'Oh we have the piano too. Mama and Kai play, and Marianne is learning now too. There's always someone making a noise. Pa and I just put up with it all.'

Katje sat down on the edge of the bed, next to Elise.

'So do I, just about. My brother Werner is such a misery these days. Don't you ever want to play anything?'

'No. I wanted to be a ballet dancer.' Elise bent and stretched her weak leg with her hands, then touched her head to her knees. 'You've never asked what happened to me,' she said, twisting to look at Katje.

'I really didn't know how to, in case I upset you or something.'

'I can tell you're always wondering. I had polio you see, when I was nine. Afterwards I couldn't move my left leg, and everyone thought I'd have to be in a chair, or on crutches for the rest of my life.'

'That's terrible. But they were wrong, weren't they? You can walk as well as anyone else, kind of anyway.'

'Pa did a lot of research and found this lady called Sister Kenny – she's an Australian who helps people to move again with exercises. She was working in England, so Mama and I went over there to a hospital near London for a few months. By the time I came home I could stand and walk a few steps. Then Pa found Hedda's school for me. Before I was ill I went to a classical ballet school, but they wouldn't have me back. Hedda saved my life, in a way.' She stretched her arm towards the ceiling and moved her hand in the candlelight so its shadow fell over the wall. 'Sometimes I lie awake in the dark and I dream that I can dance again properly. I want so much to run and jump, and to dance so nobody ever knows there's anything wrong.'

Katje reached her arm out until her hand made a shadow too. The ceiling was decorated with plaster mouldings in the corners and round the light fitting. Their fingers entwined and moved apart again, like strange underwater creatures.

'I'm sure you'll be able to one day. I'm sure you can do anything if you put your mind to it.'

'Do you think we could learn to fly?'

Katje giggled.

'Maybe. Shall I try to lift you? Like that picture of the ballet dancers on the wall.'

Elise slithered off the bed and Katje put one arm round her waist. Without a word, they began to move, Katje gliding Elise round the room to the long notes played beneath them.

'We're dancing. We're like real ballroom dancers.'

She spun Elise around, and half lifted her from the floor, until they collapsed back on the bed breathless, laughing with exhilaration.

'Help me to balance.' Elise struggled to her feet again. 'Now let me hold onto you.'

They stood facing each other, Katje with her arms out, Elise clinging to her and attempting to take the weight onto her weak leg.

'Ah it's so difficult.'

'Try again. I'm holding you. I won't let you fall, I promise.'

They held each other's gaze, smiling. For a moment Elise loosened her grip, and balanced.

Part Two
1940

March

On Elise's fifteenth birthday Hedda strolled with Marten and Julia Hoffman along the esplanade at the seaside. The sun shone between banks of pearly cloud, but the sharp wind caught the sand in sudden flurries that made them turn away to shelter their eyes. Across the beach Marianne was lying flat on her back and moving her arms and legs to make a sand print. Elise sat on Katje's coat and watched as she ran towards the waves and then back again before they broke on the sand.

'That girl is irrepressible in her zest for life,' Julia said. 'Who else would play in the water on a chilly day like this? Even Marianne has more sense.'

Silhouetted against the light, Kai and his girlfriend, Ida, held hands and turned towards the sea. Hedda liked Kai. Since first meeting there'd been a sense of ease between them. She understood his restlessness and intensity, and despite that, there was a light-heartedness about him that was soothing.

'They all look so happy,' she said.

She shivered and delved in her pockets for her gloves. One spring day six years ago in England, on a beach in Devon, she'd fallen in love with Kurt. She'd realised in one elated moment as she watched him walking along the shoreline, bending to pick up shells – then the weeks that followed, awkwardness and longing and jealousy. She'd never told him, but he must have known. It was obvious to the other dancers. I took myself so seriously, as if I was the only person who'd ever been in love. How tiresome I must have been. Kurt mattered to me more than anything or anyone in the world, but I recovered, thank goodness. She thought of him now with deep affection, and recently with concern. She'd heard nothing from him since England had been at war with Germany.

'You're far away, Hedda,' Julia said.

Hedda turned and smiled at her.

'Ida seems a nice girl,' she said, unwilling to share her thoughts.

'Yes. I'm afraid she's completely smitten with Kai.'

'Don't you think he is with her?'

'Kai's a free spirit. The girls come and go. He's like his father.' Julia laughed.

Katje ran up to Kai and Ida, her hair streaming out behind her, and they saw Kai turn towards her, their heads almost touching before both set off, racing across the sand towards the esplanade. Kai easily overtook her, and stopped to wait until Katje, laughing and panting, caught up with him.

'I think the young Katje is also a little smitten,' Marten said.

'She's just a child. She's awestruck, as well she might be. He must seem very glamorous to her.' Julia pulled her coat closer round her and leant towards Marten. He circled her with his arms, kissed her cheek. 'It's cold when the sun goes.'

They began to walk. Hedda stayed, watching the activity on the beach. Kai had left the girls together on the sand and was walking in her direction. She realised, with surprise, that he was coming to join her.

'Hello, my friend,' he called when he was within her hearing. 'My parents left you on your own.'

'I don't mind. I was watching you all.'

'Well I'm glad. I have you to myself for a moment.'

She smiled at his confidence. He knew he was attractive, but it didn't make him less so. He reminded her of the familial banter she'd shared with the dancers in the company – so unlike the erratic relationship she had with Erik.

'What are you thinking, Hedda?'

'I'm trying not to think. I'm sick to death of my thoughts.'

'I know that feeling.' He stood close to her, his back to the sea. 'Since we heard Germany invaded Denmark I can't stop thinking. It keeps me awake at night, so I end up getting up to practise the fiddle, as quietly as I can, hoping none of the family get woken too. Germany will invade us before long. It's inevitable, isn't it, whatever anyone says?'

'Yes. I think it is.'

'Are you afraid?'

'Afraid? Not for myself. I'm angry, and I'm ashamed these days to be German. I'm sad too.'

'Perhaps I shouldn't say, but my mother told me what they did to your father. It must be very hard for you.'

She nodded. For a moment neither of them spoke. She watched a gull buffeted by the wind, landing by a stretch of water.

'We're the same, you and me, with our revolutionary fathers.'

'Yes. I suppose we are.'

'I hardly knew mine though. He was never a father in the usual way. Marten is more like my father. But I wish I could talk to him now.'

'You were young weren't you when you left Spain?'

'Seven. My mother couldn't live with him. He was impossible. But he wrote from time to time, sent me pictures. I met him just in time, before he was killed. I went out to find him but by then he was caught up in the fight against Franco. I was of passing interest.' He paused, kicked at the railings. 'Oh I don't mean you to feel sorry for me.' He gave Hedda a little smile. 'It's just that when it happens, when we're taken over by Germany, where then do we stand? And what do we do about it? Do we fight back like they did? Do we give everything for freedom, even our lives? They set high standards for us.'

'I've never seen it in that way. As far as I'm concerned my father suffered terribly and achieved nothing. He felt he

71

had to speak out, but I've never reconciled losing him in the way I did. His revolutionary ardour didn't balance.'

'But can you measure it like that?'

'I know no other way, yet.'

He was looking at her keenly. She met his gaze briefly.

'My father was courageous,' she continued. 'In another way you could say he was reckless, even naïve, though he accused me of that the last time we saw each other. You can't publish anti-Nazi articles and expect to get away with it. Especially when he knew we'd all left for daring to disobey Nazi policy.'

'You often seem sad, Hedda.'

'Oh I'm all right really. I'm pretty tough, you know. My work here gives me stability and a lot of happiness.' Over the sands she saw a yellow kite flying, and a little group of children with a dog.

'Sometimes I have dreams of killing Hitler with my own hands,' he said with anger. 'I wake wondering if my father's spirit has taken me over. I don't feel like a violent person, you see. Not normally.'

'Perhaps it's not so much about fighting as finding a way to resist. Fighting back can't be the way for everyone. It wasn't for me, when I left Germany. Though I admit, I often think I was a coward. My sister said as much to me.'

'That's unfair, cruel even.'

'I don't know. At the time I saw no other way of surviving and continuing to dance, and now I won't adhere to any Nazi rules, either about my choreography or the people I teach, and how I teach them. That's my only resistance, small though it might be.'

'You're amazing, Hedda.'

She laughed. 'I'm not. But it's very nice that you think so.' She saw Ida walking towards them. She waved and Ida waved back. She was such a pretty girl, her round dimpled face.

'Oh dear, I wanted to carry on talking to you.' Kai said.

'But I think Ida wants your company. We'll talk again another time. Let's walk to meet her.'

Katje helped Marianne to set the table in the Hoffmans' dining room with the best linen, and silver cutlery, and the bowls of red tulips. They lit the candles and stood back to admire the table. Hedda passed the door and looked in.

'It looks lovely, like a painting – The Hoffman Family Party, a twentieth century Rembrandt. Beautiful, girls.'

She was wearing a burgundy silk dress, and a jet necklace and drop earrings.

'You look lovely too, Miss Brandt. So romantic, like a film star.'

'You'd better call me Hedda tonight, or I'll never be able to relax. Let's forget I'm usually your dancing teacher.'

She left a faint scent of roses behind her.

'She's the most glamorous person I've ever met since my Aunt Minna,' Katje said to Marianne. But Marianne was pouring wine into two glasses and wasn't listening.

'Let's have our own toast.' She giggled and passed a glass to Katje. 'Let's make a wish. For something we want in ten years time.'

They sat at the corner of the table, and looked into each other's eyes.

'You first.'

'I wish to be a dancer as wonderful as Miss Brandt.'

'And I want to be as beautiful as Greta Garbo, and live in America in a big house by the ocean.'

Solemnly they raised their glasses and drank.

'It seems an awfully long time away. I'll be twenty-three.'

'And I'll be twenty-one. We'll both be grown-up.'

'We'll still know each other do you think?'

'Sure, shake hands on it.'

'What are you two doing?' Elise came in, disturbing them. 'If you're both drinking, then I must too. It's my birthday.'

It was the loveliest night. Katje turned from one to another, watching with admiration. How beautiful everyone looked in the candlelight. Elise and Kai were so like each other, even with their different fathers. They had an absorbed intent way of listening. Hedda was no longer the stern demanding person who taught class, but happy and full of stories and laughter. After they'd eaten, she danced with Elise, holding her lightly and skilfully, one hand around her waist, the other on her arm. They dipped and swayed, and turned around the room, as Kai played and Ida sang.

'Now you dance, Hedda,' Marianne said, clapping her hands.

'No solos tonight,' Hedda replied. 'We'll all dance. I'll teach you a circle dance I do with my small ones. It's easy.' She took Marten's hands and he stood up, smiling and embarrassed.

'Papa's dancing,' Marianne cried out in delight, so there was no getting out of it. They danced in a line round the room, then led by Julia, through into the sitting room.

'Dancing and music is for everyone,' Hedda said when they all sat down again, breathless by the fire. 'Art was nourishment and life for the Russians during the revolution, and that's how it will be again for us under fascism. We won't be oppressed. But I'm becoming maudlin. Now where's my glass?'

'It's in the dining room.'

'I'll fetch another bottle.'

Kai returned with the glasses and another bottle, and poured.

'Let's drink to Elise, Marianne and Katje, to the future, whatever it brings; may the children create a better world,' Julia said.

'To the children.'

'And to doctors who must look after us all,' Elise said.

'To all of us.'

They hugged and kissed, and sang to Elise. Elise cut her chocolate cake and handed it round.

'And now,' Kai said suddenly, 'we must all of us ask ourselves a question.'

'And what is that, dear brother?'

'I'm serious.'

They all fell silent.

'I know, speak.'

'If, or when, we're taken over by Germany, when we have to live by the rules of a bunch of barbarians – forgive me Hedda for slandering your country – but you said as much yourself. Do we submit to save our skin or do we give everything for freedom, even our lives?'

Someone coughed. Julia stood up and went to the piano.

'Nobody has answered me.'

'Well you have rather changed the tone of the evening,' Julia said, lifting the lid and settling on the stool.

'We fight with everything we have,' Hedda said quietly. 'We fight and we live.'

Julia played a few notes on the piano and called for Marianne to turn pages for her, and it seemed to Katje that she wanted to stop Kai talking about the future.

'I love you, Hedda,' Kai said. But Hedda had turned towards the piano, and only Katje heard.

'I never wanted the night to end,' Katje said, as she and Elise brushed their hair and changed into their nightdresses. 'My family are so different from yours, I don't think I ever want to go home.'

'What's so different?'

'Everything. Well you've met my mother, so you must have some idea.'

She got into her camp bed beside Elise's, and straightened out the blankets.

'We do quarrel at times, you know. You saw the very best of us today.'

'Even you and Kai?'

'No, I suppose we don't. Marianne and I do though. All the time.'

'I think he's wonderful, your brother. Like a film star.'

Elise looked at her sidelong, and smiled.

'Don't give me that knowing look. You'd understand if you knew my lot. I've never seen Papa kiss Mama, and seem happy, like your parents. I suppose, now I think about it, everyone in my family is miserable these days, especially Werner. He's the worst of them. Wait until you meet him. I'm the only person who can honestly say I'm happy.'

April

'How are you?' Erik Weiss walked into Hedda's office, took off his coat and sat down.

She looked up from her desk in surprise.

'I'm very well. Are you?'

He'd paid her scant attention since they'd finished their tour of concerts in the autumn.

'You must forgive me for neglecting you.' He paused, as if waiting for the response she didn't give. 'I've been pre-occupied with work, as I've mentioned before. I find it impossible to think of anything when I'm composing. I'd like to make amends now I'm less busy. Are you free on Monday afternoon?'

'Yes.'

'Then do come to my apartment. For tea.'

'I'd be glad to.'

How absurdly formal we're being, she thought, and he's giving me that appraising look of his. I mustn't let him unnerve me. Neglecting me – the gall of him.

Later she lingered at the flower market. 'One doesn't take flowers to men. It's the wrong way around.' Karole, one of the dancers, had said that to her when she'd bought bronze chrysanthemums for Kurt – so long ago it seemed. 'He's not your lover.' The scent of chrysanthemums reminded her, with bittersweet pain, of Kurt.

Flowers for Erik must be white – lilies or jasmine – exquisitely perfumed. Erik and I are not lovers either, Karole. I wish I could get your bossy voice out of my head.

On her way to Erik's on Monday, Hedda bought a spray of jasmine from the market, enjoying the giddy confusion of colour and perfume as she walked alongside the stalls. The first stirring of spring made her glad.

Leidsegracht, where he lived, was lined with elm and linden trees, the buds just breaking. She wore a new dress patterned with green leaves on dark blue silk. Pausing on the bridge over Prinsengracht, she saw herself distorted in the canal. A scum of feathers and decaying twigs floated on the brown water.

The façade of the red brick house where Erik lived was dominated by bay windows, one above the other for four floors. The ground floor bay was most ornate, with panes of curved glass and white arching window frames, above a balcony with a stone balustrade. On each of the floors above, a simpler version of the design was repeated; it was the only ornamented building on the stretch of canal from Herengracht to Marnixstraat.

There was a long delay after she rang the bell of Erik's apartment. She wondered whether to ring again, and stepped back to look up to his window, when the door opened and he appeared in a grey suit.

'Hedda Brandt, are you spying?' He looked her up and down, from hat to shoes, to the flowers she held to him in her confusion, and smiled. 'Such a gorgeous perfume,' he said, taking the flowers and putting his nose to them. 'And such a glorious day.' He led her inside and up a flight of stairs to his rooms.

'Please sit and be comfortable.' He gestured to a sofa covered in cream brocade. Beside it a low table was laid with tablecloth, white china cups and a silver sugar bowl. A plain cloth covered what must be cake or biscuits.

'I'll bring the tea.' He placed the flowers on the table beside her and left the room.

It was sparsely furnished – the sofa and table, another chair upholstered in the same brocade, and a large bureau bookcase of walnut wood, intricately inlaid with motifs of flowers and urns. A chandelier hung from the centre of the ceiling. The white walls were bare, the window undraped. Light streamed in a long diagonal over the marble floor.

'It is a beautiful room,' she said when he returned.

'Thank you.' He poured tea. 'Like the English I take tea with milk and sugar. I presume you drink it black.'

'Yes.'

'I bought apple tart.' He took the cloth and folded it up. 'I know how you like your sweets.'

'That's very thoughtful.'

He cut a slice and handed it to her.

There was an uncomfortable silence. Eating seemed too gross an activity, so she put the plate down.

'That's a very nice dress you're wearing.'

She glanced at the silk skirt falling over her knees.

'Thank you. Tell me about your work, how is the composition?'

'Almost complete. I'd like you to hear it when I've finished. In fact I wanted to talk about our future work.'

'I'd be delighted. I assumed you'd lost interest in any further collaboration.'

'Not at all. To the contrary.'

There was silence. She was aware of the scent of the flowers he'd neglected to put in water.

'Do you have a piano here? I can't imagine you only play in the studio.'

'Correct. I have my music room across the hall, devoted to nothing else – a piano, my scores, my books, reserved for me only. I never teach from home. I can't bear to have inadequate students thumping at my own piano.'

He raised one eyebrow. He looked so ridiculous that she laughed. She sipped at the tea, feeling lighter-hearted now that they'd relaxed.

'I will only consider teaching the most promising pupils, and even then they disappoint me.'

'I'm glad you don't teach me. How on earth do you decide who's talented and who isn't?'

'Oh I can tell in one lesson who to take on and who to dismiss. Wasting my energy on people with no ability for any longer than an hour is tiresome. After all I've devoted years of my life to music. Why should I bother with mediocrity?'

'But you never know how people might develop with hard work. What about Katje de Jong – nothing very promising there, or so I thought, but look at her now, such vitality she practically blows me over.'

He sniffed and pulled a face.

'Too clumsy and uncontrolled for my taste. Heavy on her feet when she lands.'

'Oh Erik, be fair. She's had all but six months training.'

'No sense of refinement.'

She glanced at him to see if he was provoking her, but he appeared to be serious.

'I don't think we're going to agree over this,' she said after a moment. 'Anyway you wanted to talk about our work.'

He folded his hands on his lap and gave a little nod.

'I never could tolerate chaos. When I was a boy it seemed to me that cities were never finished, all that mess of rubble and earth and ugly machinery. I had no idea then that they never would be, so I decided I'd become an architect, as well as a great singer – I'd design magnificent buildings of steel and glass, cathedrals, temples, palaces. I made drawings, many drawings.'

'It sounds wonderful, Erik,' she said, wondering what it had to do with his plan for their ballet. He closed his eyes briefly, as if irritated by her interruption.

'Music would somehow emanate from the structure of the buildings, as people moved by – such music that would transform humankind into Gods. Can you imagine? There would be no mindless chatter, no obsession with sex and money and trivia. They would move like dancers to the incredible music surrounding them.' He brought his hand up to crush a tiny fly in his fist. 'But alas, life is very harsh and most human beings are monstrous. '

She had no sense of how to respond. She found she was staring at his face and beyond, so the tones of his skin became one with the wall behind him. Everything for a moment seemed pointless.

'I still dream of a world where all the ugliness is contained under the ground, all the machinery for living. Only my palaces of steel and glass would exist on the surface. Everyone would have worthwhile work to aspire to. No illness, or grotesque old age or deformity. A good dream don't you think, Hedda Brandt?'

Startled, she realised she'd stopped listening. She'd been imagining his world as an opera, with a huge set, chandeliers hanging from crystal caverns.

'I don't know. I think the world is probably meant to be messy and chaotic as well as beautiful. Kindness and love are the only things worth living for, as far as I'm concerned. And art.'

'And art – yes. We artists dream, we have ideals.' Broken from his own spell, he was animated again. 'Our new ballet will be rather splendid, and the beginning of something truly great I believe.'

'I'm afraid I haven't given it much thought yet.'

'I've been busy with it many months, as you know, night and day.'

'Then it's not really a collaboration, is it? Not yet anyway.'

She picked up her plate, broke off a corner of the pastry, toying at it with her fork, aware she felt some trepidation about embarking on a major work with Erik. He looked as if he was about to reply, but instead continued to verbalise his own train of thought.

'As far as I'm concerned music is the only thing worth living for.'

'What about love?'

'Love is merely an illusion.'

'I wasn't talking of romantic love. I mean friendship too, and love parents have for their children, familial love.'

He looked at her a moment, his head inclined.

'Since I lost my parents and have no siblings I have no idea what you're talking about.'

'I'm sorry.' But why was she apologising? That way he had of eliciting her sympathy.

'You're a romantic,' he said. 'I should have known from the first time I watched you dance – those flowing arms, that lovely back.' He crossed the room to sit beside her. 'You're not beautiful, but there's something so pleasing, so clean and defined about you. You would be fine in my city of glass.'

'Erik. You say the most extraordinary things at times!'

He took her hand, turned it over and traced a cross with his fingernail over her palm. 'I've never told anyone this. I don't know if I'm capable of love. Since my mother died I've never loved anyone. I'm sure that I loved her, but somehow I lost the ability.'

His face was so close she could see the pores on his forehead.

'Do you think that's sad?'

'I don't know.'

'It seems to me a waste of time – love. It's unbalanced, untidy. People behave irrationally – over what? Someone who'll betray or disappoint them in the end. I'm telling you how I am. Only music will not let me down. But I've always admired you – even when I've disagreed with you – which I do over many things, not least some of the hopeless cases you teach.' He looked her straight in the eyes. She drew back.

'What do you mean? I don't teach any hopeless cases.'

'What about the crippled girl?'

'Elise Hoffman.'

'What?'

'Her name. She is not 'the crippled girl.' She has a name.'

'Elise Hoffman has no spark of energy. No physicality at all. She can hardly cross the room. She bores me.'

'She's one of the most beautiful young dancers I've ever taught. You have no idea how to see beyond the obvious.'

But then, in another way, she saw he was right, and her spirits sank. Elise was so light and frail she scarcely embodied her movement. Had she become one of those teachers, beguiled by her students? Had she lost her critical faculties?

'Don't be angry with me. I've been honest with you.' Erik smiled. The look he gave her was one of fondness. 'Oh Hedda, I know I'm different from other people. It's not easy. No not easy. Pity me if you like, but don't be angry.'

He put his head on her shoulder like a dog wanting affection, and the gesture was so surprising that she felt sorry for him. There was something so vulnerable about him behind his ridiculous pomposity and arrogance. She touched his head tenderly with her lips. His hair smelt clean, scented.

'I wonder if I'm missing something?' He sighed. 'I needed to tell you how I am. When we work together we'll become very close.' He looked up at her again, took her hands. She was unsettled by the thought she'd had before, that he manipulated her.

'But every time I think you value my friendship, every time we're intimate, you turn cold again,' she said. 'What do you expect me to do? For weeks you scarcely speak to me.'

'And yet as musician and dancer we're like twin souls. I've told you the truth – told you how I am. I'm not capable of love. Isn't that the most intimate thing anyone can admit? I wanted to tell you all that before we began our work. To ensure all is clear between us. We will never be lovers, except in the greatest sense – as artists.'

She heard footsteps outside. Someone broke into a run. A bicycle bell rang. Outside the world was ordinary. Inside, light glanced off the chandelier so rainbows danced over the white walls, oddly disturbed.

'The Netherlands is about to be invaded by our country. That's what we should be concerned about.'

He looked startled, then gave a bark of laughter.

'And if it is, will you run away, Hedda, as you did before?'

She pulled her hands away from his.

'There was little choice. The alternative was unthinkable.' She flushed with anger.

'Forgive me for provoking you, but you must understand – I've tried to tell you before. Hitler is a nonentity, as far as I'm concerned. I'm only interested in his vision for Germany as far as it serves my vision as a composer, no further. Let's not quarrel,' he pleaded. 'I'll show you around my apartment. Let's enjoy the rest of the afternoon together.'

The starlings swirled over the trees, filling the courtyard garden with their chattering. Hedda opened the window to let in the fresh air. Lights were on in the rooms across the courtyard. Small comfort – the warmth of other people close by. She shivered with cold despite the mild damp April evening, and closed the window again. Stiffly she went to the kitchen, boiled the kettle, and sat on her bed under a blanket, sipping tea and brandy. It was too late to visit the Hoffmans, or even telephone them. Hoping it might distract her from thoughts of Erik and the disturbing afternoon she'd spent with him, she reached for her notebook and pencil. She would attempt to write notes on the ballet she wanted to make with her students – work she was certain he'd have nothing to do with since Elise and Katje would most certainly take part – the cripple and the girl too heavy on her feet. She sat with the page open, pencil in her hand.

She sketched, from memory, the bureau bookcase in Erik's room – walnut wood with exquisitely intricate inlaid flowers in dark wood, ivory and gold – a magnificent piece of furniture. How expensive it must have been – more than she earned in a year. He'd inherited it from his aunt, he said. The entire room was beautiful, as she'd imagined it would be, not an object out of place. He'd encouraged her to look, but not to touch the bureau. I'll show you, he'd said, and slipping on silk gloves so as not to mark it, he opened it up.

There was its red velvet-lined interior, all those tiny drawers and shelves – empty, not a thing inside. He'd stood very close, touched her lips with his gloved fingers. For a moment she thought, he's big enough, strong enough to kill me, but he kissed her, before turning back to the bureau. She'd felt weak, hollowed out.

She scribbled out her sketch and wrote.

Erik, neither music nor dance, nor poetry, nor any lovely thing can stop human beings tearing each other apart. Your city of glass is a fantasy, your Utopia a sick dream. Art has no power beyond the moment. Kurt knew this when he made The Green Table. My ballet is never going to prevent war, he said – how can it? All it can do is express of the horror of war.

Art isn't dangerous. How can music change us, for better or worse? It's dictatorships that are dangerous – and Germany, my lost home.

She ripped the page from her notebook and screwed it up.

Invasion

Waking to the rumble of thunder, Katje wriggled onto her back and blinked her eyes open. She waited for another flash of lightning and the sound of a storm, but strangely it didn't even seem to be raining in the streets. She twitched back the curtain to let in the rosy light of early morning. It was almost six.

She was sure she could still hear the sound of rumbling, could feel the electric thrill of anticipation before a storm, and now it was impossible to go back to sleep. She got up, put on her coat over her nightdress and turned the bedroom doorknob with care. She carried her shoes as she made her way downstairs, and sat by the door to pull them on. Listening for the stirring of her parents upstairs, she pulled back the bolts, unlocked the door and stepped down into the street.

The bakery was opening, and a tram rattled by on Rozengracht. It was a beautiful May morning, the sun burning bronze through haze over the water.

A man in a long black coat came towards her across the bridge. He lurched from side to side as if drunk, so she tried to slip out of his way. Seeing her, he shouted out.

'They've landed. Dropped out of the sky like black angels. Do you hear me missy, do you understand? Deventer, Rotterdam, Utrecht, too many to stop.' There was a gleam in his eyes as he loomed up. 'I tell you black angels have landed to feed off our country like vermin.' He spat at the ground.

For a moment she was transfixed, seeing the ball of saliva spread into a wet patch on the stone. Then she looked up into his face.

'The Germans have invaded. By parachute!'

'How do you know?'

But already he had swung past her and away down the street.

Back in the house she galloped upstairs, two steps at a time, shouting to her family.

'Get up. Germany has invaded us. Soldiers have fallen from the sky in thousands – in parachutes. They've fallen into Utrecht, Rotterdam, Deventer. I told you it would happen. We are at war with Germany!'

Her mother appeared at the bedroom door, dazed and dishevelled.

'Stop shouting, Katje. Do you realise how early it is?'

'And do you realise that we are at war?'

Over the next few days her parents listened to the radio and waited for news. At school everyone talked about the invasion. Would the Dutch be able to defend their country? Not a chance, Katje's history teacher said.

Every morning Katje went straight to the window, looking out at the sky, waiting for a sign. On the fifth day she knew the world was coming to an end. It was eerie – that red glow. Hell has risen up through the earth, she thought. I won't be surprised to see black angels floating on the canal – and what then will Mama think? She'll reach for her crucifix and pray over the cooking.

She went out onto the landing and raised the sash window. There was an acrid smell in the air as if the clouds were burning. A crowd had gathered outside the little grocery store, and more people were crossing the canal to join them.

She tore up to Werner's room.

'Werner, can I come in? Have you seen the sky? It's so strange.' She listened, but there was no sound. 'Are you still asleep? You're so boring always hiding away on your own.' She pushed open the door.

His body was a hump of blankets turned to the wall. For a moment she thought he was dead and her heart jumped. Then the blankets twitched.

'You can't still be asleep on a morning like this. What's the matter? Why are you all covered up?' She stood looking down at him, perplexed. 'Why aren't you talking?' She sat down, squirmed round nestling into him like an animal with the crown of her head. 'Are you afraid we're losing the war? I am. I'm quite sure we have too. I can feel it in every one of my bones.' He didn't move. 'Speak to me Werner. I can't bear it if I don't know what's wrong. Is it your music practice again?'

His face emerged from the blankets, eyes swollen.

'Oh no.' She sat up, looking at him with tragic eyes. 'Surely you're not crying because we've lost the war?'

He rubbed his face and blinked.

'I haven't slept all night.'

'Has Papa been at you again? You really shouldn't take any notice of him. I don't.'

'No.'

'Then what? What?'

'You won't ever turn against me?' He mumbled into the blankets.

'Well why would I?'

'You don't know me,' he said in a voice so low she could scarcely catch what he said. 'You don't know my thoughts.'

'Well you don't know mine. You need a handkerchief.' She found one in the drawer and stuffed it into his hand. 'I promise I won't turn against you. But whatever you're crying about, it feels like the end of the world out there. I'm going out to look even if you're not.'

Katje couldn't stay at home with her mother who was weeping about the poor queen who'd had to flee the country. The fact was Rotterdam was in ruins, and the Netherlands had surrendered to Germany, and that was altogether a far worse tragedy than the queen moving to a palace in England. As she set off on her bicycle to visit Elise, there was the smell of burning in her nostrils, fragments of charred paper floated through the air like clouds of black blossom.

'Elise's in a really bad mood,' Marianne said. 'She was crying, and now she's in the garden pulling things up.'

What a funny time this is, Katje thought, with everybody lying around crying. Yet I don't feel sad at all, I feel more alive than ever.

She found Elise sitting on the grass, stabbing the earth with a trowel. She didn't look up when Katje called out. Katje squatted down beside her.

'Marianne said to come out to find you.'

Elise nodded without looking up. She gathered up the weeds she'd dug and threw them into a bucket. There was a box of seedlings beside her.

'What are you doing?'

'Planting things. Marianne grew them but she never bothers to plant them out. It's as if they don't matter once they've appeared.'

'Werner was crying this morning. Have you been crying too?'

Elise didn't answer. Katje tried to take an interest in the seedlings and help by taking them out of the box and lining them up on the grass.

'What's wrong?' she asked, when Elise sighed and put down the trowel.

'I'm scared – for Kai's friend, Benjamin, and for all the people in Rotterdam who were bombed, the children, the old people. It's terrible.'

'I suppose it is,' Katje said. She hadn't thought of it in that way before. 'What about the poor animals too, the dogs and cats and pet rabbits and things? And the animals on farms. They won't understand what's happening. They'll be so frightened. Perhaps it won't last for long and Hitler will get fed up with us Dutch.'

'I don't think so. Neither does Kai.'

'Maybe if we get up and dance it will help. That's what Miss Brandt would do. After all we can't give in and just go to sleep and die. We must dance for our life.'

Elise looked directly at her for the first time.

'You're very strange at times.'

Katje felt her face reddening. She bit her lip and looked down. An ant was struggling over the huge blades of grass.

'I'm sorry, but don't you understand?' Elise said. 'I don't want to scare you, but actually it's going to be awful for lots of people, and this is only the start.'

'Then maybe I should cry too,' Katje said. But she found she couldn't cry to order, despite all the suffering around her.

Katje was supposed to be shopping for groceries, but there was always much to watch in the city on a sunny morning. If she crouched down, the world was different from a cat's eye view – the boots and legs of a man who sat reading under the trees, and there the roots of the tree pushing up the paving slabs so they were all uneven and the café tables wobbled precariously. Sitting, bold as anything, with the crust of a pie in its tiny hands, was a rat. Nobody else had seen him. He must have sensed her watching and turned his bright eyes towards her. A dog trotted into view and in an instant the rat vanished. What would the world seem if you were an ant or a giant? The ant would never know or care whether Germany ruled the Netherlands or not. The giant could crush Hitler with one fall of his boot.

She stood up quickly and everything swam in front of her eyes then settled back to normal, and now she was aware of noise and commotion coming from the direction of Dam Square. How could she have missed it? It was curious how you could miss something so big just because you were paying attention to something small. The rhythm was fast and harsh like a machine, the sound of feet thudding the pavement, the swell of voices singing.

She crossed Rozengracht and slipped down a side street, following the roar of singing and cheering, across Kloviensburgwal, until she emerged onto the square where they gathered in front of the palace – rank upon rank of German soldiers in their grey uniforms. Oh goodness – she had never seen such crowds; members of the Dutch Nazi Party, the NSB, and ordinary people celebrating with flags and banners and the Nazi salute. Behind her people surged forward, pushing and nudging her, so she was swept along in the flow.

It was too difficult now to turn back against the crowds, but she could scarcely breathe, and she was scared. She pressed herself into the doorway of a shop and covered her eyes with her hands.

Oh Lord, I hope Elise hasn't come out in this. She'd be trampled on if she fell. It helped to think of Hedda's studio – a long empty room to turn and leap across, to reach her arms up to the ceiling, to stretch and slide and roll.

'Hey, girl! Wake up. Celebrate!'

A fat man prodded her. His mouth smelt of onions and beer.

'I don't see anything to be happy about,' she said, wiping his spit off her dress. 'Hitler marching in and taking over as if he owns us.'

He shoved her hard so she fell back against the wall.

'Watch what you say. You might regret it.'

He moved away, one arm saluting Hitler and Germany, and was swept along singing.

Winded, she tried to stand. She could still smell the earthy sweat of him. She trembled, on the edge of tears. Her head felt bruised where he'd pushed her. How dare he? How dare this stranger hurt her?

The crowds had thinned. She looked all around, unsure which way was safest. Through a gap between two shop fronts, she thought she saw her brother. Could it be? She kept losing and then finding him again – yes it was Werner.

In the lee of the buildings he was walking quickly, away from the action. He turned a corner and was lost for a moment. She stopped to release a stitch, then off again, following him along Kalverstraat and down a narrow lane to the Spui.

He had stopped to talk to a man who'd just emerged from the Begijnhof into the square. Katje hung back to watch. It seemed as if they'd met by chance, but when they turned and walked together, and she saw it was Herr Weiss, she knew it must be a planned meeting. She caught sight of Werner's face gazing at him before they went into Café Hoppe. It was more than a look of admiration. It was like the faces of the marble saints in church. She'd never seen Werner look that way before. She laughed, feeling sick in her stomach. It was ridiculous looking at Herr Weiss like that. She sat on a bench where she could watch the door of the café, willing Werner to come out alone, knowing that he wouldn't.

Herr Weiss had said it was important that Werner witness, at first hand, the gathering on Dam Square. There will only be one such day in the history of your country, he'd said, and I want you to be there. So Werner had left the house early to find a place to stand, across from the palace, by the doors of the Bijenkorf department store. The square had filled with people singing and chanting Heil Hitler, as they followed the German tanks. Werner, looking on with a sense of awe and wonder as the noise rose and fell, couldn't believe so many people had come out to welcome the Nazis, their plain faces radiant with hope and joy. He'd worried then that it would be impossible to reach the Spui in time to meet Herr Weiss, yet he'd been drawn towards him, instinctively, as if magnetised, until – surely it was a miracle – Weiss was there, emerging through the door at exactly the moment Werner reached it, greeting him with a little bow of his head, then taking his arm and leading him towards Café Hoppe. He didn't dare to mention that his parents didn't like him to go into bars. It would sound childish and ungrateful.

Herr Weiss led him to a dark corner at the back of the narrow bar, with a low window that looked out onto an alleyway and the bakery opposite. Werner had no idea why Herr Weiss had wanted to meet him, but now he felt quietness settle over him. Nothing mattered but this encounter. He felt more at peace than for a long time.

Herr Weiss drank red wine, and although it seemed early in the morning and he didn't care for the taste of wine, Werner agreed to join him. It was an auspicious day that should be marked.

'Change is not necessarily a bad thing,' Weiss said, as he raised his glass to his mouth. He took a couple of sips, then neatly dabbed his lips with his forefinger. 'They will try to tell you otherwise, but believe me, there will be great opportunities before long. It's not that I wholeheartedly concur with Nazi ideology, but it's time the old ways were shaken up, and the dead wood eliminated.'

The back of his head was reflected in a stained mirror on the wall behind him. Their knees touched under the table. Werner drew back, but Weiss put his hand on his thigh. His pupils catching the light, gleamed with intensity. Werner could smell the starched cotton of his shirt. Herr Weiss talked, his voice low and urgent.

'I prophesied all this long ago and I've been preparing. I want to be remembered as one of the great composers of our time. I very rarely tell anyone that, Werner, but I know I can trust you. It goes beyond Nazism – the Nazis are just the heralds of something much greater.' He smiled. 'Yes. I can see you understand.

'In practical terms there will be a new ministry for the arts under German Occupation, with specific rules, and I will play along with them. Nothing will stand in my way. I don't have to agree with everything they stand for, indeed I don't, but that's irrelevant.'

He glanced around the bar, drained his glass, and poured himself another.

'You and I are different from other people. I saw something special in you from the moment we met, and it was confirmed when I heard you play. Let's say I recognised you.' He gave a perfunctory smile. 'I'm working day and night on a new composition. I envisage an immense choir of movement and voice, the organ, a full orchestra, layers and textures of sound. It's essential – our meeting today. I need to explain my ideas to the few people I know will understand. I need the right encouragement for them to take root and grow. You do understand, Werner? You won't let me down.'

Werner tried to express the admiration he felt in the look he returned Herr Weiss. He answered, his voice full of gravitas.

'I do understand, sir. I hope I'll never disappoint you.'

Weiss reached across the table and took his hands, holding them in his own and looking Werner straight in the eye.

'My dear boy,' he said, with tenderness that made Werner's heart ache.

Hedda dreamed she stood on the tree platform as a sheet of fire rushed through the leaves. It was the platform she and Gitta had built as children, high in the branches of the chestnut tree, with a pulley to carry their basket of dolls up and down. Kurt stood on the lawn below, but she was afraid to jump. It can't be helped, he said, looking to where she clung.

She woke in terror, and in the grey light of dawn she sat on the edge of her bed hugging her knees.

No news from Kurt for a long time – they had written every few months until Britain declared war on Germany.

Now he'd be interned in England as an enemy alien, unable to work as a choreographer any longer. Poor Kurt. He'd escaped a dangerous situation, only for it to catch up with him later.

She washed her face in cold water, dressed, and ate toast and jam with tea, though she had little appetite. With the Netherlands under German Occupation, how long will it be before I'm unable to work without Nazi interference, she wondered? Will my choreography be dismissed as alien or degenerate? My work is my life. I must keep working as long as I possibly can.

She pressed her palms to the window feeling the cold glass against her forehead, as she watched her neighbours, two elderly and beautifully dressed Jewish sisters, on their way to the bakery. Whatever I'm threatened with I won't give up teaching my Jewish students, she thought, with a flare of rage.

She cycled to the studio early. She had a rehearsal with Erik at ten and looked forward to the distraction of work, but it appeared that Erik, scrupulous about time-keeping as he usually was, had forgotten to come. Or perhaps he was sick? Should she telephone him? She went into her office, began to dial his number, and changed her mind. She made coffee, sorted through papers to file and put them down again. She picked up a duster and wiped it over the desk and windowsill, pausing to look out at the barges and houseboats on the river – a fine sunny day, the shadows of clouds on the water. The morning passed. Half-heartedly she made notes for the ballet she planned with her senior students.

After lunch she went into the studio and warmed up, marked through a sequence. Step, turn, extend, pause, fall, run, tilt – so good to move, to forget everything else – to run with long strides, leaning into the angles of the room, spinning, leaping.

Erik, holding his music case and a bunch of yellow wallflowers, was standing in the doorway. She stopped, reaching for her shawl from the barre.

'I'm so sorry, I got caught up in events in the city,' he said, neglecting to remove his outdoor shoes and walking across the studio.

'What events?'

'They've come out in their masses to greet the enemy.'

'Then everyone has taken leave of their senses.'

He handed Hedda the flowers. She didn't take them.

'Where did you get them? Picked from some person's window box?'

'Don't be angry with me, Hedda,' he said, putting the flowers down on top of the piano and smiling in his attempt to placate her. 'I encountered one of my students. He was in some distress. I felt obliged to calm him down.'

He smelt of drink.

'It doesn't matter,' Hedda said stiffly. 'I've kept busy with work all morning.'

'I brought pastries too. Pear and almond. They're on the desk.' He smiled again. 'Your favourite.'

'Oh for goodness sake, Erik, stop creeping round me. I suppose we'd better go and eat your peace offering so I can recover my temper.'

They sat in her office. She made more coffee. She realised she was hungry, and didn't speak until she'd eaten.

'Truly delicious,' she said, picking up the crumbs with her fingertips, and looking at him directly for the first time. 'I'm glad to see you actually. It felt so bleak here, alone. I didn't know what to do with myself.'

'Yet I find you working.'

'Not very successfully.'

'If ever we missed Germany, our country has caught up with us. But besides that, for me it's a great day. I completed the first section, a sonata, of my new work last night. May I play it for you?'

'I'd be delighted.'

Hedda sat on the floor of the studio, her back against the wall.

'Is there a title?'

'The first sonata is called Anthem for a Dying Age. The second will be called New Dawn.' He opened his case and took out the score. 'The third is untitled as yet, and then I shall need an over-arching title. I'm arranging them all for full orchestra as well as for piano and organ. It enables more flexibility.'

She was aware of his sense of gravitas as he placed his music on the piano and adjusted the stool. He sat down, his hands poised over the keys as if he'd frozen mid-thought.

She closed her eyes and hoped she'd put him at ease. He began to play, single notes with long pauses, followed by a sequence of loud descending chords in a minor key.

She imagined his city of steel and glass – the sounds created a kind of architectural structure. How would a choreographer work with it – vast choirs of dancers, slow moving, like Greek drama? Or a solo dancer? Perhaps that would work theatrically, small gestures, pauses – discordant with the grandeur and pomposity of the sound.

The music segued into a clever pastiche of ballet music of the Romantic Period – she could almost hear the entrance of The Queen of the Wilis, followed by echoes of other German composers, before returning to an elaborated repetition of the opening section.

It was odd, disappointing even. It scarcely hung together. She opened her eyes.

'Now you've heard me play, you must dance. I need to see how it will be danced.'

He spoke with urgency. What could she do? She got to her feet and paced round the studio, hoping for some impulse to take her in any direction, as he started to play again. 'It's possible to dance to anything if you let yourself go,' her first ballet teacher had said.

She found, and held angular tortured positions, moving slowly through the chords. In the pastiche section she danced fragments of enchainments from Giselle, she'd learnt so many years ago, linking them with light running steps in the manner of Isadora Duncan. It was all as inconsequential as the music itself. She had to get through it somehow.

She stood in the centre of the room when it was over, waiting for him to say something. He sat with his head in his hands. Lord, was it that bad, she wondered? Well, she'd done her best. He stood up and gazed at her across the room. Surely he hadn't shed tears? He had been drinking. He opened his arms as he crossed the room to her. She took a step backwards.

'You understood so well,' he said, his voice quavering with emotion. 'You felt the music with your whole body, the grandeur and majesty of it. Oh Hedda, I look forward to a great collaboration with this piece. We must begin working immediately.'

'Immediately?' She was so taken aback that she laughed.

'What's the matter? Don't you agree?'

'I'm glad you liked what I did.' She picked up her shawl and wrapped it round her shoulders. Her body ached. She'd danced hard.

'If we're to make something together,' she said, 'I think we need to find a mutual starting point, the way we used to when we improvised. It's as if you've imposed the theme this time, and I'm just commissioned to make something of it.'

'Is that a problem? You commissioned me to play for your every concert, and even complained the one time I altered the speed.'

She looked at him in amazement. Surely he wasn't still upset about that?

'There's a world of difference, Erik, between being my accompanist, and collaborating to create a ballet together,

98

as surely you know? If you're talking about commissioning me to interpret your sonata in dance, then I'm not sure I'm the right person.'

He looked shocked. His face flushed. He walked back to the piano. She followed him.

'Why?' he asked. 'I've just given you my verdict on your interpretation.'

'Your piece is very original,' she said, searching for ways to be kind. 'I'm just not sure that it's music for dance, or not dance that I feel I want to choreograph. Perhaps we can spend some time working more freely together, to see what emerges, before fixing anything so definite.'

'You're dismissing the whole of my work?'

'Of course not. You know I respect your work immensely. Anyway, whatever we do, it will have to wait, I have my ballet with the students to prepare over the next few weeks, and I'm not sure your music is quite right for what I have in mind.'

'No, indeed, I don't want your students to have anything to do with it.' He closed the lid of the piano. 'Don't dissemble. I see you don't like my composition.'

'You're misunderstanding me. You're not listening. Perhaps I need to hear it again.'

He picked up his score. He didn't look at her.

'Please Erik, be reasonable. Don't take offence.'

'I expected more of you. I can't believe you disregard me so.'

She didn't follow him out of the studio. She could see there was no point. He was exhausted, overwrought, and he'd drunk too much. It unsettled her, though she couldn't see what else she could have done.

Katje had given up waiting for Werner, and had wandered off thinking she would visit Elise. But she found nobody at home. She sat on the edge of the pond in the park. She supposed she should start to walk back or there'd be trouble. She could hear the uneasy crowds in the distance. She got up, still dazed, and wandered in the direction of home.

'Is Werner back?' Katje called to her mother, who was sorting the groceries in the kitchen.

'He came in just before you. He's gone up to do his homework.'

Oh goodness, he's always working, she thought, or brooding about something. But at least he was back from his meeting with Herr Weiss. She didn't say anything to her mother. She'd be sure to tell her father and then there'd be trouble. She scampered past the kitchen door and on upstairs.

She tapped on Werner's door and went straight in. He was sitting on the floor writing.

'What do you want?' he asked. 'You made me jump.' He didn't look up, so she sat down beside him. He sounded so grumpy she didn't tease him by pulling the paper out of his hands.

'I want to talk.'

'What about?'

'Today. Everything.'

He turned a little away from her.

'I haven't got anything to say about today.'

She shuffled closer, nudging him.

'Just leave me alone. Please.'

She tickled him, but he pushed her away.

'Stop it. I'm trying to write.'

'Listen, I had a horrible time. I was shopping and I got caught in all those flag waving crowds.'

'So? You're still alive. What's the problem?' Werner stood up and walked away from her. She got up and followed him.

'I saw you and I tried to catch up with you but you were with Herr Weiss. What were you doing there with him, going into a bar together?'

'It's none of your business. Now get out.'

'Not until you tell me.'

Werner turned on her. She rooted herself to the spot. He put down the page and manoeuvred her by her shoulders towards the door. She tried to pull out of his grasp, but he pushed her so forcefully that she lost her balance and crashed into the low beam. She crumpled, clutching the side of her head.

'I'm sorry,' he muttered. 'I didn't mean to push you. But you were making me mad.' He knelt on the floor beside her. 'Are you all right?'

Pain made her giddy with shock. She looked at his hand resting beside her – that hand she had known all her life with its long sensitive fingers and prominent knuckles.

'Are you in love with Herr Weiss or something?'

He recoiled, stared at the floor, rigid.

'You are!'

Still he neither moved nor spoke.

'How can you love a person like him? He's horrible. You should see how he looks at people in class, as if he hates them. And he makes you so serious and miserable.'

Werner got to his feet, picked up a book and opened it. His actions were slow, deliberate. She began to cry.

'Talk to me!'

When he looked up it was into space, not at her. It was as if she wasn't there in the room.

At the Hoffmans'

Julia Hoffman invited Katje's family for tea. She was keen to meet them, she said, since Katje had come into their lives. Werner didn't want to go but there was no getting out of it.

'You'll love them, Werner,' Katje told him as they drove over. 'They're so different from us, thank goodness. You'll see what I mean soon.'

He sat in the window seat of the Hoffmans' living room. She was right, they were different. They were so pleased with themselves, and now Katje was gabbling nonsense, and whispering and laughing as if she belonged with them all.

Everything seemed pointless. What were they all doing sitting in that hot room with its old worn furniture and untidy shelves of books? Why had they been invited to peer into this smug little world? Didn't everyone realise a new order was about to be born that would smash their world to pieces?

His mother sat with a reserved smile, nodding in response to effusive Julia Hoffman with her wild curly hair and gummy smile. His father was talking in a self-important voice about his business and how he may well have to amalgamate with a German company in due course and how that would bring new opportunities. German occupation might have its advantages after all, and they may well come out better in the end. Werner could tell Dr Hoffman found this distasteful. Well it was all very well being a privileged doctor. Hoffman could afford to have principles. He didn't have to make his way in the world – there were always sick people in abundance for him to tend. Then there was the crippled girl, and a child with a fat face and brown pigtails, and finally Kai. He hoped that Kai, a fellow musician, would continue to ignore him. Whilst this was galling, it would be worse to have well-meaning attention turned in his direction.

He moved closer to the window and sat looking out at the crows in the trees.

'What's your favourite colour?' Marianne asked as she sat down next to him. She had a box of crayons.

'Blue.'

'What's your favourite animal?'

'A wolf.'

Resting a pad of paper on her knee she began drawing, singing under her breath.

'There.' She showed him the picture of a wolf shaded in light and dark blue. 'Now you draw me something.'

'I can't draw.'

'I don't mind.'

She was as persistent as Katje. She leant her small warm body against him, watching as he took the pad of paper and a red crayon and began the outline of a horse. She smelt of biscuits. Perhaps it would be all right if he could stay with this little girl until it was time to leave. He flushed with shame at the horrible things he'd thought about everyone earlier. His misery turned everything ugly.

He heard his father's voice, raised, and then Kai.

'Oh dear,' Marianne said. 'Your papa and Kai are arguing.'

He concentrated on his drawing, hardly daring to look up.

'How can you believe that?' Kai was shouting. 'Why don't you look at what's going on in front of you? Or are you like the rest of them, keeping quiet whilst you're lining your own pockets at the expense of the Jews?'

His father's face flushed with a stupid smile as he tried to splutter out his defence.

'Why do you think so many got out of Germany?' Kai continued. 'For a holiday?'

Julia was telling Kai to calm down, and apologising, and his father was saying it didn't matter.

'Young men are entitled to opinions. We were all young once.'

Katje was sitting rigid, studying her hands. Werner had to get away. He asked Marianne where the toilet was.

'I'll show you.'

'No, just tell me, I'll find it.'

Marianne told him there was a toilet downstairs in the hall, but a bigger bathroom upstairs that was much smarter, so that's where he went, intending to stay away for as long as possible. I feel a little sick, he would tell them, if it seemed he'd been away too long, though they were probably too caught up to notice.

He took time washing his hands, letting the bubbles of soap form between his fingers, then plunging them into the warm water again, swilling it up his wrists till his sleeves were drenched. He heard the front door bell and now someone else had arrived, and there were merry voices from the drawing room, so everything must have been smoothed over. I wish I were sitting with Herr Weiss far away from them all. He would understand how I feel.

The sound of gypsy dance music sounded from the living room, followed by laughter. He knew he must have been missed by now, and that if he stayed longer his sister would take it into her head to search for him. He tried to dry his shirtsleeves with a towel, unlocked the door and went down.

The woman who'd just arrived was sitting on the sofa with her back to the door as he opened it. He hoped to slip in unnoticed as they watched Kai play, but his sister turned and smiled and came over to him.

'Oh Werner are you all right?' she whispered. 'Never mind, you're back now.' She waited until Kai finished and everyone had applauded. 'Come and meet my dancing teacher.' She tapped the woman on the shoulder. 'Miss Brandt, this is my brother, Werner.'

'I've heard a lot of good things about you,' Hedda said, twisting round to greet him. 'I've heard from my colleague, Erik Weiss, that you're a most talented pianist. It's nice to meet you, Werner.'

Disarmed by her kindness and interest, he sat beside her. He couldn't bring himself to ask what Herr Weiss had said, though he longed to hear.

'Werner must play the piano for us now,' Julia Hoffman said, and everyone turned to look at him.

He felt his cheeks grow hot. He looked down at the carpet.

'Come along, what do you think I pay for all those lessons for?' his father boomed.

'Yes come on, you must,' Marianne clapped her hands, and echoed her mother's voice. 'We know how good you are because Katje's told us.'

'But I haven't brought music,' he mumbled. 'I can't remember anything well enough without music.'

'We have music here.' Mrs Hoffman opened a cupboard behind the piano. 'Do you have a favourite composer?'

If he closed his eyes the room and all the people in it might disappear. He felt the lightest touch on the back of his hand. Hedda turned towards him, blocking off the others.

'Would you really rather not play?' she asked.

He looked at her with desperation.

'Leave Werner to think about it,' she said, standing up. 'I'm a pathetic pianist, so I'll go first to get it done with, if Kai you could play, I can improvise along with you'

Werner watched Hedda as she skilfully directed attention away from him. She took a sip from her glass of wine, and stood by the piano.

'I'm going to choreograph a new ballet. I'd like you and Katje to dance in it,' she said looking at Elise. 'I need some musical ideas to get started.'

'Us dance!' Katje said. 'Oh brilliant. Where, when?'

'In July, in the Rozentheater. This is where I am with my ideas so far, just fragments – I see my dancers – that's all of your class – sitting on stage on chairs – isolated from each other. Your movements are repetitive, ritualised. You're waiting for something to redeem you. Then there is music and everyone comes to life.' She played a few notes with one hand. 'I'm hopeless. I can hear it in my mind, almost feel it in my body, but I can't play it on the wretched piano.'

'It's not the fault of the piano,' Kai said, teasing her.

He picked up his violin, and Katje sprang up from her seat and whirled about, and Werner's father watched, smiling with approval. It was all so embarrassing Werner couldn't bear to look. He felt his skin prickle with heat.

Julia took her place at the piano, and Hedda returned to sit beside him. She smiled.

'I thought they were rather bullying you,' she said. 'You must ignore them – lovely people but they can be overwhelming.'

Frozen, he couldn't smile in response.

Rehearsal

May 1940, sitting outside Café t'Smalle, sunshine on the water.
Note for ballet – untitled.
Students – eight from senior class + six from elementary.
Professional dancers (Gonne and Mischa Klein)
Music – Kai Hoffman + soprano (to commission)
Note 1. Three dances of oppression and release. Bound/flow,
stillness/quick movement, grounded/elevated. Use of chairs?
Note 2. Dancers bound in white silk sheet. When unbound,
fabric forms angelic figure, animated by dancers.
Note 3. Love duet, dancers separated by fabric, pushing
against it in attempt to reach each other – no physical contact
until the end.

June 1940. France has fallen and Britain stands alone now. If
Britain is conquered it will be the end of civilisation – those are
Kai's words. The Hoffmans are inclined to think the worst.
First week of rehearsal.

Hedda's bicycle had a puncture. She sheltered under the
trees as the rain pooled around her, sliding from the leaves,
and bouncing off the surface of the river. Kai's gypsy
rhythms still played in her head after last night's rehearsal,
and she smiled, thinking of Katje's solo with the chair –
Katje peering from underneath it with her droll expression
– and how she danced with such verve and joy. Hedda
always relished the first weeks of rehearsal, before pre-
production stress, seeing the work take form – her sense of
vitality and purpose, the days when she could think of little
else.

The rain ceased, and as she neared the studio, she saw
Werner de Jong come down the steps, music under his arm,
and turn in her direction. He didn't see her at first. As he
walked towards her, she thought how beautiful he is – that

exquisite ephemeral beauty, on the cusp between boyhood and man. He's so unlike his brash, self-important father with his opinions.

'Good-morning Werner. Have you had a good lesson?'

The boy's anxious face softened as he recognised her.

'Yes, thank you.' He smiled, then looked down at the ground.

She would have asked more, but his shyness made her hesitate, and he walked on before she could speak.

Hedda arrived in the office and put down her bag. She had barely time to hang her coat up to dry, when she heard the studio door open. Erik Weiss entered the room without knocking.

'Oh you made me jump. I thought you were downstairs teaching.'

He didn't answer. His expression was blank. He appeared to look right through her.

'What on earth's the matter, Erik? You look as if you're in shock. Do sit down.'

She was discomfited, then irritated at his silence, the way he stood rigid, without explaining himself. She took the water jug to fill it at the tap. When she returned he was still standing. She poured the water into the kettle, and turned to him. He wouldn't look at her. She put her hand on his arm.

'Please tell me what's wrong.'

He brushed her away.

'I've been usurped by that gypsy fiddler,' he said.

'What do you mean?'

'Werner de Jong happened to tell me in passing, unaware I didn't know. I suffered the humiliation of asking him to explain what he was talking about.'

'Erik, what are you trying to say? You're surely not upset that Kai Hoffman is playing for my new work?'

He stood tight-lipped, staring at the wall.

'You were very clear you didn't want anything to do with it.'

'To the contrary, you were adamant you couldn't work with my sonata.'

'Adamant is too strong a word.' She tried to speak clearly as if to a troubled child. 'I recall telling you I needed to think about it, I had ideas already for my present piece, and your music wasn't appropriate.'

'You are wrong and misguided to employ Hoffman. I trusted you.'

'But surely this isn't about trust or lack of it. It's an artistic decision. You of all people should understand that. I have trusted you too – on artistic matters above all.'

'I saw a great partnership between us, but you have toyed with me.'

'No. Believe me, Erik. I've respected you and valued every moment we've spent working together.'

'Yet you treat me with contempt.'

'Contempt. What are you talking about? This is a relatively unimportant matter – a festival of new dance work involving my students. You and I have a season of concerts this autumn, if we agree to take it on. We work very well together, as you've often said. You're completely over-reacting.'

'You have betrayed my trust,' he said, with more force.

'I'm very sorry you see it like this. It was never intended. I'd never hurt you deliberately,' she said gently.

He turned to look at her, his expression so cold that she felt the blood drain from her. He can't have been drinking at this time in the morning?

'Oh, I see,' she said, 'There's no point in talking. I think you should go. Believe me I'd never upset you intentionally. We'll talk another time.'

He didn't move. He stood barring the door, repeating how he'd been humiliated and betrayed.

'For goodness sake, Erik, stop this. Now.'

The expression on his face frightened her. Nobody else was in the studio; nobody was scheduled to arrive for another half hour. She was trapped in her office.

'If you want the truth, I hated your work. There's no way I'd ever want to dance to it. It's nothing but sentimental schmaltz, when it actually gets going. The Nazis will lap it up, you can be sure of that. Is that what you want? Is it?'

He'd gone. After a moment she heard the street door close. Turning to the window she saw him charging towards the swing bridge, and away.

She collapsed over the desk, shaking.

'What have I done? Oh God, what have I done?'

After teaching her little ones without an accompanist, Hedda went for the first rehearsal in the theatre. Entering the auditorium she discovered her students lying on the stage pretending to warm up as they watched Kai.

'Who am I?' he said. He strutted up and down with his chest stuck out like a cockerel and his heels striking the floor.

'You could be any old Nazi,' Elise answered.

'Right, which one? Here's a clue.' He jerked his arms and head as if he'd been electrocuted.

'You just look ridiculous!'

'Commissar Seyss-Inquart, Hitler's puppet!' He dangled as if from a noose. 'Hitler's puppet, strung up, it'll happen to him one day, sooner or later.'

Hedda strode up the steps onto the stage.

'Stop immediately,' she shouted. 'You should be warming up. Kai what do you think you're playing at? Do you imagine you're invincible?'

Shocked by her rage, he stopped abruptly, and turned away without a word.

And now I've offended another musician, she thought with irritation. But she saw he was sitting in the wings with his violin, playing quietly.

'We're going to walk through the first scene – chairs. Find your places, please.'

The girls scampered up, silent and obedient, exchanging glances with each other.

At the end of the rehearsal, Hedda dismissed everyone, and sat on the edge of the stage to write her notes for the next day. Her head ached. She was unable to shake off the thought that, regardless of how much he'd provoked her, she'd wounded Erik terribly. What was she to do to make amends – write to him, or just leave it and wait? They had their concerts to consider. Such temperament was irksome. Weary and dispirited, she gathered her notes into her bag, put on her outside shoes and made her way to the stage door.

The sun had come out whilst she'd been working, and she blinked in the sudden light. Kai was sitting against the wall beside the door, his violin at his feet, so she nearly fell over him.

'Hello, you're still here.'

He scrambled up.

'I wanted to apologise for earlier.'

'Really, it was nothing.'

'I was unprofessional. Sometimes everything gets to me and I act stupidly.'

'But I shouldn't have shouted at you, especially in front of the students.'

They stood awkwardly a moment, before walking towards the main street. Hedda was aware he wanted to say more, but a tram rattled by and he waited until the noise had passed.

'You seemed unhappy in rehearsal. I didn't want you to have to walk home alone.'

'That's very sweet of you. It's been a difficult day.'

111

It was a mild evening. They walked down Prinsengracht to Egelantiersgracht. The tables and chairs were out in front of the Café t'Smalle now the rain had cleared.

'Shall we stop for a beer?'

'Oh that would be most welcome.'

They sat down by the water, and watched the waiter wiping rain from the tables and chairs, and a scruffy grey dog gnawing a bone in the gutter. Now the rain had stopped the canal was deep green and gold and silver, and smelt of the sea. You can look at the surface of water where the leaves and scum float, or at the rippling reflections, but never down to the bottom, Hedda thought, as she gazed into the water.

Kai waved at a man passing on a bicycle.

'Someone I know from university,' he explained. He took a long drink. 'Ah, beer! It was a good rehearsal. Were you pleased?'

'Yes, I suppose it was in the end. I'm afraid I had a difficult time earlier, with my accompanist.'

'Erik Weiss?'

'Yes. Do you know him?'

'I've met him once or twice, and I hear about him. He's quite well known as a pianist. He teaches in Utrecht a few weeks every semester. Elise told me he played for you. Difficult man to work with, I imagine.'

He pulled a face that made her smile. She couldn't tell him about Erik's jealousy, but she found herself talking about his composition.

'To be honest, I didn't like his work, but I shouldn't have lost my temper like that. He scared me though, and now I'm afraid I've hurt him very badly.'

'He shouldn't be so ridiculously sensitive.'

'No – but sometimes we are, about our work, don't you think? It's like a personal affront isn't it, when someone doesn't like it?'

He shrugged.

'I don't feel like that myself. If people don't like my work, well too bad. I won't die over it.'

She laughed. The memory of Erik standing by the door, his cold blank expression, stopped her short.

'There's something about Erik Weiss. I always end up feeling sorry for him, regardless of how difficult he's been. I suppose it's inevitable when we've worked together so closely. He can be so arrogant and pompous, but there's this pitiful little boy in him, and I find myself falling for him every time.'

'You should dismiss him,' Kai said, surprising her with his vehemence.

'What makes you say that?'

'He's not good for you.' He leant towards her, elbows on the table, hands clasped round his beer glass. 'Dismiss him and work with me. I'll treat you with respect.'

'Oh Kai. I'm sure you would. But I can't just abandon the man. We've concerts lined up for the autumn. It's not only that – we're friends. At least I thought we were friends. We're work colleagues anyway.'

She sat back and took a long drink of beer.

'He's like this with his students, the ones who aren't his favourites. He's destructive.'

'Destructive?' She was flooded by a sense of desolation. She put her glass down on the table, carefully so he wouldn't see her hands shaking.

'Hedda, are you all right?'

His voice was distant and she thought she was going to pass out. A chair scraped on the paving slabs, a woman's laughter – sounds coming towards her again. Kai's hand on her arm. She moved away, not wanting to be touched.

'I'm just very tired,' she said. 'It's hit me harder than I thought.'

'I'll walk you home.'

They walked in silence until they reached the door. She took her key from her bag. When she turned to say goodbye, she saw he was reluctant to leave her.

'I wanted to say how much I love your work,' he said. 'The movements aren't like any ballet I've seen before – quirky, I suppose, even a bit grotesque, but funny and tender too. I'm ever so glad to be part of it, Hedda. I can't wait to see what it's like in costume, with the set.'

'Thank you. It's a pleasure working with you.'

Still he stood beside her as she turned the key and opened the door.

'But particularly the way you've created Elise's part. You've made her so beautiful you forget she can't walk easily. I've told my parents. They can't wait to see.'

'Elise just is beautiful.'

'Till tomorrow then.' In a rush he embraced her and walked away.

Performance

Katje stood alone on the stage. Dress rehearsal over, the other dancers had run back to the changing room. Dazzled by the glowing warmth of the footlights she looked up into the vast fly-tower. Silver dust motes floated round her. It was like being a small child again – the times when she had made a whole world out of sheets draped over a table, with the torchlight shining amongst the folds of fabric. The theatre made real the magic. She flapped her arms and ran and leapt a circuit of the stage.

'Katje, can you make your way backstage this instant,' Hedda shouted from the gloom of the auditorium.

'I'm just off.' She peered out. 'I can hardly see anything. Where are you, out there in the dark?'

'I'm here.' Hedda stepped up. 'No more excitement now. You need energy to dance. Off you go, my angel.'

'I'll dance as if my life depends on it.'

But it was essential not to get carried away. Miss Brandt shouted with impatience when she let her imagination run away.

'Concentrate, Katje, otherwise I won't have you in the company.'

Every gesture had meaning. In performance it became clear to Katje for the first time. Her focus was divided. She turned, twisted, lunged and jumped, remembering to dance exactly as Miss Brandt had rehearsed it, but at the same time, she ran through streets of immense buildings, darting away from the marching of soldiers coming nearer. The Puppet Master loomed up and she cowered, oppressed by his brutality and dominance. When Kai walked onstage and his music soared through her, she danced with joy. Knowing she was watched, it was as if, for a moment, she stood outside herself, watching too.

She heard the applause, and, giddy with happiness, she laughed as roses fell from the fly-tower and littered the stage. She wanted to shout and jump. The curtain rose and fell for the final time.

'Well done Katarina.' Kai stood behind her. She spun round and hugged him. Immediately she wished she hadn't. Already he had turned to speak to someone else.

She needed to be on her own. Overwhelmed, she ran behind the cyclorama and down metal steps, to a room that smelt of drains, where rails of costumes were stored. Crouched on the floor between two wicker trunks, she burst into tears. Oh the wonder and complexity of everything. It was impossible to go up and meet everyone when she felt like this.

After a while she dried her eyes and looked around the room. A mask of a donkey hung on the wall, gazing down at her, one ear flopped over. It looked so sad and comical. She was already feeling better, and contemplating who might have danced the donkey role, when the door opened. She heard the sound of heels striking the concrete floor.

'Katje! Oh dear. Someone said they thought you were here.' Hedda stood beside her.

'I was having a little cry.'

'I sometimes feel like hiding away and crying too,' Hedda said, crouching down beside her.

'Tonight, dancing, it's the best thing that's ever happened to me.'

'So good that you must cry about it.' She patted her leg. 'I've felt the same sometimes.'

'You have?'

'Oh yes.'

'It was as if I could hear and see and feel everything at once, and for the first time ever I understood, but now I've forgotten what it was I understood. I've forgotten.'

'I know, I know. Perhaps when everything is quiet and you're in bed remembering this night…but now you must come upstairs. Your parents will be waiting to see you.'

'Oh you look so beautiful,' Katje said. Hedda was wearing a dark blue evening gown; a red rose in her hair. 'And your lovely clothes! You shouldn't be sitting on the floor, you'll get dirty.'

Hedda smiled.

'Yes, for once you're telling me what to do. Now are you going to dry your eyes and come and get changed?' Hedda got up, smoothed out her dress, and put out her hand to Katje. 'You danced beautifully tonight. Come on now.' She pulled Katje to her feet, and led her back up the metal stairs to the stage.

A boy had just finished sweeping, the lights were low, the auditorium in darkness. Nobody else was around.

'Go on up to your dressing room,' Hedda said. 'Leave your cloak here, and the rest of your costume on the rail upstairs. I'll follow you in a moment.'

When Katje had gone, she checked the chairs were stacked in the wings, all the costumes hanging on the rail, nothing torn or damaged, the silk laid out ready for ironing tomorrow. Satisfied, she paced to the centre of the stage and gazed out into the darkness.

Time was nothing. It seemed so recently that she'd sat next to Kurt with the dance company in the bar of the American Hotel, all of them giddy and wild after the performance – the night they'd laughed at everything and anything, and later Kurt had walked her back to her lodgings on Willemsparkweg.

She walked with small deliberate steps down to the edge of the orchestra pit. There was something about an empty theatre; the air seemed still to ring with music, the rustle of satin, static friction of fur. Absorbed by the sense that her whole body was dissolving into the darkness, she floated through the walls of the theatre, into the summer night, back into her past – September 1933, walking through the park with Kurt.

Someone was watching her.

'Who's there?' She turned and stared into the wings.

No answer.

She couldn't explain the terror that made her rush from the stage – there was nothing, nobody. I am a fool, she thought, as she reached her dressing room, jinxed by my own mind. She paused to calm her heart, tidy her hair, and put on lipstick, and then gathering up her bouquet of roses, she left to join the others in the bar.

Katje sat at a table with her fellow dancers, amidst the press of people – parents and friends. The girls were eating ice creams. Kai drew up a chair and sat beside her.

'Great dancing, Katje.'

She beamed at him, and put down the spoonful of ice cream she was about to put in her mouth.

'Did you ever think you could dance like that?'

'Oh yes. I was sure, in one way. But in another way dancing in a real theatre is different from anything.'

She wanted to tell him how she felt transformed by it, how for a moment she seemed to understand everything. It began with dancing – with the exhilarating sensation in the body that carried her away, that made her want to laugh for joy, then that blinding realisation. The words choked her, and they both laughed.

'It's changed my life. I feel grown up now, Kai. Do you think perhaps dancing can change the world? If everyone danced there could be no Nazi Occupation. Everyone would just be too happy.'

He'd stopped listening. She followed his gaze to where Hedda, carrying a bouquet of white roses, was weaving through the groups of people, stopping to smile, and shake hands with parents, stooping to speak to a small child. She saw Hedda catch sight of someone, a look of surprise and gladness in her face. Herr Weiss was standing alone in the corner of the room looking straight at her. She began to move towards him, then stopped short. There was no recognition or warmth in his expression. As if he hadn't seen her, he turned and left the room.

The Review

The telephone call came at eight the next morning. Hedda was summoned for a meeting at the theatre in an hour. No further explanation.

The call had come too early for comfort. The assistant director had been perfunctory, offering no explanation. It could be anything, a triviality. It hadn't felt like that. She dressed in a dark blue suit, and hat, was careful with her makeup, and drank a cup of black coffee. She couldn't eat.

Dr Hoffman would be up early. She telephoned him so that somebody at least would know where she was.

'It was a wonderful evening, Hedda. It will be some triviality they want to discuss.'

She knew by his hesitation and the tone of his voice that he didn't believe this. Neither spoke for a moment.

'Julia and I will walk up to the theatre to meet you,' he said.

'No. I'm probably over-reacting. I'd better go and get it over with, whatever it is. Thank you Marten.'

'Come straight here afterwards,' he said. 'Come for lunch.'

The main theatre was still closed. She was told to wait at the stage door. The assistant director, a man who'd shown her friendly interest whenever they'd met before, was called down to escort her upstairs. He seemed nervous, and kept brushing his hair from his forehead. When they reached the director's office, he hesitated.

'I'm really sorry, Miss Brandt.' He avoided her eye. 'It's probably only a formality. Try to keep calm.'

'I've no intention of being anything other than calm.' She spoke sharply. She didn't need his sympathy.

The office, a long room at the top of the building, was large, untidy, and airless. Morning sunlight slanted through the diamonds of stained glass, in bands of yellow and blue, across the walls, and the long table. Van Nooten, the director, sat at one end of the table, and on one side; a man in his mid-forties with yellowish skin stretched over sunken cheeks, and a sweep of thin hair over his baldpate. He wore a Nazi NSB badge on his lapel. Behind him was a poster of Alicia Markova as Giselle, rising from her grave, still wearing her shroud.

Nobody looked up. Hedda, knowing that courtesy was no part of their game, waited for instruction. The NSB man gestured her to sit. The only chair was opposite him. She sat, arranging her skirt over her knees, her hands folded on the table. The assistant director remained standing, as if forgotten.

'Passport.'

She took her documents from her handbag. The official looked at them in detail. His hands were small for a man, bony.

'Why are you living in the Netherlands?'

He had a quiet toneless voice.

'I was engaged to be married to a Dutch man,' she lied.

'Name?'

'That's not relevant. He left me. We never married.'

'I decide what is relevant,' the man said, looking at her for the first time. 'Name?'

'Pieter Van de Veen. I have no idea where he is now. He married someone else.'

Her mouth was dry. She knew her neck had flushed. She tried to keep her breathing even.

'Why didn't you return to Germany?'

'I had started to teach. I didn't want to let down my students. My school was successful.'

'You've travelled. France, Belgium, America.' He scanned the pages of her passport. 'You were in England for a year. Why?'

Her heart beat hard and fast, sounding in her ears.

'I was in a dance company, briefly. I had a back injury and had to leave.'

'Yet you perform here in the Netherlands.'

'The solo work I make is less demanding. I choreograph to suit my strengths and weaknesses.' She looked him in the eyes. That much was true. 'I have four solo pieces in concert at the moment. Perhaps you are interested in ballet?'

A flicker of annoyance crossed his face. He put her documents down and turned to address Van Nooten.

'From now on, until the Reich Arts Chamber is fully established, we require listings of all future productions – artists' name, date of birth, nationality, history if any, details on performance – theme, composer, writer, duration. You will then wait for official approval. Nothing must be staged without official approval. Is that understood? I will have the official documents sent to you.'

'But forgive me. Many of our productions are scheduled two years in advance. We've already advertised our autumn programme. As well as being an immense administrative task, it won't be possible to put companies on hold at this stage.'

'The entire programme must be put on hold until passed by the Reich Minister for Arts. The current production must be cancelled immediately.'

'Not possible.' Van Nooten spoke emphatically. 'There are two more nights to go. Tickets are booked. We have full houses.'

'Then make it possible.'

His command rang in the silence that followed. Hedda heard the rumble of someone's stomach, the assistant director shifted his position.

'I don't understand what the objection is,' she said, trying to stop her voice rising. 'My students performed well, the audience was enthusiastic. It's outrageous – without even an explanation.'

He ignored her as if she hadn't spoken. She looked at Van Nooten for support. Almost imperceptibly he shook his head, and she realised he was warning her. She had no voice. To lose her temper, as she was so close to doing, would be futile, even dangerous.

'We will continue this discussion in private,' the official said. He pushed Hedda's documents across the table and addressed the assistant director. 'Escort Miss Brandt out of the building.'

Hedda put the documents in her bag, her fingers clumsy with trembling as she tried to fasten the clasp. She stood up, and pushed the chair under the table with deliberate control.

'How can you agree to this?' She looked across the table at Van Nooten, speaking as if they were alone in the room. 'Don't you see what you're doing? It's not about me, or the dancers, or even the audiences. How can you let petty bullies like this destroy your theatre?'

As she was led out of the room, she saw his face, weak with fear and embarrassment. His eye twitched. He looked pathetic. Strange what happens to the face, to the body too, when people are afraid. Distantly, she hoped her own face had not betrayed her.

Hedda Brandt is not only content with expressing perverse and dangerous political views, but she also denigrates the world of dance and theatre arts. In her new work The Waiting Room, performed at the Rozentheater, she presents a series of contorted images, a puppet master masquerading as Der Führer, and glove puppets made to resemble German soldiers. A vagrant shambles around with a violin, and a group of girls dressed as peasants, playing with chairs, are accompanied by vulgar and uncontrolled gypsy rhythms. The two professional dancers make the best they can of the choreography. Her students, several large girls in ugly costumes, repeat a limited repertoire of graceless movements, exaggerating everything that is unattractive and malformed. These dancers are girls with minimal training, including a cripple who struggles to cross the stage. This work provokes pity and disgust. Work of this nature has no place in the Theatre of the Third Reich.'

Part Three
1941

Werner

Werner imagined walking into a field of newly fallen snow, lying down, staring up into the night sky, his head sinking into the drifts. He would feel only the numbing intensity of cold.

Hunger pangs twisted his stomach, but the messy activity of eating, of chewing and swallowing and digestion, disgusted him. Looking up and seeing his father's mouth working as he ate, with that absent look on his face, made family mealtimes a torment. Katje always watching him too, with her worried expression, as if she was trying to read his mind. It was easier in school to make excuses and avoid lunch all together – there was his music, or extra mathematics to hide behind. People ignored him. He was the good-looking unobtrusive boy, likeable enough.

In the kitchen he cut a slice of bread into four squares. He nibbled two squares, and drank cold mint tea sweetened with half a teaspoon of honey. Bread was innocuous, and the sharp freshness of mint was akin to snow. He craved sweetness and allowed only this indulgence in small measure. The other two squares he left for later.

Weiss had demanded single-mindedness and efficiency from him. His life, from now into the future, must be like an arrow focussed on the target of truth. Werner ached for more time to listen to Weiss, so he might understand better. He stared into the dark at night and tried to fathom Weiss' teaching, until it seemed as if everything fragmented into smaller and smaller pieces, and he had to reach for the bedside lamp in terror. He felt as if he clung to a rock face, neither able to climb higher or to go back.

He swept the breadcrumbs into the palm of his hand and threw them out of the window, then rinsed the plate under the cold tap and turned to go upstairs.

Dearest Herr Weiss,

I don't know what the truth is. I only know that when I'm with you, when I play the piano well enough to please you, I am happy.

I feel alienated from my family, even from my sister. She's just a child. I know that I'm different. I don't understand or fit into the world as it is. I know you are different from other people too and that only you understand me and can help me.

All my life I was waiting to meet you. It's as if I'm like a moth now and you are the light. I can't bear to be in the darkness any longer. My father tried to talk to me about women. I think it's time you knew about these things, young man, he said. He gave me a book to read. As if I don't know already. There are diagrams. It's horrible, like a medical book. I can't look at it.

He read the last line and crumpled up the paper. He took another sheet of paper.:

Dearest Herr Weiss…

The tyres of his bicycle were worn to shreds and it wasn't possible to buy new ones. It meant he took more time walking home from school, and he delayed his return still more, taking a detour to Leidsegracht where he knew Weiss lived. He stood, looking up at the window. When the light was on in that first floor window, how brilliant and warm it looked. He drifted into a trance. It was peaceful feeling so near, not having to do anything. He dared not ring the doorbell. He didn't post his letter.

Dearest Herr Weiss, I would like to lie down in the snow. I would close my eyes and think of you. I would be glad to die.

Katje stood in the doorway, holding a bunch of daffodils wrapped in paper. She and Werner glared at each other.

'Why do you have to follow me around all the time?'

'Because I don't know what's wrong with you and I'm worried.'

'Nothing's wrong.'

He pushed past her and out of the kitchen.

'Be happy Werner,' she shouted after him. 'Why can't you just be happy?'

Katje put the flowers down on the table. She heard her mother's footsteps on the stairs.

'I'm here. I got flowers for the house,' she said as Wilma came into the kitchen. 'They smell lovely. I was going to put them in the big glass vase but I can't find it.'

'It's still in the dining room with the flowers you got last week. You're always buying flowers. Would you run round to the shop for me, there are a few things I need? I've written a list.'

'But I've already been out shopping.'

'Not for anything useful.'

'Flowers are useful.' She thrust them at her mother. 'Just smell them. I always forget daffodils smell so nice.'

Wilma took the flowers and sniffed.

'You're looking lost, just standing there,' she said.

'Well I'm not. I'm worried about Werner.'

Wilma unwrapped the paper, and took the scissors from the drawer. She cut the stems and scooped the clippings into a pile.

'Werner's not a child anymore.'

'Of course he's not. What's that supposed to mean?'

'I mean that he's a young man and your father knows best what to do for him.'

'But he doesn't, he doesn't at all. Papa just bullies him and tries to make him what he isn't. Can't you see that?'

'Calm down.'

'But why don't you do something?'

She saw the tense lift of her mother's shoulders.

'I need you to go to the shop. My purse is on the hall table.'

'But you haven't said why you won't do anything.'

'Because I don't know what to do, Katje,' she said with exasperation. 'Werner's going through a difficult phase. I know he's unhappy, but we are all unhappy at times. That's the way life is. I don't know what to do to help. I've tried but I might as well not exist. All I can do is pray.'

'What good will praying do? Everyone in this house is unhappy and your prayers do nothing. I'm sick of unhappiness.'

Katje stamped out of the house in a fury. Nothing had been normal for ages. If her mother had no idea what to do other than talk to God, then everything was lost. How could her mother be so defeatist? When she had children of her own she would be quite different.

She sat dangling her legs over the edge of the canal. Werner frightens me these days, she realised. No, it's not exactly that he frightens me – after all he's my brother. It's that I'm frightened for him. He's become cold as stone, and untouchable. It really is as if Herr Weiss has bewitched him.

She'd found a page of writing in his room, and she'd taken it to look at later. She took it out of her coat pocket and unfolded it. There were diagrams, a cross, a six-pointed star, a face in the middle of a sun, and another cross, drawn in thick black ink, and underneath and above, the Nazi symbol in finer red pen. The words were written in beautiful italic hand she scarcely recognised as Werner's. It could be Herr Weiss' handwriting.

There will be the dawn of a new world, an end to everything we know now. You can be sure of that, and then you will all come begging for a place in the new order. Too late.
God is on our side.

God again. Whatever side was God meant to be on?

She would talk to Elise and ask her to get her father's advice. A doctor should be able to help. Or was Miss Brandt a better solution? She had been so kind to Werner that day at the Hoffmans'.

She studied the sheet again. It was horrible. She wanted to tear it up and throw it in the canal, if only that would make it go away.

February Strike

Katje loved to hear the bells of the Mozes and Aaron Kerk on Waterlooplein ringing out as she walked towards Hedda's studio, as if they were calling out to her that everything was still fine and well. Waterlooplein was closed to non-Jews now, and she missed pottering round the market. Elise had been angry with her when she'd said so. What about all our Jewish friends and all the places they can't go, she'd said.

Katje remembered this now as she made her way early to Hedda's studio, hoping to talk to her about Werner. She felt stupid beside Elise – stupid and thoughtless and naïve. Her mother often criticised her for opening her mouth and speaking without thinking, and she knew it was true. Elise's family were so much more aware of what German Occupation really meant, and how bleak the future looked. Katje's own parents, like so many Dutch people, pretended everything was just as it had always been. Even she knew this was not the case. Every week there was some new change. She'd grown out of her shoes, even though she thought she'd stopped growing, and now it was hard to find new ones that fitted properly, and she'd not had any new clothes for ages, not even a winter coat – her old one was worn enough to let the wind through. And school was impossibly tedious with all the new books about Germany they must study, until you were sick of everything German. When would it end?

She had quite forgotten Werner as she neared Hedda's studio, and saw Elise coming towards her. She waved, called out and began to trot towards her, when she heard the sound of an army truck behind her, and Elise's reply drowned out in the roar of engines. There was more than one German truck, hurtling towards the swing bridge, throwing muddy water over her stockings. She stepped back into the doorway of the nearest building.

'You nearly ran me over, you oafs,' she shouted as they drove on and over the bridge to the Jewish quarter. They wouldn't hear her, wouldn't care that they might have dragged her along in their haste.

Elise sat on the street with her crutches beside her. Katje ran up to her.

'Oh goodness, are you all right?' She crouched down. 'Are you bleeding? No, you look all right, thank goodness.'

Elise's face was white.

'Something terrible is going to happen. I can feel it, can't you? We'll have to go to the studio. We mustn't be seen out in the street. Hedda will know what to do. Help me get up.'

Katje pulled her to her feet and handed her the crutches.

'Hurry, hurry.' Elise's fear was infectious.

'I am hurrying. Wait, don't go ahead without me.'

'I'm scared.'

'Me too.'

They reached the studio, and stood for a moment on the bottom step, Katje's arm around Elise.

'Can you make it upstairs? Shall I ask Miss Brandt to come?'

'You go ahead. I'll be all right.'

Katje ran up the stairs, and stumbled breathlessly into the studio. Hedda was standing by the window overlooking the river.

'Something terrible is happening,' Katje cried out.

'I know. I'm trying to hear,' she said. She opened the window wide.

'Elise is coming too, Miss Brandt. She's making her own way. She fell.'

Hedda didn't seem to register what she'd said. The bridge over the river had been raised, so the Jewish quarter was cut off from the rest of the city, and soldiers were stationed at the end of every street.

'They're stopping anyone getting out.'

Katje went to the window. German voices shouting orders, people scattering, a scream, a gunshot, more running.

'I can't look any more.'

'What are they doing? Why are they hurting them?'

'Those poor people, those poor people,' Hedda covered her face with her hands.

'Oh Miss Brandt. What can we do?'

'I don't know.'

Katje heard Elise at the door, turned to see her take an awkward step towards them, then sway for a moment. There was a thud as she fell. For a moment Katje thought she'd been shot. Instantly Hedda was across the room, kneeling beside her.

'She's fainted. Fetch the blanket and pillow,' she demanded. 'They're in the basket in the office.'

Elise was conscious again when Katje returned. Hedda had turned her onto her side. She'd been sick. Without a word Katje cleaned the floor around her with the towel.

'Ssh, darling, you're all right now, you're safe. Katje, would you bring a bowl of warm water. The kettle is on the table in my office.' Hedda sat on the floor with Elise's head on her lap.

Katje's hands shook as she filled the kettle. Waiting for the water to boil she stared at the blue and green flowers on the wallpaper. It had torn in the corner by the light switch.

'Dear father in heaven, help us, please help us all.'

February 1941.

I saw a woman running, holding a tiny child by the hand, the child tripped and howled, other people were running in all directions. I lost sight of her. I saw a girl in a green coat clinging to a young man. A soldier battered the young man with his rifle and he staggered and tried to run, but more soldiers blocked his

134

way. The girl was kicked to the ground. The man was dragged away.

News from the Jewish neighbourhood – German soldiers took men and boys away from their families. Over a hundred were taken. They made them crawl on hands and knees through the streets. They were driven away in trucks.

The city is on strike. There are no trams, no trains. The dockyards and the factories, many shops, and even the offices have closed – my school too. Strange quietness, tension and agitation in the air.

Third day of the strike. Tried to telephone the Hoffmans, no answer. Cleaned, baked bread, mended a pile of clothes, prepared classes for the whole month. Made a casserole of vegetables, and the girls from the apartments next door ate with me. Impossible to sit around any longer – this electric atmosphere, too much alone, too disconnected from everyone. The last two nights I've woken with a start, pitch dark in my room with the blackout blinds. In the bleak hours I lay awake, thinking of Essen. Germany is still my home, despite everything.

Hedda put on her coat and scarf and set off towards the old city. It was a relief to be outside, to feel the chill air on her face, the soothing rhythm of walking; re-assuring to pass other people, to exchange a glance, understanding.

She walked quickly, past Westerkerk, along Keizergracht and up Leidsestraat towards the centre. Crossing the bridge, she was startled by gunshot, and someone screaming in a street nearby. She hastened over and stepped back into the doorway of an office.

Moments later a group of young men rushed towards her. A brick hurled from across the street, missed the side of her face by a fraction before it crashed into a window. More gunfire – an old man in a brown coat arched backwards, a look of amazement across his face. His hat rolled from his head as he hit the ground. A woman started to wail. Everywhere people were running and screaming.

Hedda closed her eyes. This is what it's like to drown, she thought, after the moments fighting for life – the surrender, the white calm, release into the flow of water.

She came round lying at the foot of a tree beside the water. She had no memory of running there. Her hands were cut and smeared with mud and grit. She struggled to sit. Her stockings were torn and her knees bleeding. Clutching the trunk of the tree, she staggered to her feet, took a few steps, stood still to regain her balance. Dazed with shock, it took a long time to reach home, moving slowly, aching with cold, her body sore as if beaten.

Too cold to take off her coat, she put Brahms Violin Sonata on the gramophone. She lay on a blanket on the floor and listened to the opening movement, watched the slight movement of winter branches through the window, a crow, its feathers puffed out. She had no strength. She moved her hand, her fingers, tracing the smallest dance on the floor by her face.

In the Face of Oppression

Hedda lay sleepless through the bleak hours after two, haunted by a vision of the old man, his bewildered expression, his wife's cry of despair – so desolate a sound. She heard the intermittent sound of planes crossing to Britain and thought of Kurt and his family. She tried to pray. She fell asleep as morning came, wanted to stay sleeping. She dragged herself exhausted from the warmth of bed.

'My days teaching dance are numbered,' she told Marten Hoffman one morning when she'd called for coffee after classes. 'They'll make demands I can't go along with sooner or later.'

Kai had just come in and overheard.

'You can't let that happen, Hedda,' he said.

She turned to answer. He was so emphatic, as if he actually thought she had any choice. Tiredness gave an edge of anger to her voice.

'Rozentheater was closed and Van Nooten was dismissed straight after my production was cancelled. I got away lightly – apologising for my depraved work.'

'Apologising!'

'What else could I do? Put myself in prison?'

'You actually apologised? You never told me this before. Did you know?' He turned to Marten.

'Your parents are the only people I told,' Hedda answered for him. 'You were away at the time.'

'God, I hate Weiss for writing that review.'

He stormed out of the kitchen, banging the door.

'I'm sorry,' Marten said. 'Kai's in a bad way since the strike. And he cares about you. As we all do.'

'He's right though. I think of my father, Marten, and I'm scared. I try to make the right decision, to be clear of my motives. Maybe I am just weak.'

'You know it's not as simple as that.'

He got up to pour her more coffee. Kai had started to practise in the next room. It was a sweet sound.

She'd asked herself the same question about the review and Weiss. She hadn't seen him since the night in the theatre, when he'd walked out without a word. She'd missed the best of him. Their partnership had never reached the potential it might have done, but work was easier without him.

'Even so, I don't think Erik Weiss wrote the review,' she said when Marten sat down again.

'Don't you?'

'He's too sharp for such crudeness. He'd have damned me with satire if he'd been up to it at all. He looked sick with despair that night. Pitiful.'

'Can't despair be a motive?'

She glanced at him, then away. Outside the sun had just come through. A flock of sparrows fluttered from the shrubbery. She felt exhausted. If only she could sleep.

'But in the end it wasn't the review that damned me. It was the work itself. I was naïve to think I'd get away with it. The review was merely the public face.'

In the studio Hedda paced around, demanding more from her students.

'In the face of oppression you will dance,' she shouted, and banged the flat of her hand on the piano.

Afterwards she sat in her office, clutching her coffee cup for warmth, nibbling biscuits, and thinking how foolish she was to lose self-control. At times the girls, except for Katje and Elise, exchanged glances, as if to say she'd gone mad. Why should they feel oppressed when their families were doing very well under Nazi rule? In the face of oppression you will dance – what on earth was she thinking?

Katje knocked, and peered round the door.

'May I ask you something, Miss Brandt?'

'Come in.'

'I wanted to show you this. I found it in my brother's room, and I think Herr Weiss might have written it.'

She unfolded the paper and handed it to Hedda.

It was indeed Erik's handwriting, a lot of nonsense. What was he doing giving it to the poor boy? No doubt he filled his head with notions of the city of glass and such-like.

'Herr Weiss talks a lot of nonsense,' she said. 'Tell your brother to ignore it and just get on with his music. Herr Weiss is an excellent pianist, but if Werner's unhappy I suggest your parents find another teacher.' She didn't want to discuss Erik further. It wouldn't be professional to interfere. 'You danced very well in class today.'

Katje's face lit up, Erik Weiss apparently forgotten. She pushed the hair from her face and balanced on one leg as she answered.

'It helps me to jump high. Did you see? I imagine I'm leaping away from all the evil, trying to reach the ceiling when I jump.'

'Oh yes, Katje, your jumping is much improved.'

'Miss Brandt, I think of you like a strong tree, with the wind rushing through it when you dance.'

Hedda had to turn away, suppressing her laughter, hiding the unexpected tears that filled her eyes.

I'm no tree, dear girl. I'm like dead leaves, maybe, or dust, she thought. Then smiled at her sense of melodrama.

The Dunes

Hedda's doorbell rang in the middle of the evening. Outside it was dark and moonless. She'd prepared for bed early. She listened, hoping whoever it was would go away, thinking she was out. The bell rang again. She put on her dressing gown and ran downstairs.

'Who is it?' She spoke through the closed door.

'Kai.'

He'd never called at night before so she knew it must be serious. She let him in.

'What is it, Kai? What's happened?'

She could smell tobacco smoke in his hair and feel the damp cold of his clothes.

He was shivering violently and struggled to speak.

'Dear Kai, you're in shock.' She held him for a moment. 'Let's go upstairs. You need to get warm.'

She helped him take off his wet coat and led him to sit on the sofa. He put his head on his knees and howled.

She sat beside him and felt for his hand. It was still ice cold. She held it in both hers, trying to rub warmth back. Brandy – that would help. She was about to get up, but he held her back.

'Stay.'

'I'm here. I'm here.'

'I had to come, Hedda. I couldn't be alone.'

'I know.'

He clung to her and sobbed, and she held him, rocked him until he was exhausted and lay still, leaning into her chest like a child.

'They shot him. They shot Piet, my oldest friend.'

'Oh Kai.'

'How can they take young men who've done nothing but defend the Jews? How can they do such things to the Jews in the first place? I don't understand the world, Hedda. I don't understand anything.'

There was nothing she could say to comfort him.

'I'm going to fetch the brandy. I'm coming straight back.' Gently she disengaged herself and went into the kitchen. She returned with the bottle and two glasses.

He drank, and she poured him more. He was still shivering. She fetched a blanket and put it round him, then knelt at the stove, firing it up to a blaze.

'The organisers of the strike were discovered and arrested last week,' he said, when she was beside him again. 'There's a place, a café by the Concert Hall. We have a contact there. He told me they'd been taken to the Oranjehotel in Scheveningen – that's what we call the prison. They were interrogated, then taken to the dunes and shot. What can I do, Hedda?' He threw off the blanket and stood up. 'They deserve to hang. I've got to do something.'

She went to lead him back to the sofa, but he turned to her, embraced her hard.

'I remember …when I heard my father was dead…I understand.'

He grew calmer.

They lay facing each other on the narrow sofa. He wrapped the blanket round them both.

'We were friends from ten years old. Every year his family took me to their summer house on the island.' He laid his head in the crook of her neck. She felt his breath, warm and moist on her skin. He cried quietly. 'One year we built a den, so fine it was, out of those long grasses that grow by the sea. His father showed us how to weave them together, with driftwood supports and a few nails. It was warm that summer and we slept out. We made a fire and we'd sit out there in the dark, listening to the sea.'

His words were like a low vibration. It seemed to Hedda, as she floated into sleep, that he drew the dead man to them and they were consoled.

141

'We stole a bottle of wine from his parents one night and drank it all. I remember the sky spinning, and waking freezing cold. He was going to live in America. He had it all planned. He'd met a girl, Helen…'

She slept from desperate exhaustion, though she had meant to stay awake for Kai – she slept more deeply than she had for months, reassured by the warmth of him beside her.

When she woke in the morning he'd gone. She had no recollection of hearing him leave.

Elise

Katje rushed through her household chores. Elise had telephoned her. It was urgent, she'd said. Wilma was out at a meeting of church ladies so there was no need to do the housework perfectly. She put the dusters into a bucket to soak, then ran to brush her hair and put on a clean jersey.

She knocked on the study door, opened it a fraction, met by the fusty smell of her father and his cigarette smoke.

'I'm going out to visit Elise,' she said.

He looked up from his papers and smiled.

'I'll be back by five, tell Mama.'

She closed the door before he had time to object, put on her coat and hat, and left the house.

She cycled alongside the canal – not so quickly that she'd be conspicuous – turning towards Leidseplein, over Stadhouderskade, and through the park, until she was standing outside Elise's house panting to get her breath. She fastened her bicycle to the railings, pulled the bell, and listened for Elise's uneven steps along the corridor.

'It's you at last. I thought you'd never come.'

'I told you I had all the damned dusting to do. At least Mama was out at a church thing so she couldn't stop me.'

'Come upstairs. I've got chocolate in a flask and some biscuits Marianne made, and I laid out the table specially.'

Katje followed Elise to her room.

'Oh I like your bedroom so much,' she said, and threw herself down on the bed. 'Now what is it? Why did I need to hurry here? Not that I didn't want to come, of course. I'd much rather be here than home.'

Elise eased herself down on the bed beside her.

'I heard my parents talking last night. I shouldn't have listened, but I couldn't help it. They were whispering and I know they didn't want me to know, and that made it even worse. I'll go mad if I don't tell someone, and Kai's never

143

home these days. Do you know what doctors are doing to their patients in Germany?'

'How could I?'

'Children who have something wrong with them are taken away to have medical experiments done on them. It's worse than torture. Then, when the Nazi doctors have finished they gas the children.'

'Gas them? What do you mean?'

'Kill them. They do the same to mad people.'

'But that's terrible, evil. How can they?'

'How do I know? I heard Papa saying it could happen here if the Dutch doctors join the Artsenkamer.'

'What's the Artsenkamer?'

'It's new. All the doctors are supposed to sign saying they'll obey the Nazi medical laws. Some people, even doctors, think babies should be killed if there's anything wrong with them, and it's the law in Germany now. Papa said it's only a step away for us.'

'What if the Dutch doctors don't obey?'

'They'll be put into prison.'

'What can we do?'

'I don't know. Kai has ideas about resisting and fighting, but he won't talk much. Then I get scared for him too.'

Katje reached for Elise's hand. They held so tightly that Katje thought their fingers looked like white worms, twisted together. Nothing feels safe anymore, she thought. Nothing is what it seemed to be when I was little, or even last year.

Katje was late. Her parents and Werner were at the table when she rushed in.

'The soup will be tepid,' her father said.

'I'm sorry. I so wish you would just start without me.'

'Have you washed?'

'Of course.'

She'd forgotten, but it would only delay things even more.

Her father said grace. She folded her hands and muttered thanks to God. They began their meal. Katje stirred the soup round and round.

'I'm really not very hungry.' She pushed away the bowl, and looked round at her parents concentrating on the task of eating. Werner, as usual, was messing round with his food. 'Do you know what the doctors are doing to their patients in Germany?'

Her father carried on slurping the soup. Her mother dabbed at her mouth with the napkin.

'Why is nobody answering me? You should know. It's important.'

In a rush she told them everything.

'People are spreading rumours,' her father said, in a reassuring tone. 'Perhaps founded on partial truth, but there will be an awful lot of exaggeration and scare-mongering.' He tore a piece of bread and smiled at her. 'Your friend will pick up bits of the truth and because of her condition she will be more sensitive and easily upset. Facts will be twisted. You mustn't believe everything you hear, Katje.'

'But what if it's true? What if doctors here have to do the same thing?'

'We must pray they'll be guided by God,' Wilma said.

'Oh Mama, what's God going to do about it?'

'Maybe they've already been guided to do what's best?' Werner said.

'What do you mean?' It was rare for Werner to say anything.

'Aren't people like that better off dead? They're only suffering, as well as giving their families a life of suffering?'

Katje looked at him in astonishment.

'But these people are someone's brother or sister, or little baby,' Katje said, her voice catching in her throat. 'They are loved.'

'That's just sentimentality.'

The room stifled her, the heavy wooden furniture, the drapes, the way everyone sat there complacently. She got up, dragging the tablecloth with her, so her bowl slithered to the floor, spilling soup over the carpet.

'Calm down, Katje.'

'No. I won't calm down. I'll never be calm again. It's a terrible opinion. If that's God guiding people, then God is even more hateful than ever.'

Her father got up to lead her out of the room, but she pushed him away and rushed out.

'Leave her alone,' she heard Werner saying. 'She's bound to be upset. The cripple is her best friend.'

She ran upstairs to her room. She wanted escape from them all. The cripple is her best friend.

Elise had said something to her before she'd left. She hadn't been able to make sense of it, hadn't dared to try, but now she understood.

'In their eyes I'm deformed because I can't walk properly, remember. I'm not perfect.'

'Stop!' Hedda shouted across the studio. 'Katarina, what is the matter with you? These sad eyes and drooping head! You dance like an English pudding.'

'It's not possible to be happy,' Katje said.

'I'm not asking for happiness. I want concentration. Where are you? I can't teach if you refuse to work.'

'I so much wanted to get here and dance. I came here as quickly as I could and now I can't dance at all. I can't help that I'm like a pudding.'

Hedda turned her round by the shoulders.

'What is it child? You wanted an extra class, but you're doing nothing but wasting my time.'

Katje gulped, then sobbed.

'I need to talk to you.'

'Oh dear, oh dear,' Hedda said more gently. 'Come, I'll make coffee, I have the smallest amount left for special occasions, and this must be such an occasion. Go and put on your warm jumper and come into the office.'

Katje huddled, sniffing, on the chair by the window. Hedda handed her a handkerchief.

'It's too pretty to spoil with my crying,' Katje said, folding it over and smoothing it on her lap. She wiped her eyes with the back of her hand.

'Now, tell me what's wrong. Is it your family, is it your dancing, or school perhaps?'

'It's everything. It's been terrible since your performance was stopped. One minute I was happier than I'd ever been in my life, then everything was destroyed, and now it seems to get worse and worse.' She told Hedda everything she'd heard from Elise. 'Is that true about Germany?'

'Yes. I'm afraid it is.'

'But what about Elise? What will they do to her?'

'The Dutch are naïve in many ways, they've let the Germans get away with far too much, but even so, I trust there are limits.'

'Do you remember Elise's birthday, Miss Brandt, when Kai asked us what we should do. Fight, and live, you said.'

'I say very foolish things at times, especially if I've had a drink.'

'It wasn't foolish. Kai said he loved you for it.'

'Did he? Then he is foolish too.'

'No, you were right. We must do something.'

'Oh Katje, it's hard for you, troubled with questions like this. Sometimes you remind me of myself – when all my anger fuelled my dancing.'

'Doesn't it still, Miss Brandt?'

Hedda turned to look through the window.

'It's not as simple as that any longer.' The light caught the edge of her face, the wave of hair falling over her temple. She looked so tired. 'When you're older you'll have more choices. You can work in secret organisations to overthrow the government, you can speak out through your work as an artist, or you can try to live a good life despite everything. For now you must do your best to be happy, Katje. Elise has good parents, and she's strong.' Hedda finished her coffee and stood up. 'Now we'll work again. Oh the Nazis are clever at marching in their great boots, stamping their way through the streets, but they have no brains and no grace and in the end they'll fall from power. You'll lift your head and dance as if each step defeats them. Come on now.'

Katje was still holding Hedda's handkerchief. It was cream silk, edged with lace. Absent-mindedly she put it in the pocket of her jersey and forgot about it.

Brothers

Herr Weiss was unwell. Werner's mother had taken the telephone call early one Saturday morning in July.

'Yes Herr Weiss, I am sorry. I'll tell him.'

Werner tried to hide his sick desperation, but he caught Katje watching him as she cleared the breakfast table. He wished she'd leave him alone.

He left the house. There was a carefree air in the street – people sat outside the cafés in the leafy shade. He walked not knowing where he should go, or what he should do. All week he'd practised, anticipating his next lesson, counting the days, the nights, and finally the hours. He would write a letter to Herr Weiss, wishing him health, saying how he missed their hour together, tell him he intended to practise even harder for next week.

He stopped outside a little gallery. In the window was an oil painting of a single lily in a vase on top of a piano. The piano stood in a white room with long windows. It was a beautiful little painting — perfect. He'd like to buy it for Herr Weiss. But that was impossible – he had no money, and it would surely cost a great deal. He thought of giving him a gift, of seeing the flare of light in his eyes as he looked down at the painting, then into Werner's own eyes. *That's the most beautiful thing, Werner. So few people understand what I really like*, he would say. *I always knew that you would.*

'Hello, there.'

He turned to see Kai, leaning on the handlebars of his bicycle, smiling at him.

'You're Katje's brother, aren't you? We met at my parents' house last summer. Kai Hoffman.' He held out his hand. 'I saw you from across the bridge and thought it was you. Which way are you walking?'

'I don't know. I was just wandering,' Werner mumbled.

'I meant to tell Katje to say that if ever you feel like working on any piano and violin duets together, that would be great. I'm always looking for good pianists to play with – other than my mother, of course.'

Werner nodded. He began walking, hoping that Kai would cycle off and leave him alone. But instead he fell in beside him, wheeling his bicycle alongside.

Werner glanced sideways at him, this dark, graceful young man with girlishly curly hair, in a short-sleeved green shirt. His arms were sunburnt, muscular.

'Do you play anything else?' Kai asked.

'No. I only want to play the piano.'

'I'm learning too. My third instrument. I hear that Erik Weiss is your teacher.'

'Who told you?' Werner felt his face flushing.

'My sister, I think. What's he like? Not everyone gets on with him. Not entirely to be trusted.'

'He's a wonderful teacher.'

Werner realised, too late, that he'd spoken in vehement defence of Weiss. He caught Kai's amused look.

'Well I'm glad you get on with him.'

'Who said he's not to be trusted?' Werner couldn't help asking.

'One of my friends had lessons from him for a while. But really it doesn't matter, if you find him satisfactory that's all that counts.'

He smiled at Werner.

'I must go,' Werner said.

He darted away down a side street without looking back. It doesn't matter what Kai thinks of me. It doesn't matter what any of them think. He ran, not knowing where he was going.

Katje sat with Elise on a rug in Elise's garden, drinking lemonade. The glass doors were open. Julia was singing in the kitchen. Marianne practised somersaults on the frame of the swing.

'It's worse and worse at home now Werner hardly speaks. He just plays these awful dirges all the time,' Katje told Elise. 'I feel as if I'm going mad living there. Then we had a quarrel last night. All I said was how much I hated the new ID cards, and doing my fingerprints, and he said it was for our safety. What safety I said? He looked at me as if he thought I was stupid.'

'Do you think it's anything to do with Herr Weiss?'

'Why do you say that?'

'Kai saw Herr Weiss in a bar with two men from the Nazi Party. He doesn't think he's to be trusted. Perhaps you should tell your father to stop Werner's lessons.'

'Oh no, he'd hate me forever.'

Elise was looking at her in that serious way she had. Katje looked away, scratched at a scab on her knee, hot with panic at the thought of the trouble that would cause, if her father would even take any notice.

'Oh God, Elise, I wish Herr Weiss would just disappear. Fall in the canal, or just die of some deadly illness.'

'Can we light a candle for Werner?' Katje said later, when they were up in Elise's room getting ready for bed. 'Like we do for people in church.'

'I've never been to church, but I suppose so, if you like.' Elise struck a match and put it to the wick. They watched the light flicker a moment, then flare up. 'A candle for all of us.'

'Yes, for all of us, but especially for Werner.' Katje draped a blanket over her head, and sat cross-legged on the bed. 'Remember those weeks we rehearsed for Hedda's ballet? Then the performance? Sometimes I'm scared now, Elise. I wish things were the way they used to be. Everything's changed for the worse since Hedda was banned from the theatre.'

'I know. That night we danced I felt amazing, as if I could do anything.'

'Me too. I'll never forget going to the theatre the next day, so excited, thinking we'd have two more performances, then seeing everyone crowded round that notice. I thought Hedda must have died.'

'I think she did in a way,' Elise said after a while. 'Pa said she was depressed for a long time. There was nothing she could do. Being German she has to be even more careful than the rest of us.'

'I wish we could do something for her.'

It was all so troubling – Werner, and now Hedda. Katje got off the bed, and walked to the window and back.

'What are you doing? You look like a nun with that blanket over your head.'

'Thinking. I think better when I walk about.'

Elise stopped watching her, and lay on her back in bed.

'I had an idea last week,' she said, so quietly that Katje almost missed it.

'What?' Katje stopped pacing, and knelt down, her elbows resting on Elise's bed. 'Are you going to tell me?'

'If I do you mustn't tell anyone.'

'I promise.'

'We can tell the truth. That's what some of Kai's friends do, secretly. We can write down the terrible things that happen, as if we're writing a letter to the world, and then we leave the things we write in cafés, anywhere we can think of. It will be different coming from us, because we're young. We can write so that people see it all as if for the first time.'

'But do you really think this will make a difference?'

'Not to begin with. Kai says it's like a dripping tap that fills a basin – at first it's nothing, then it grows in volume. Someone will read and understand, and they'll tell other people, and those people tell more people. I'm sure he's right.'

'So how do we begin?' It seemed such an enormous task.

'We have to watch and remember, until there are enough things to say. You mustn't let your family know. Kai says that whatever happens, no Nazi can rule our thoughts. One day it'll all be over. Hitler will be dead.'

'I hope it's not us dead instead.'

'It won't be. We're going to survive, and Kai and Hedda too. Think of the celebrations we'll have when it's over.'

Katje didn't answer. Would Werner be dead? Elise hadn't included him.

'The end of the Nazis! I feel as if my heart missed a beat thinking of that,' Elise said. 'We'll have chocolate again! I do miss it more than anything, don't you? I miss chocolate, and cake, and coffee, and all those good things. Sometimes I go to sleep dreaming of them. And we'll dance again. Katje, why are you crying?'

'I'm imagining things. I can't tell you. Horrid things.'

Elise peered down at Katje huddled on the camp bed. She tugged the blanket away from her face.

'Oh I shouldn't have gone on so. Forget my stupid idea. What can I do to comfort you? Let's make a list of everything we'll do when it's over.'

Katje grew quiet, listening to Elise's soothing voice as she whispered about summer days swimming in the sea, and the magical lantern-lit winter skating parties. The candle burnt low, and Elise's words intermittent. Katje heard her breath lengthening, and knew she'd fallen asleep.

The clock struck each quarter, on through the night, until the birds sang in the garden. Katje churned round in bed, the sheets tangled. She was hot, then cold. She half dreamed she was trying to write, but the words kept jumbling. Waking again, she made up dances to the songs she knew. She kicked her feet. She had to keep moving to keep away that vision of a black bottomless hole, of Werner slipping over the edge before she could catch him, Werner falling forever.

Kultuurkamer

As Hedda opened the door of her studio one morning in the early winter, she caught the faint scent of Erik Weiss' cologne, and with it the potent memory of their long evenings working together. But he was so often censorious and exacting, there was no reason to miss him, she reminded herself as she went on up the stairs. It was only when she reached the first floor she questioned why the scent of him should be lingering when he'd moved out of the building months ago? Uneasy, she went on up the stairs. She found him standing just outside her office door.

'Good-morning Miss Brandt.' He smiled and put out his hand, as if his presence in the early morning was normal. 'I should have made an appointment, but I took the opportunity to come and speak to you as I was passing.'

'I didn't realise you had a key,' she said, her unease turned to irritation.

'The caretaker let me in, of course.'

'He shouldn't have done.'

'Please don't be so hostile. I've done nothing to deserve such treatment,' he said.

'I'm sorry,' she offered him a chair. 'It's just that you gave me a shock. I haven't seen you for a long time. You haven't exactly kept in touch.'

'I'm sorry. I would never want to disturb you.' He smiled, sat down without taking off his coat, and crossed his outstretched legs at the ankle.

She noticed that he'd lost weight, his face finer, less flesh round his neck. It suited him. She took off her coat and hat and hung them on the peg.

'How are you?'

'Very well indeed.'

Rather than give him attention, she leafed through the papers on her desk.

'I've only half an hour before teaching. What can I do for you?' She spoke in a business-like manner.

'I came to give you some advice.'

She glanced at him in surprise.

'I'll get straight to the point. I came to discuss the Kultuurkamer.'

'I'm afraid I've nothing to say on matters of bureaucracy.'

'I anticipated as much. That's why I'm here. I care about you, whatever you may think. These are important times. Have you signed up?'

'That's my own business.'

'Well, yes and no. You'd be foolish to be pig-headed about this. Forgive me, but I know how stubborn you can be. You must be aware that if you don't sign, you won't be in a position to continue the school, or your dance career. Membership is a requirement of the new law.'

She stared down at her papers. He waited.

'Why aren't you speaking to me?'

'You know well how I feel. Now please go away. I've much to do.'

'I wish you would let me advise you. You're very foolish. It's a small matter but an important one.'

'Small, it is not. Are you really here to advise me to join a Nazi organisation that encourages propaganda rather than art – an organisation that won't allow any Jewish artist to work again? Have you ever sat through one of those hideous films they're promoting?'

'Have you? I don't believe you have. You're talking from a position of ignorance.'

'I know enough about Nazi ideology.'

'Then you should use your intelligence and recognise that there's much to admire. To be part of the machine that gives life to such ideals, surely as an artist you understand the power of that?'

'Like the oppression of the Jews?'

'That's but a small part of it.'

'Small – the brutal elimination of thousands of people?'

'You inflate the facts.'

'My father saw it coming long ago.'

'Your father was blinkered by prejudice. I saw that the moment you told me about him, and so would you if you let yourself be rational. The Jews are their own worst enemy, and always have been. As artists, as German artists indeed, we both have a great future in this country. On the other hand, there's no possibility of fading away unnoticed if you continue to work without signing up. There really is no choice.'

'If it ever crossed my mind to sign the Kultuurkamer, which it hasn't, your recommendation would make me determined not to. I'd rather die.'

His laugh was short and sharp.

'I love your passionate vehemence, Hedda. I always did.' He stood up, buttoned his overcoat. 'We were friends once. I was very fond of you. I still am, so I'm sorry for you now.' He held out his hand.

She ignored his gesture.

'Let's part on friendly terms.'

She turned away. His hand fell. He shrugged.

'You are very foolish. Good-bye, then. I hold nothing against you. I reiterate – I only wanted to advise.'

She listened as the studio door closed, his footfall dying away down the stairs.

A week after Weiss' visit to Hedda, Katje arrived for class in time to have the space to herself. She changed hurriedly, flinging off her coat and shoes, and leaving them in an untidy heap. She ran around the empty room to get warm, her arms flung wide, hands outstretched. How good to be away from her family, to dance in the half-light of the winter afternoon. From the corner of the room she practised turning across the diagonal, trying to focus on the edge of the window frame to keep her direction. She stopped after a while, giddy and breathless. She hoped Hedda would come into the studio and see her practising. After a while, impatient, she went out into the lobby to see if her office door was open, and then she might call out hello. Instead she heard Kai's voice. He'd begun to accompany classes and must have arrived early too. She pressed her ear to the door. She knew she shouldn't listen.

'How can you sign up to something you are so opposed to? This is the beginning of the end for us,' Hedda said.

'Because I have to work, and no petty organisation or government will stop me.'

'So you're willing to give up all your big ideals in order to compose and play wretched little marches and anthems? You'll no longer be allowed to play anything by a Jewish composer, or with Jewish musicians. No, they're being systematically eliminated from society, as you know. There'll be nothing but sentimental schmaltz, that's what the Nazis love. How will you hold your head up, Kai?'

'Because I'll be working from the inside to bring the government down. It's safer to look as if I agree with them. Don't you see that? How can you give up everything you've worked for all these years? That's what it amounts to. As well as that, you're making yourself a target.'

'It's not like that and you know it.' Her voice sounded desperate. 'Weiss was here last week full of warnings and what ifs. I shouldn't take any notice of him, but I know what I'm faced with. And now you're saying the same thing.'

There was a movement towards the door, and Katje scuttled back to the studio. Should she walk into the office, pretend she wanted to ask something? But they'd just do that adult thing of going silent. She was desperate to know what it was all about.

She loved to jump, to work her knees and feet, and push herself until her body seemed to hover in the air before landing again. Only jumping would stop her feeling so anxious and afraid.

The studio door opened and Kai came in.

'Don't stop, I don't want to disturb you,' Kai said. His voice and the way he moved betrayed his anger. He began to tune his violin. 'Katarina, get on with it. Just pretend I'm not here.'

He played a few notes, then launched into such a vibrant tune that she had to dance, hesitantly at first, then galloping, and twirling in circles and spirals round the room. Faster and faster he played, and she laughed with exhilaration. Then he stopped abruptly and put his violin down on the piano.

'Bravo. I bet you didn't know you could dance like that.'

She staggered towards him in mock exhaustion, and he took her face in his hands and kissed her on the forehead.

'What are you two doing?'

Hedda stood in the doorway.

'I was playing for Katje. She managed to keep up with me.' His voice died away when he saw her expression, and he picked up his violin and left the room.

'I'm sorry,' Katje mumbled.

'Continue your work,' Hedda said, and followed Kai, closing the door behind her.

The other girls came into the studio and began to warm up. Elise was absent with a cold. Katje heard the outside door, and the sound of someone running down the steps into the street. Hedda came into the studio alone. She was late.

'No accompaniment today. To the barre, now, quickly.'

She set the first exercise, and progressed brusquely through the class, giving little correction and no praise. The girls glanced at each other, disquieted.

'Go and get changed, then come back to the studio,' she said when class was over. 'I need to speak to you all.'

They pulled on warm clothes and ran back to the studio. Hedda was sitting on a chair by the piano. They sat at her feet. Katje hugged her knees and put her head down. She couldn't look at Hedda.

'I've taught some of you since you were very little, and I know you very well and I trust you,' Hedda said. 'I've decided I must be truthful to you all, as I've always been.'

Yes, Katje thought, Hedda had been so honest at times, that often a girl could be found crying in the changing room after class.

'Perhaps you are aware of the changes to our lives since the German Occupation, but you won't necessarily know the details, so I must tell you now that, as a dancer and teacher, I'm required to sign a document to register with the Kultuurkamer.'

It was unsettling. She gave a nervous laugh, then continued as if she'd rehearsed a speech.

'The Kultuurkamer is a Nazi organisation for the arts and professional artists of all disciplines. I have to sign in order to continue my profession as a teacher and choreographer.'

The silence that followed was uncomfortable. Katje looked up. Hedda was staring vacantly across the studio. It seemed to Katje that she'd lost all sense of time and place.

'But you haven't signed it, Miss Brandt?' she burst out.

'Of course I haven't. I see it as an insidious move towards propaganda of the worst kind. Everything – poetry, art, and theatre will have strict rules that must be adhered to. I won't any longer be allowed to teach you, Mirjam, or your sister, and many others. How can I dance to their tune? I can't, can I?' She looked at them all. 'People have tried to persuade me to sign and continue, from the inside, to work in my own way. But duplicity is not a choice for me. I wanted to tell you all face to face, because you're good students. I've loved teaching you. You must know that, even when I've been hard on you.'

Nobody moved.

'I don't want to put myself, or any of you and your families, into an awkward position. We have a week left before the end of term. After that my school will be closed until further notice. I will send letters to your parents. I don't want any fuss, or big farewells.' She was going to say more, but her voice caught as if she was choking. She coughed, took a handkerchief from her pocket. 'Thank you girls. That's all. You can go now.'

Nobody moved. She stood up and walked out without another glance.

As soon as she'd closed the door they broke into whispering.

'I think Miss Brandt was nearly crying.'

'Well she would. It's awful for her.'

'For all of us. It's terrible.'

'I'll ask my father to speak to her.'

'As if that would do any good. We'll have to find another teacher, like she said.'

'There's no-one like Miss Brandt.'

Katje buried her head in her arms.

'Are you all right,' someone asked?

'Just leave me alone.'

The door closed on their agitated voices.

Twilight turned the sky deep blue. Katje supposed she should go before night fell and the blackout. If she didn't get home soon, Werner would be sent out to look for her, and there'd be such trouble. She clambered to her feet and went to the changing room. The others had gone. Someone had left her a note. *We're meeting tomorrow, 3.00 usual place. Tell Elise.* In a daze she put on her coat and shoes, and packed her bag, then sat down on the bench, head in her hands. It was impossible to leave without a word to Miss Brandt.

She hesitated outside Hedda's office, tapped the door, and opened it wide enough to see Hedda sitting at her desk staring into space.

'Oh, I thought you'd all gone home,' Hedda said.

'The others have.'

She stepped into the room, and closed the door behind her.

'It's late. What do you want now?'

'I couldn't go without seeing you.'

'Well here I am.'

'How can you give up? You can't do it. You can't close your school and just let us go like that.'

Hedda said nothing.

'There must be a way?'

'Don't you think I've had this conversation, gone over it in my head until I'm exhausted?'

'You said you would fight.'

'Go away, Katje. You don't know what you're talking about.'

'I can't go.'

'You're behaving like a spoilt child.'

'You mustn't close the school. People need you. I need you. I'll die if I don't dance.'

Hedda got up and took hold of her hard by the shoulders.

'Katarina, listen. Listen to me. These are terrible times – Jews are being rounded up, kept in ghettoes, and transit camps, then sent away, Lord knows where. Everywhere the Nazis oppress us. There's far worse to come. In the face of that how can I think of dancing?'

'In the face of that, what can we do but dance? That's what you said, day after day. You made it all seem bearable. I believed you. You've betrayed us.'

'Do you really think I do anything lightly? I don't need my students coming telling me about betrayal. Now leave me alone. I've much to do.'

Hedda manoeuvred her out of the room and closed the door.

Katje opened it again and was about to argue.

'Get out, now.'

Katje stumbled down the stairs and out into the street.

She walked without knowing where she was going. She turned the next corner, walked again, counting her steps to stop her thoughts. She didn't care any longer that it was growing dark. Nothing much mattered. She stood with her back against the damp trunk of a tree and stared down at the earth, then up into the empty sky. A few dead leaves rustled.

She'd lost her bag with her dancing clothes. She must have dropped them in her distress. She remembered she'd had the bag when she left the studio. Or had she? It felt terribly significant that the very clothes she danced in had gone.

Hedda sat at the table in her apartment. She had letters to compose to parents about closing the school, but she hadn't been able to eat since returning home, and her arm was limp with the effort of writing, her mind weary with thinking. Had she been too reactive after Weiss' visit? She had known she'd have to close the school, but should she have waited longer before telling her students? She pulled her shawl around her and shivered. Recalling her quarrel with Kai, and then Katje's despair, she put her head down on the table and closed her eyes, wanting oblivion, knowing it would not come, even in sleep.

She'd been still for some time when the doorbell rang. Who else turned up so late at night but Kai? She felt too weary to move. After a moment it rang again. She'd been holding her breath. Slowly she exhaled. She got up and went to the window, peered through the crack in the blinds, forgetting it would be impossible to see anyone in so little light. A flurry of grit hit the glass. She put on her shoes and went down to the outside door. As she reached the lower stairs there was another gentle tap.

'Hedda. It's me.' Kai's voice, muffled against the door.

Of course it's you, dear boy, she thought.

She let him in, closed the door and leant against it for support. Without a word, he embraced her, so hard her arms were pressed to her sides, her face smothered against his shoulder. She could feel his heartbeat just above her own. For a moment she yielded, then pushed him away.

'You'd better come in for a while.' She spoke without looking at him. 'But I must try to sleep soon, so you can't stay long.'

'I'm sorry I rushed away earlier,' he said, quickly. 'I had to come back to see you again, to see what you decided to do.'

'I told them I'm closing the school, your sister's class – although she's away sick, as you know. It was only fair to let them know. Now I'm exhausted, I can hardly think.'

The room was scarcely warmer than outside, she realised. She lit the candles, and offered him tea, which he accepted. She sank down on the chair rather than the sofa, so there was no room for him beside her, but he moved to sit on the floor. She looked down at his curls – the kind of hair she'd longed to have as a child.

'I'm sorry, I'm so sorry we quarrelled,' he said.

'It doesn't matter. It's over now. It feels to me like the end of the world – closing my school. No doubt I shall feel better when I've slept.'

He grasped her hand and kissed her palm.

'Kai, you're young,' she said, softly, disengaging her hand. 'You mustn't get involved with me.'

'But I am already, Hedda. Surely you know? I've loved you for months.'

'I've known, and not wanted to know.'

'Why?' he turned to face her. 'Why not just give in? I would make you happy. I'd look after you.'

She smiled.

'How can you look after me, my gypsy boy, my young rebel? You have your own struggles. Of course I love you. I

163

love all your family.' She was struck by the tenderness of his gaze. Her eyes filled with tears. 'I've been careful for years not to get involved with anyone, Kai. I always intended to go home to Germany. Now there's no home to go to, I find I'm used to being alone. And I'm at least fifteen years older than you. Consider that.'

'I have, endlessly. What does it mean? Just that you've lived a few years longer. It doesn't matter. None of it matters if we love each other.'

'There are other considerations. I don't want to get you into danger. Remember I've already been called up to explain myself. I can't join the Kultuurkamer – even though all of you are right, and I should, for my safety. I can't make false work, and I can't dismiss my Jewish children. I think of my father and Kurt – how they never gave in, and it's not possible for me either.'

'I know. I understand now.' He looked at her intently. 'After I left you this afternoon I walked around, the whole of Amsterdam, it seemed, until I'd exhausted all my frustration. And it's only because I'm so scared for you that I was angry, believe me. I understand. But I'm certain that it'll be over one day, and we will survive. It's only a question of time, and hanging on until that time. We must have faith. I'll help you Hedda. My love will help you. There is no argument, you see.'

She shook her head and laughed. It seemed absurd that they were discussing it all so solemnly. She fell silent.

'All arguments exhausted,' she said at last.

They looked at each other and smiled. His eyes seemed very dark, the light of the candle a tiny blaze in the black of his pupils. I have never really seen this face before, she thought. Not in this way – so defenceless and tender and beautiful.

Winter

Katje scattered the contents of her jewellery box over the bed – a string of pearls from her parents, a silver bracelet engraved with leaves from her grandmother, and Aunt Minna's brooch.   She held the brooch to the light, and brought it close to her eyes until the brilliant ruby, framed in a band of gold, was all she could see. It hurt to part with something so pretty, but that only made her more certain that Miss Brandt should have it. Trusting her mother would never ask where it had gone, she put it into a box lined with white silk, and wrapped the box in tissue paper.

Dear Miss Brandt,

I'm really sorry for being so rude to you. People always say I should think before I open my mouth. It was just that it was a terrible shock, your school closing. It's like the end of the world, for me. I'll miss you and my dancing almost more than I can bear, but I promise to keep practising. I'll work hard every day on my own. One day you'll open the school again, I'm sure, and I won't have forgotten anything. In the box is a present to say thank you for everything you taught me. My Aunt Minna gave it to me. It was because of Aunt Minna that I saw you dance when I was little.
With all my heart, thank you.
Love,
Katarina.

Ps did I leave my dancing clothes in the studio?"

She dropped the box and letter through the door of Hedda's studio on the way home from school, then crossed the road and peered up at the windows. She cried a little, rubbed her eyes and put her handkerchief back in her pocket. I was so happy, but I won't stop dancing. I'll find a way, she decided. She hitched her school bag onto her shoulder and, humming one of Kai's folk tunes, turned towards home.

Dear Katje,

Thank you for your letter and most beautiful gift. Yes, you left everything here in your rush to leave! Your bag is safe with me.

I have a plan, and we will talk. Would you like to visit on Saturday afternoon? My rooms, as you will see from the address, are very near your house. It's funny we've never bumped into each other in the grocers on Leliegracht. Come around 3.00.
I look forward to seeing you.

Hedda Brandt

Saturday came, wild and blustery, with squalls of icy rain. Katje rushed out of the house and down into the street, the door slamming behind her. In moments she was drenched, the hem of her coat dripping rain onto her ankles and shoes as she crossed the canal, into Egelantiersgracht and past Café t'Smalle. She wore her best woollen skirt and cream blouse. She hoped to look as different as possible from the child who had screamed at Hedda only days before, but strands of hair escaped from their pins, and she was windblown and dishevelled by the time she reached Hedda's house.

She had rehearsed many times everything she wanted to say to Hedda, but when the door opened, and Hedda stood smiling, she forgot everything. She blinked, unable to say a word.

'Welcome, Katje. Come in quickly and get warm, it's so cold outside.'

Katje followed Hedda up two flights of wooden stairs, where she opened the door into a long room with gable windows either end.

'This is my home, my attic apartment.'

'You must love it, Miss Brandt, being so high above the street looking out into the trees.'

'I do. Take your coat and gloves off and I'll put them by the stove to dry. You're shivering. I'll get you a towel for your hair.'

Hedda left, and Katje looked round the room. One side overlooked the trees that lined the canal, and the other down into the courtyard with its patch of grass surrounded by low hedges and path, a little cherry tree leaning over a seat, and across to the windows of the surrounding buildings. The room was full of things to look at even though it was sparsely furnished – an upright piano against one wall, the gramophone player, a radio, a bookshelf full of books and plants filling almost an entire wall opposite the piano, a small round table covered in a red cloth, and three chairs. There were drawings too, so many, pinned wherever there was space. She saw many of them were by Hedda. Red velvet curtains were half drawn across an alcove, and behind them Katje saw the edge of a bed.

Hedda returned with a tray of cups, tea, and a cake. She lit the candle under the teapot stand and put the pot down.

'Mint tea, and I made an almond cake.'

'That's very kind.'

Katje tugged her skirt, twisting the fabric in her fingers.

'We parted badly, didn't we? I'm sorry you were so upset.'

'Oh, and I'm sorry too,' Katje blurted out.

'You sent me a beautiful gift. I was very touched, but I can't accept it.'

'Why? I have to give you something beautiful. To say everything I can't say in words. It seemed right too, because it was Aunt Minna's. Remember I told you about her?'

'I can't take Aunt Minna's gift away from you. You may regret giving it away, and I would hate that.'

'No, I'm sure, Miss Brandt. I want to think of you wearing it, when I don't see you any longer.'

The brooch was on the top of the bookshelf. Hedda took it down and opened the box.

'It's very pretty.'

'You must have it.'

She looked at Katje again and smiled.

'You always were a very determined young lady. Perhaps you will let me keep it on loan, as a kind of symbol of affection between us, as I see you're not going to relent. Then, one day, when I can go home to Germany, or sooner if you change your mind, I'll give it back to you.' She held the brooch against the collar of her shirt.

'Well if you're sure you won't take it for good, I have to agree.'

'I'll take great care of it, on loan.' Hedda fumbled with the clasp.

'I'll fasten it for you.'

It felt strange to be so close to Miss Brandt that she could feel her breath, and the warm skin of her neck under her fingers.

'There, it looks lovely.'

'Thank you. Until the war is won, you and your aunt will be with me. Now, what is this silliness about not seeing me any longer? Are you going away somewhere?'

Katje looked at her, puzzled.

'No, it's surely you who are going away, Miss Brandt.'

'I'm going nowhere. I'm staying in Amsterdam and teaching German language for a living. That, and my savings should keep me afloat for a while. I have told the bureaucrats that I retired from dancing with a bad back. I hope to God they never investigate. Now, I have a proposition to make. How old are you? Nearly fifteen, I think.'

Katje nodded.

'I'm fifteen next February.'

'You're not a child any longer. Now that I'm no longer your teacher, I'd like us to be friends. We have dancing in common. I have few people I trust to share that with now. What do you think?'

'I think that would be the best thing in the world. I can't think of anything better.'

'Good. I'll write to your parents and suggest something to keep them happy. Now you see I have very little furniture in here so there's room to dance. I just push the table and chairs back. Perhaps we could dance together sometimes. You could help me with the ideas that buzz round in my head all day and night. I could watch you dance, and sometimes give a little criticism that will help you. For an hour or two we can forget Hitler and the master race! This, you understand, is not teaching. Just sharing what we both love best.'

Katje laughed.

'I can't believe you're telling me this. I can't think of anything better than to dance here with you.'

'Well then, that's good. There's been too much sadness recently. Marten Hoffman often talks about the seed of creativity. We must imagine we are keeping the seed safe, until better times when it can grow at last.'

When Katje left Hedda, two hours later, the rain had turned to sleet stinging her face as she ran home, but she wanted to smile at everyone she passed. The naked trees, the gables rising up to meet the darkening sky were beautiful, even with the blacked out windows. Behind them people would be lighting lamps and candles, and the city hummed in the warm glow of Advent. She would like to see Elise if only evening wasn't drawing near. Never mind, she would go tomorrow, as soon as she could get away after church.

Singing, she let herself into her house. Werner was standing in the hall holding the post. She let the song fade away and smiled at him as she hung up her coat.

'Hey, Werner.'

'Hello.'

He put the mail down on the hall table and went on upstairs. Damn him, she thought. She would follow him to his room, sit on his bed and make him listen to her news.

'I'm home,' she said, peering round the door of the living room where her mother sat sewing. 'I'll come in soon, just got to tell Werner something.'

Her mother would never understand how important her dancing was, and father would look up from his work and smile, but he wouldn't have heard a word she said. She raced upstairs, two at a time.

She stopped short as she reached the ladder to Werner's attic. He'd pinned a poster on the wall – angular black words, on a grey background of fighter planes. She sank down on the lowest rungs of the ladder.

Waffen SS

With Adolf Hitler in a New Europe

She stared until the words became a jumble of black shapes.

'Werner.'

He came out of his room. She saw his feet in grey socks, toes curled over the top rung of the ladder.

'This isn't true. I must have got it wrong?'

'What are you talking about? Oh that. It's just a poster.'

'I know it's a poster, stupid. Why is it there? It makes me scared.'

'What of?'

'Have you turned into some kind of Nazi?'

'It's just a poster. Don't make such a fuss.'

He turned back to his room, closed and locked the door.

'Werner. I'm not going to let this happen. Listen to me.' She scrambled up the ladder and banged on his door. 'Stop hiding in your room.'

'You don't know me,' he shouted. 'You just think you know, and make your own stupid conclusions.'

'What am I supposed to think? Open the door and tell me.' She waited. 'All right, don't then.'

She tore the poster off the wall, ran down the stairs, and burst into the living room.

'Papa, Mama, look.' She flapped it in front of her parents. 'Look. You've got to stop Werner.'

'Do quieten down, child.' Her mother glanced up from her sewing, reached for the scissors and snipped at a thread. 'Whatever you two are quarrelling about it's not worth all this shouting.'

'It's not a quarrel. It's far more important. Papa, listen to me.'

'What is it, my chicken?' He put aside his newspaper and smiled at her.

She thrust the poster into her father's hands.

'I found this on the wall outside Werner's room. You've got to stop him.'

'Waffen SS,' he gave a short laugh. 'I'm sorry to say I don't think the poor boy would last a moment with the Waffen SS.'

'But it's a Nazi poster, Papa.'

'Well I can see that. I don't think you need worry about it.'

'How can you say not to worry? How can everything be fine if he sings and marches for Hitler and Seyss-Inquart, and Mussert? One day my best friends might be locked up or killed because of people like him. That's not fine! And the other thing is, I don't want him to leave for the army. It's hateful.'

She opened the door.

'Where are you off to now?' her mother said.

'If neither of you can listen, I'm going.'

Still wearing her indoor shoes, and without a coat, she ran out into the garden, not caring about the cold. She stood on the sodden grass and lifted her face to the sky. No moon, no light, only rain trickling down her cheeks and neck into her collar.

'Oh God, are you there, are you somewhere? Where are you? If you exist, if you're on the side of the good people, not a Nazi, dear God, help Werner. Please help him.'

Artsenkamer

'I decided that because you're one of the family you need to know what's happening,' Elise said to Katje when they met the Saturday before Christmas. 'I'm sure Ma and Pa would agree if I asked them.'

They turned off the main street into the park.

'Are you leaving Amsterdam?' Katje asked, her voice betraying her fear.

'Not yet. I hope never. No. Pa has made a decision not to join the Artsenkamer. I want you to know, because anything could happen.'

'Anything? Like what?'

'He could be arrested.'

'Oh no. That's worse for you than I could have guessed. That's terrible.'

'I'm only telling you so you know. It probably won't come to that. So many people have refused to sign. They can't arrest all the doctors in Holland – can they?'

They walked slowly, down the avenues of winter trees to the ponds, then sat down on a bench.

'The other thing I need to tell you – Kai's in trouble for not complying with the Nazis when he was a student, so he might have to go into hiding. I think he should cut his hair. I told him he's too noticeable with hair like that. I never understood how he got away with it at school. He never got teased, never told to cut it off. Oh it's just Kai, people said.'

'Where will he go, if he has to disappear?'

'I don't know. He's with Hedda as much as he can be. They're so in love.'

'In love. But she's years older.'

'Why should that matter?'

'I don't know. I suppose not. I knew Kai was in love with Hedda, anyone can see that. But I didn't know she loved him. I can't imagine her loving anyone, not in a romantic way.'

'Pa says she's the most emotional person he's ever met, underneath all that pride.'

Katje looked out across the half-frozen pond. A duck skittered along the ice and plopped into the dark water.

'People are never what they seem, are they?' she said. 'I think all sorts of different characters live in us all the time, going round and round in our heads as if they're dancing in a ring.' She pulled her scarf up around her neck and huddled into her coat. 'I had such a row with Werner last week, just horrible. He won't speak, or look at me. He has Nazi posters up on the wall. I don't think he's a Nazi at all, not really – it's that horrible man, Weiss.' Katje spoke in a rush, trembling. 'So in the end I told Pa that Herr Weiss is a bad influence and he should stop Werner's piano lessons. Perhaps I shouldn't have, but I couldn't think what to do. Werner hardly eats, he's getting thinner every week, and I'm sure he doesn't sleep either.'

'You did the right thing. I don't know why you have any doubt. Herr Weiss is a cruel man.'

'Pa said he'd talk to Werner. Talk talk talk. Even if he does, it'll be useless. I should have known. I don't suppose he'll stop the lessons. The thing is Pa has never understood Werner.' She looked along the path to check they were alone. 'We should start to write our stories. That's almost the only thing that will make me feel better.'

'Stories?'

'You haven't forgotten? You can't have done. You know – it was your idea to write all the bad things. You said it was a way of resisting. Remember – that night?'

'Oh Katje, I never thought you'd take me seriously.' Elise said lightly, and picked at a loose thread in her gloves. 'I thought about it afterwards. It was just a stupid idea, the kind of idea you can have in the middle of the night.'

'How can you say that?'

'Because it's true.'

174

Katje looked at Elise with incredulity, but the expression she was met with stalled all argument. She got up and stamped away towards the edge of the lake.

The grass lay in pale fronds, trapped under the ice. She bent and picked up a stone, threw it so it bounced along the ice and sank into the dark water at the centre. She turned around. Elise was gazing into space, as if she hadn't even noticed that Katje had left her side. Something has been said, she thought. It's as if she's decided not to trust me. It made her feel so alone.

Christmas

Kai leapt onto the crowded tram and stood in the doorway, pressed against the damp cold bodies of fellow passengers. Someone sniffed and breathed down his neck. He shifted his position. The tram moved too slowly. He looked down at his scuffed boots, working the fingering of a new violin piece in his mind, impatient as the minutes passed.

He jumped from the tram just before it reached Museumplein; saw Hedda standing on the steps of the building where she'd been teaching German. He was reminded of the first time he'd ever seen her, cycling past the Tea House in Vondelpark, and the look of recognition that had passed between them. She'd been radiant later that evening, with her stories of childhood in Germany. He remembered how she'd suddenly stood up and sung like a cabaret artist, some saucy German song, and Elise had giggled helplessly. Now she looked so small and strained. His heart soared with love for her. He dashed across the road, dodging bicycles. Catching sight of him she smiled and waved. He bounded up the steps, flung his arms round her.

'Guten abend meine leibling. How is the German going?'

'Horrible. Please don't attempt to speak German to me. I'm tired beyond belief. All those fat Dutch officials stumbling over their words. My first day and already I've had enough. Horrible horrible.' She smiled. 'But I am happy to see you.'

He put his arm round her waist and she leant into him.

'I'll take away all your tiredness.' He bent to kiss her, tilting her face towards him with his gloved hands. 'A surprise for you at home – your home I mean,' he said, between kisses.

'What surprise?'

'If I told, it wouldn't be a surprise.'

'You can stay tonight then?'

'Yes.'

Her eyes shone with delight. She closed them momentarily, and he kissed her eyelids.

'A few hours with you – perfect. Now the dreary day falls away as if it never mattered. Let's not wait for the tram, let's walk home.'

They crossed the square under leafless plane trees, towards Van Baerlestraat, where the Concert Hall and the Skating Club loomed out of the December twilight.

'Have you ever been skating there?' Kai asked.

'No. Have you?'

'Yes, I went every weekend for a while, with Benjamin and Piet. Ben is forbidden entry now. It makes me sick thinking of those Nazi parades in the summer, Seyss-Inquart ranting on. Makes me want to blow the place up, with all of them inside.'

He took Hedda's hand and held it in his own, warm in the pocket of his coat. They walked by in silence, left the main street and wandered zigzag down side streets to the Jordaan.

'I've been scared to ask you before, about the work you're doing.' Hedda stopped, her fingers tightened round his. 'Then I couldn't sleep last night, many nights I can't sleep, thinking of you.'

'Ssh. Not here.' He kissed her cheek, slipped his hand under her coat to caress her warm body. 'Wait until we're home. We'll talk there.'

They reached the house, and Kai bounded ahead of her up the stairs and stopped outside the door to her apartment. 'I'm going in first,' he said. 'Wait here for a moment.'

'What are you up to now?'

'I told you. A surprise.'

'Ah but it's so cold, Kai.'

'You'll be warm soon. I won't be long.'

Inside her room he lit white candles on the table he'd already laid with a bottle of Claret, cheese and bread and apples, and the cherry cake he knew was her favourite. Fir branches and red ribbons decorated the windows.

'Now come in,' he called.

He picked up his violin as she stepped inside.

As he began to play, he saw the tears that glistened in her eyes, and how she brushed them away. Her skin was pale gold in the candlelight. He wanted the image of her, at this moment, standing in her overcoat looking at everything with such delight, to burn into his memory, so that he'd always remember.

He put down his violin and humming the melody he'd been playing, he took her in his arms. She laughed in surprise as he danced her round the room.

'Oh and I brought vegetables too. Things I found cheaply at the market.'

'You're so very resourceful – and at the same time so romantic.'

'The perfect combination. Do you agree?'

'I do, Kai. Indeed.'

They stopped dancing, stood holding each other. She had closed her eyes. Her touch on his skin was gentle and intent.

'I'm mapping your face, every muscle, so my hands remember forever,' she said.

Later Hedda woke with a start as Westertoren clock struck one-thirty. She had slept too briefly, and now she remembered how yesterday she had taught German to three Nazi officials, and as far as anyone knew, her life as a dancer was over. She sighed, so deeply that Kai stirred, without waking, and reached for her hand. She lay a while longer before slipping out of bed. She felt her way to the window overlooking the canal. She peeled back the edge of the blind. The moon gleamed on the water, through frosted branches.

She thought of the conversation she'd had with Kai, too late in the evening. It had clouded her joy.

'I work for an anti-Nazi organisation,' he'd said, at last, when she insisted he told her. 'We collect and publish information, forge identity papers, help people disappear, that kind of thing. Hedda, I don't want to say more. It's safer that way.'

'Do Marten and Julia know?'

'Of my family Elise knows the most. I've never been able to keep secrets from her.'

'How long?' she'd asked. She'd taken his hand, held it to her lips.

'I began in a small way as a student; demonstrations, petitions and that kind of thing. After Piet was murdered I knew I had to do more, I knew I couldn't rest if I didn't.'

'I know. I understand. I'm feeling so many things, now you've told me. That I should do the same, of course – as my father did. That goes through my mind often. But there's fear for you too. I'm scared that you'll be harmed. It's a kind of agony to love, at times like this.'

He'd held her hand in both his, and told her that he knew he'd be safe – that he'd always been a survivor, like the cat with many lives.

She heard him calling her now, alarm in his voice.

'I'm here, darling. I couldn't rest any longer.'

She stumbled back. He was sitting up, his body still warm and soft with sleep.

'I dreamed you'd gone. Come back to bed, Hedda. It's so cold without you.' He reached for her arm, drew her close, his mouth reaching for hers. 'Don't ever go.'

Part Four
1942

Dancing Party

2nd May 1942 My fortieth birthday. The sun shines over my yellow cup, and across the blue checked tablecloth. White lilac Kai brought yesterday fills the room. Outside the sparrows chatter in the trees, and I can hear children playing.

A new law – all Jews are forced to wear the yellow star. A star must be stitched to every article of clothing, not only the overcoat. They must use their coupons to buy them. I'm sure Kai's organisation is responsible for the messages that fluttered down from the roof of the Bijenkorf yesterday – Jews and non-Jews unite – but I mustn't ask him.

Last night we shut out the troubled world. We climbed through the gable window and into the little space between the rooftops, and watched the moon rise. The bats were flying round the trees. Kai can still hear them, and I asked him to describe it. It's so impossible to imagine the unknown. We have no reference. The sound of a bat – high pitched, beyond anything I can hear.

Katje sniffed – what a gorgeous scent of flowers. Hedda's room was full of tulips and narcissus, in jugs and vases on the bookshelf and floor. On the table was a vase of white lilac, its heavy blooms drooping over her pile of books.

'Today I'm celebrating the colour yellow. A small gesture of defiance. I can't afford to be outspoken as I used to be.' Hedda's eyes met Katje's.

'Celebrating yellow?'

'In solidarity with the Jews. We're going to some friends of mine, musicians and artists. They've taken over my old studio. Kai will be there too. How long can you stay?'

'Until evening – maybe.'

'Good. Then that's decided. I'll be ready soon.'

Katje sat by the window and watched Hedda combing and pinning up her hair with deft movements, and humming under her breath. She seemed so happy these days. A red silk dress and long white scarf lay on the chair. Hedda folded them into her knapsack.

'We can go now.'

'What are you taking those for?'

'Wait and you'll find out. We'll go by bicycle. You'll have to sit on the back of mine.'

Hedda cycled along Prinsengracht and across bridges to the river, with Katje perched on the back.

The potent scent of beeswax, and river water that seeped from the basement, met them as soon as they opened the door.

'Ah that smell takes me back. I feel so much older than that day I first came to your school.' Katje said, as they climbed the stairs.

'Well so you are. Not a child any longer.'

'I've really seen life in the two years I've known you, haven't I? The most terrible things, and the most wonderful too.'

A young man greeted them at the top of the stairs, kissing Hedda, and turning to shake hands with Katje.

'This is Jan Schuyler, a great friend of Kai's and a most talented artist.'

'Welcome, both of you. Come and look around.'

'I must say, I can't wait to see what you've done with the old place.'

He led them through into the studio.

'I'm indebted to you, Hedda, for passing it on to me.'

One wall was hung from ceiling to floor with a length of yellow silk shot with silver thread, pooling like water on the floor. On it stood a life size bronze statue of a dancer on demi-pointe, arms raised over her head. A grand piano stood in the corner where Hedda's upright piano used to be, and tables and chairs were placed around the edges of the room – a single yellow tulip, and a white candle on each table.

'Oh goodness, it's quite like the grandest hotel.' Katje said. 'And how did they get such a big piano up those stairs?'

Many of the people who had gathered there had the obligatory yellow star sewn to their overcoats, but they shed these as they sat down at the tables. Kai hurried over, hugged Hedda and turned to Katje.

'Our friends hold private concerts in this room. This is Hedda's birthday gathering, so it's a concert for her. I don't suppose she told you that?'

'She told me nothing!'

'Well now you know. My family should be coming over later if the message reached them. It's all very last minute though, and I'm not home often these days, so I won't be surprised if they don't show up. Excuse us, Katje, we'll be back in a moment. Make yourself at home.' He took Hedda's arm and led her off to meet someone.

Katje sat down at a table in the corner where she could watch everything. An old gentleman brought her lemonade and asked if he could sit beside her.

'For an afternoon we can forget about our yellow stars, and the world out there,' he said. 'Are you Hedda's student? You're a fortunate girl.' He raised his glass. 'She's a marvellous teacher.'

'I know.'

His smile was so sad that for a moment Katje was transfixed. She realised she was gazing too long into his tired, red-rimmed eyes, and looked away. The room had filled with people. A young man made his way to the piano and began to play. The sun beamed through smoke and dust, the warm scent of flowers and ladies' perfume.

'I do wish I'd known to dress up, or at least to wear a yellow flower.' She looked at the man again. He smiled and said nothing, and she flushed, wondering if she'd offended him.

Kai was playing the violin, accompanying the pianist, and she turned to watch, her lips parted in admiration.

'Chocolate, a gift from Benjamin.'

Hedda held out a silver plate with pieces of chocolate.

'Oh delicious.'

A girl with red hair and a long green gown sang. It was a sad sweet song. It seemed, to Katje, to come from a world far away, to speak of possibilities far from the reality of life under German Occupation. She closed her eyes, drifted in the enchantment. When the song ended, the singer shook out her hair and bowed, and the room filled with the sound of talking. If only Werner had friends like this he'd never have to hang around with Weiss like a sad puppy. She nibbled the corner of her chocolate, trying to make it last. Her fingers were sticky, so she sucked them too.

'Silence everyone.' Kai clapped his hands. 'To celebrate her birthday, Hedda's now going to dance her solo – the Partisan – from Kurt Jooss' ballet, The Green Table. Benjamin will play the piano.'

There was shouting and applause. Hedda stood up.

'No applause, I haven't danced a step yet,' Hedda said. She untied her shawl. Underneath she was wearing the dark red dress she'd bundled in the bag earlier, and she took the white silk scarf from the chair behind her. 'And you will all have to imagine the soldier, and Death dancing with me.'

'Oh we imagine death all the time,' somebody teased. 'Death, in the form of a Puppet Master, haunts us all Hedda.'

'Don't jest, don't tempt fate,' she called back as she walked to the middle of the floor. 'Now I am a rather rusty dancer but I know today you'll forgive that. And Kurt, wherever you are – safe in England I hope – you would forgive me too, if you knew.' She took her place and nodded to Benjamin.

Katje watched, entranced, as the music began. Hedda leapt in a circle, her scarf held above her in both hands, and spun round pulling her arms into her sides, twisting the scarf into her belt. She looked younger, more powerful than Katje had ever seen, with her lilting sideways steps, interrupted by electric pauses, her body taut and alert.

Everything came back to her – the autumn night years ago in the theatre with Aunt Minna by her side – time was nothing – a whole life might be lived in one moment. Katje saw a clearing in the forest where the Partisan Girl watched and waited, knowing her death was certain. Her scarf was the symbol of her power, and as she threw it over the invisible soldier, the figure of Death appeared, forcing her back to meet the firing squad. She arched her spine, twisted and fell slowly.

Someone sighed. There was a second of silence, before everyone broke into applause and stood up.

Benjamin bowed to her, then took her hand.

'Hedda you are amazing, you will always be.'

She seemed dazed for a moment. She smiled, and thanked everyone.

Kai picked up his violin and someone began to dance. More and more people joined, holding hands in a chain, and stepping forward and back, swaying and spiralling around Hedda, closing in on her, until Katje, at the end of the line, saw her lifted above everyone's head, laughing. She slithered down to the floor, and everyone applauded again.

'Oh I am so happy,' Hedda said, sitting down, breathless beside Katje. 'For this one afternoon it's possible to dance, to forget.'

'Thank you so much. Your dance made me cry it was so beautiful,' Katje said. 'And I suddenly remembered the very first time I saw you.'

'Yes, I remember too, funny how memories sometimes return so clearly, out of nowhere. You had a little green coat with a velvet collar, and your aunt was a tall lady, rather flamboyantly dressed, some kind of deep pink hat. You jumped up and down waving – you must have loved to jump even then.'

They met each other's eyes and smiled. Behind her the whole glittering room shone in the mirror.

'But I have to leave soon,' Katje said. 'I wish I could stay forever.'

'I'll take you back.'

'No, it's all right.'

'I insist. I brought you here and I'll take you back. The party will have to stop anyway, it'll be evening soon.' She went off to find Kai.

As they left, Hedda broke a yellow tulip from its stem and pinned it to her collar.

'I'll be back soon, another day,' she called out to the party. 'I'm taking Katje home, and Kai is escorting us, for our safety.' She seemed to find this amusing, and ran down the stairs ahead of them.

They rode back with Kai just ahead. As they turned away from the river and started the stretch alongside the canals, a young Dutch policeman stopped Hedda. Kai, not noticing, rode on.

'ID cards.'

They took them out. He scrutinised them, handed Katje's back, and held on to Hedda's.

'You're German.'

'Yes.'

'How long here?'

'Nine years.' She stared ahead.

'Why do you wear this flower?'

'It's called a tulip'

'Why do you wear it?'

'Because it's yellow. In support of my Jewish friends.'

Katje heard the anger in Hedda's voice. She fumbled for her hand and felt the firm pressure of Hedda's fingers back.

'You should be ashamed of yourself.' He ripped the flower from her collar and stamped it into the ground. 'This time I'll let you off. Next time you won't be so lucky.' He gave her back her card.

Katje tugged Hedda's arm, knowing how close she was to erupting in fury.

In silence they rode to where Kai was waiting for them.

'What does he think he can arrest me for?' Hedda said when they reached him. 'How dare he, how dare he?'

'What happened?' Kai asked. He jumped off his bicycle, let it fall, and ran to her. She pushed him away.

'We got stopped by the police. He wanted me to tell him why I wear a yellow flower, even though he knows already. He threatened arrest. Oh how can I have been so feeble not to tell him what I think?'

'You said enough,' Katje said. 'He was close to driving you off to the police station. It was horrible.'

'I could have fought him off.'

'No,' both Kai and Katje said together.

'Oh I hate it. I hate all of it, and I hate being German. It's a sick nation. We deserve to perish in Hell.'

She walked away from them.

Katje and Kai glanced at each other. Katje saw the pain in his eyes. He went to Hedda, and again she turned her back on him, hiding her tears.

It was such a beautiful evening. The last sunlight caught the spire of Westertoren. A scent of lime blossom hung in the air.

'You were right to stop me losing my temper,' Hedda said with bitterness, when she returned. 'I must learn to keep my mouth shut.'

They walked slowly, wheeling their bicycles, until they reached the corner of Leliegracht.

'Goodnight,' Katje said. 'Thank you for the loveliest time. And for your beautiful dance.'

'Come Sunday, if you can. Try to forget all this. Don't look so sad.' Hedda touched Katje's cheek. 'Goodnight.'

Katje walked on, her feet in her scuffed old shoes moving her away from the friends she longed to stay with. It was painful to be alone with her thoughts, the bruised yellow tulip, and Hedda's anguished voice. If they'd only left the party seconds earlier. Or later. That's how it had been since the Occupation – the world swinging madly from sweetness to brutality. How hard it is to bear. But we must keep on, we must have courage. She turned to look back, to wave. She was too late. They had gone.

She saw Erik Weiss leaning against a tree and smoking. He smiled.

'Nice evening?'

He'd rarely spoken to her before. She didn't answer.

'Have you been dancing?'

She shook her head, and walked on.

'You should remind Miss Brandt that she's not permitted to dance any longer.'

His voice was odd, incoherent, as if he'd been drinking. She stopped and looked at him directly.

'We don't dance,' she lied. 'Miss Brandt has a bad back so she stopped teaching us. She teaches German now instead. Good evening, Herr Weiss.'

She went up the steps to the front door.

Kai and Hedda didn't speak until they reached the apartment and locked the door behind them. Hedda collapsed on the sofa. Kai stood beside her.

'What was Erik Weiss doing? You saw him, didn't you? He was watching you when we said goodbye to Katje.'

'He teaches Werner. He'd probably been to drop some music off. I don't know.'

'I don't trust him.'

Hedda didn't say anything.

190

'I've seen him hanging around, this last month. Early in the morning, twice he's been there outside the bakery looking up at your window. I saw him one evening too. He doesn't live near, does he?'

'Leidsegracht.' She sighed. 'I'm tired, Kai, tired beyond belief. I don't want even to think about Erik Weiss, never mind talk about him.'

'But what's he doing? He's no right to be watching us.'

'I'm sure he's not.'

'Rubbish Hedda. Of course he is. Why are you defending him? You were friends weren't you, as well as working together? You told me as much.'

'Yes, of course we were friends.'

'Were you more than that?'

With surprise, she saw the anguish of jealousy in his face, in the way he stood, arms tightly folded. He looked so young and fearful, in a way she had not seen before. I am making a mistake, she thought, he's scarcely more than a boy, what am I doing having this love affair with a boy?

'What if we were? It was before I loved you.'

'I must know, Hedda.'

He took her hands, and looked at her hard. Hedda looked away.

'Did you love him?'

'You know. I've told you all this. I respected his work, and he mine. I missed my country and there he was, another German – someone who spoke my own language. He always made me laugh. No, I didn't love him in the way you mean.'

'He's not funny.'

'No I know he's not.' Hedda spoke sharply. 'Against my better self, he made me laugh. I was very lonely. I've been lonely often since I left Germany.'

'You had friends, you had my family. You had me, Hedda, or could have had if you'd not been blinded by him. You had no right to be lonely, or to laugh at his cruelty.'

She covered her eyes with her hands, briefly. She felt so weary she could hardly think. Had she been blinded by Weiss? She'd wanted so much to trust him, when she'd always known in her heart that he was unreliable.

'Why did you push me away? In front of Katje.'

'Kai, please. I was in shock. I don't want to talk anymore.'

He went into the kitchen and she heard the tap running. It's my birthday, she thought. It was a beautiful day and now it's gone wrong. Only three hours ago I danced for the first time in months, and we were so happy. It had been brutal the way the policeman had ripped the tulip from her coat, his face so close and vicious, the yellow petals torn, and scattered on the road.

'Kai. Where are you going?'

He had his coat on.

'Out for a walk.'

He wouldn't look at her. She sat up, she couldn't catch her breath, couldn't call out. She rushed to the window, but already he'd gone. Everything had been poisoned by the encounter with the policeman, and then Weiss. She collapsed on the sofa and wept desperate tears that shook her body.

Empty and exhausted, she lost consciousness. Later she woke and remembered, and the misery flooded in. I quarrelled with Kai. Somehow we lost all sense of proportion – I cannot bear life without my work. I need to dance and teach. This stupid pointless work – teaching German to Dutch idiots.

She got up and turned on the lamp. Kai hadn't returned. Had he been arrested? It wasn't safe to walk around the city at night.

She hadn't eaten. It would be sensible to eat and drink, whatever had happened. She went to the kitchen. Mindlessly, she boiled milk and drank it, made toast and ate.

I will find him – when morning comes. Sick with anxiety, she lay down and tried to sleep.

He arrived so quietly, she hardly heard the door, didn't realise until he was in the room. He knelt beside her. She took his head in her hands, and he gripped her fingers, his body tense and desperate.

'Where did you go?'

'I walked.'

'All night. Oh no…'

'It's all right. I make sure I won't be picked up. I had to walk. You've been crying. Oh darling, I'm sorry.'

'For some reason he always made me feel sorry for him, Weiss, I mean. It wasn't love, not like you. Not like this.'

'Ssh. It's all right. Don't talk about him. Not now. I don't know where my jealousy came from. It was like being taken over by madness. I'll never leave you again, never, I promise.'

She wrapped her arms round his shoulders, burying her head in the crook of his warm neck, the collar of his coat, knowing that no promise could be kept in such times.

Stars

Papa used to say 'be happy, be grateful, Hedda, for fortune can change in a second.' I know pity alone will help nobody; it will only make me unhappy. But in the middle of the night the walls of the mind wear thin. Last night the rumble of an army truck down Prinsengracht woke me. It crossed the bridge and stopped only doors away, and I knew they had come for the two sisters.

I used to see them in the café on Sunday mornings. They would sit together, immaculately dressed in their fox furs, drinking coffee. They always smiled and asked about my dancing girls. They are so old, so frail. How will they survive? I switched on the light. Kai opened his eyes, and we looked at each other, listened to the shouts, the brutal banging on the door. We held each other. What can we do? Nothing? If Kai finds safe houses for many people, there are hundreds, thousands more.

The trees were heavy in late summer, leaves curling, tinged with gold. Katje practised staring up at the sun as she waited for Elise, then closed her eyes to watch the spots swirling under her lids. Now sounds became dominant, a child crying, a voice lost in the sound of traffic. How hard it would be not to be able to see anything. Would she give her sight to have the true Werner back? She opened her eyes to stop such thoughts.

They were going to visit Elise's old housekeeper, Mrs Goldstein. Elise said the dog had pups and she wanted to see them. Katje knew this wasn't true. There would be something else, some private errand of Elise's that she needed help with. 'Wait for me at the gates to the park,' Elise had said.

Sure enough, as she reached the gates, Elise was struggling down the road with a knapsack and two bags. Katje forgot Elise's difficulty walking, until she saw her from a distance, her face strained with effort. She waved and hurried forward.

'Do you mind carrying some of these things?' Elise said. 'They're for Mrs Goldstein's children.'

Katje took the bags from her.

'They're so poor now, the Goldsteins. Oh it's desperate, Katje. Mama doesn't know I've come. She'd stop me if she knew, but they were our neighbours once, so we have to try and help. I've found some of my old clothes to give away. The wool is still good. It could be unravelled to make new things.'

The trams were infrequent and too expensive. They walked slowly in the heat, stopping often to rest, until they reached the river and crossed into the Jewish quarter.

All around them people had yellow stars stitched onto their shabby clothes. It seemed they were the only girls without. With Elise on her crutches as well, they would be so easily noticed.

'Perhaps we should have worn stars too,' Katje said.

'What for?'

'So nobody will suspect us of anything. '

'Sometimes you say the stupidest things. How would it feel to have a great big star on everything you ever wear? Think how frightened you'd be then.'

'But I think all the time,' Katje said. 'I'm tired of thinking.'

They didn't speak again until they reached the Goldsteins' – a narrow brick house in the middle of the terrace. The street was strangely quiet. It was a poor looking house, Katje thought. The paint was peeling from the woodwork, and one of the upstairs windows was broken. The ground floor windows were obscured with houseplants, a curtain half closed.

Elise rapped on the door, but nobody came. They waited. A breeze caught the dust and litter, whirling it in a flurry against their legs.

'There's usually someone in. I hope she's not taken worse than she was last month. It's so hard for her to get out.'

Katje tried the door handle. It was locked. She reached up to peer through the window into a small dark kitchen. There was a table covered in a white cloth, laid with two plates and cups and a jug.

'It looks normal in there. She must have just gone shopping or something. We'll have to come back later.'

'I don't know. We can't wait around here, and I can't leave everything. There's nowhere to hide it.'

'We can go to the park. Or a café, if you've got any money.'

'I haven't, not enough.' Elise looked defeated. 'It's so hot.' She sank down on the step. 'Katje, I think something terrible has happened,' she said after a while. 'I don't think they're coming back.'

'I'm scared. I don't want to stay here.'

Elise looked up at her. 'They were our friends. I've got this terrible feeling.' She began to cry.

'Please, let's get away.'

For a moment nothing was quite real to Katje. She saw Elise's pale face turned towards her, the sunlight blue over her dark curls, a housefly crawling over her cotton dress, as if watching a girl in a film. Then panic crashed in. She wanted to run, back across the river, away from the Jewish quarter to the safety of home. Sobbing, she pulled at Elise's arm.

'It's all right,' Elise said over and over again, but her breathless voice betrayed her fear, as she tried to move quickly, stumbling, and catching herself again.

From the main street there was the sound of a police whistle, and dogs barking. They'll catch up with us. We can't go fast enough.

'I left the knapsack behind,' Elise said, stopping abruptly, her face desolate with tears.

'It's too late for that. I left the bags too.'

Everything – the blank windows, closed doors, and the huge imposing portico of the Jewish Council building – terrified Katje. She fixed her eyes on the distant bridge that marked the boundary of the Jewish quarter, and dragging Elise with her, she dared not look back.

The other side of the city, that same afternoon, Kai walked slowly back to Hedda's with his friend, Benjamin. Benjamin carried a wicker basket, and tried to keep it from swaying as he moved, so the cat inside it wouldn't be too frightened. From time to time he stopped to soothe the animal.

When they reached Café t'Smalle, Kai slowed down.

'You are sure you're making the right decision?' he asked.

'You know my answer,' Benjamin said.

Kai unlocked the door to Hedda's apartment. His hand shook.

'I still hope that you'll change your mind.'

'I can't bear the thought of being cooped up, or being dependant on anyone else. That hasn't changed.'

Hedda came to the door, greeted them both quietly. She took the basket from Benjamin and put it on the table. Inside the cat mewed and clawed.

'Shall we let her out?'

'She'll hide, but yes, let her out, poor thing,' Benjamin said. 'It's been a bit of a journey.' He lifted a little black cat from the basket and held her to his face. 'Elise will love you, Puss. You'll be happy in your new home.'

'We'll take her tomorrow.'

'Thank you.' He put the cat down, and she ran under the sofa.

For a moment they were all at a loss what to do or say. Ben had received orders to report at Central Station the following morning. There'd been so little time to prepare in the end. He'd said goodbye to his family.

He sat down at the piano.

'I should think it's the last I'll see of one of these for some time. I'm going to take my penny whistle with me, easier to hide in my pocket than a piano.' His voice was cheerful, but the words caught in his throat. He turned to Hedda. 'Will you dance for me?'

'What shall I dance?'

'What about the Partisan Girl, with a different ending? I know the music by heart, but I'd prefer a happier outcome for you. No soldiers, no Death.'

'The Triumph of the Partisan?'

'Wonderful.'

She had no will to move, but for Ben, for the last time, she would try. They smiled at each other.

She danced in the small space between the sofa and the window, through the beam of evening sun that fell over the floorboards, a spiralling, energetic dance, stamping her feet, rising and falling, raising both arms, her hands clenched, as he played the last notes. Kai sat on the arm of the sofa watching.

Afterwards the three of them shared a bottle of beer. Ben raised his glass.

'To us! Until the next time we meet.'

They drank, held hands, held tight. They dared not look at each other.

The Small Dance

Katje never told her family of her visits to Hedda, but between errands for her mother, and on the way home from school, she often ran across the canal to Egelantiersgracht. She'd ring the bell, and if Hedda appeared at the window and beckoned her up, she'd let herself in with the key she'd been given, run up the stairs and burst into the room. On days when she was expected Hedda would be waiting, the furniture pushed back.

'How are you, Katje? Ready to dance?'

Over the months, in their snatches of time, they began work on a solo for Katje.

'This is the small dance,' Hedda said. 'A ballet for a living room instead of a theatre. Imagine you're in a tiny dark space. That's right, let your fingers stretch from flexion, twist your wrist and then lean away from your arm, focus on your hand. If you arch back and support with your other arm...that's good, a beautiful line Katje.' Hedda paced around, watching from different places in the room. 'Your hand movements must be absolutely precise. If only your hands are moving, the dynamic is as important as the pathway of the movement. Try again, now with a darting action. Good. Soon we'll be ready for Kai to play for you. I'd like you to try with one of Vivaldi's pieces.'

After working, Hedda made tea. They moved the chairs and table to the canal side window and sat looking out at the wet leaves dripping onto the surface of the canal, the ripples of light. They watched a young girl crossing the bridge, the yellow star bright on her brown dress.

'I have this notion,' Hedda said, 'that when we dance, as you have just now, we create a powerful force that defies oppression.' She gestured to the girl outside, and they watched as she turned the corner onto Prinsengracht. 'I can't do anything to help that poor girl, oh that I could, but I can stop myself despairing.' She looked at Katje and smiled. 'I'm very proud of you. One day, soon if possible, you can dance for our Jewish friends, those who are still here. To Hell with the Nazi controlled theatre.'

Katje leant against the windowsill. The sash was pulled up, the air cool and fresh. A chaffinch sang in the trees.

'To Hell with them all,' she said, laughing. 'Tell me about when you learnt to dance, about when you were a child.'

'I was the oldest. There was Gitta next, and then little Hanna. She died when she was three. I was sent to ballet lessons with Gitta. I think my aunt thought it would be good to get us out of the house, away from my grieving parents. As far as I was concerned she was right. Even those early days it was the one thing that made me happy.'

'You were like me then.'

'Yes. I understood you very well that day you arrived in my studio, so stubborn and determined. I was clever and my father wanted great things for me, not the life of a dancer, but it only made me stronger. I studied Russian and English, to please him, but I kept up my ballet lessons, paying for them by teaching little ones. Then Kurt Jooss began teaching in Essen and I went to him and begged to join his classes. Fortunately I had a good body for his style, and I adapted quickly, and I was happy, so happy, Katje. I felt alive for the first time in my life. Those first days when I joined his company – I was walking on air.'

She stood behind Katje and gazed out of the window. How far away she looks, Katje thought, as if I'm not even in the room any longer. In the distance she heard the clock striking four. She knew she must go home soon. It was always so hard to leave, like getting out of a warm bed on a winter morning.

'I've just remembered something.' Hedda went to the corner of the room. She bent down and pulled up a loose board. 'Katje, if ever anything happens to me, please come and take these, keep them safe.'

Under the floor was a space big enough to hide a pile of notebooks.

'They're only dance notes, scribbles, ideas I have, bits of journal, but I don't want them falling into German hands.' She laughed. 'Even if they were written by a German hand.'

'But nothing will happen to you,' Katje said. 'It mustn't.'

'But if it does then you know what I want you to do.'

As she replaced the floorboard the outside door opened and footsteps sounded. She sprang to her feet as Kai entered, holding a bunch of white roses.

'Kai I wasn't expecting you!'

He put the roses down on the piano.

'Aren't you glad to see me then? Hi Katje.'

'Of course I am, but not rushing in like that when I don't know you're coming. Never like that again.'

'Who did you think I was, the Gestapo?'

'Oh Kai, please don't jest.'

Sobered, he held her shoulders, kissed the tip of her nose, then hugged her.

'It's all right,' he said. She looked so small and vulnerable, pressed against his chest, that Katje had to look away.

'If the Gestapo ever come looking for us, we'll disappear like spirits up into the rooftops.'

'You're such a child. As if it's all a game to you.'

She pushed him away.

'Come and look at this Katje,' he said.

He showed her the tiny window from Hedda's bathroom that opened onto a space, hidden by the gable, between the rooftops.

'It has a bolt on the other side, so nobody could follow us if they wanted to. And anyway the Gestapo are all too fat. They'd get stuck, and then wouldn't they look stupid, legs dangling and kicking over the washbasin?'

Katje climbed onto the washbasin, squeezed through the opening, and out onto a narrow platform. There was so much sky – the distant sounds of a tram and the people scurrying, so small below her.

'How wonderful it is,' Katje said, when she joined them in the kitchen where Hedda was washing the cups.

'I saw that miserable Weiss, on my way here,' Kai was saying. 'He was wearing an NSB badge. What do you say to that?'

'Entirely predictable,' Hedda replied shortly. 'The NSB are toy Nazis, posturing, power-hungry men. Poor Weiss will be at home with them.'

'Poor Erik!' Kai turned to Katje. 'Keep an eye on that brother of yours. If he joins up too, you can spy for us, be our ears and eyes into the enemy.'

'Kai, leave her alone. She needs to stay out of it all. I won't have her put into ridiculous situations, and I'm sure Werner has more sense.'

'But he hasn't,' Katje said. She couldn't make sense of the resistance she saw in Hedda, the lift of her shoulders, her concentrated focus on the cups. 'I haven't known what to do,' she added.

'Tell him to talk to me. I can find him an excellent teacher,' Kai said.

Hedda reached past Katje for the teacloth.

'Let's not talk about Weiss again. I'm sick of him.'

There was the sharp tone in her voice that Katje knew well – and there would be no further discussion. Hedda dried the cups and put them back on the shelf. Kai sat on the table watching her intently.

'Keep Hedda safe Katje,' he said. 'I worry she's not safe alone. Watch out for her when I've gone.'

'Where are you going?' Hedda asked, disquieted.

'Nowhere, nowhere,' he said. 'I just want to make sure you're looked after.' He opened his violin case, took out the bow and rubbed it with rosin.

'I can look after myself, Kai.'

'I must go. I'll be expected at home,' Katje said.

She went to fetch her things, listening as she put her dancing slippers in her bag, in case they said any more about Werner. But there was silence. She called goodbye. Hedda came out and kissed her.

'Til next week.'

'Will you be seeing Elise?' Kai asked. 'When you do, give her my hugs. Tell her I'll be home as soon as I can.'

They stood in the doorway, watching her go down the stairs.

She turned to look up at the window when she reached the street, but Hedda wasn't there. Slowly, and reluctantly, she walked home.

Symposium

Katje was in the kitchen clearing up after Sunday lunch. The doorbell rang.

'You'd better see who it is. I don't think your father heard,' her mother said.

Katje put down the dishcloth and scuttled down the hall, hoping it would be Elise. The bell rang again just as she opened the door, and she was faced with Erik Weiss. She drew back. He was so close she could smell him.

'Werner isn't in.'

'I have an appointment with your father.'

'He's not in either.' She knew her defence was feeble, but she was unable to stop herself.

'I hope he is since I've taken the trouble to come here,' he answered, with a tight smile.

She stood with her arm barring entrance.

'He must have forgotten.'

He laughed.

'Don't waste my time. If you would be so kind as to tell your father I want to speak with him.' He stepped towards Katje so forcefully she backed into the hall.

'Papa, Papa, come quickly,' she called. Her father appeared from his study. 'Were you expecting him?

'Good-afternoon, Herr Weiss. Do come in.' He smiled, his hand outstretched in greeting.

'Forgive me, I'm a little early, but I have a rehearsal in the church this afternoon and thought I should come before.' Herr Weiss brushed past Katje without another glance. They went into the study. Katje stuck her tongue out as the door closed.

'It was Herr Weiss.'

Her Mother was filling a jug with water. Her hand jerked and water splashed over her wrists. She put down the jug.

'I'd better make coffee then. Where's Werner? Does he want to see him?'

'Where is Werner ever? In his room or playing the piano, and as he's not playing the piano, he must be in his room. He obviously doesn't know his beloved Herr Weiss has paid a visit.'

Her mother sighed.

'This constant friction with Werner has really gone too far. I wish you would let it rest.'

'What has that horrible man come for? I hope Papa cancels the lessons now he's here.'

'If I remember correctly it was you who insisted he couldn't live without the piano.'

'But not lessons with him. He's evil.'

Katje stamped out of the kitchen ignoring her mother's complaints. She pressed her ear to the door of her father's study. She could just hear Weiss's clipped polite voice.

'These are important times. There will be enormous changes culturally, and I expect to have a part in shaping them. I have a vision of something great, something that reflects the power of the Reich. I believe only the best musicians should be trained. Anything else is an indulgent waste of time and money.'

Her father coughed.

'Do I understand that you're saying my son is a waste of time? I'm quite prepared to stop his lessons. He spends far too long at the piano as far as I'm concerned.'

'No no, I wouldn't have come to see you if that were the case. You'd have received a letter saying I no longer wish to teach him.'

He's the most pompous man I've ever known, Katje thought. I'd laugh if he wasn't so cold that he's truly frightening. Hearing her mother coming from the kitchen with the coffee, she darted upstairs, and sat on the top step where she could peer down into the hall and wait to see what happened.

In a short while, the door opened. Weiss emerged followed by her father. They shook hands.

'I'm sure Werner will do credit to us all,' Weiss said. 'I'm glad all misunderstanding has been cleared up.'

A few days later Weiss invited Werner to his flat on Leidsegracht. With a portentous manner, he ushered the boy into his music room. Werner gazed around, too nervous to speak. With deep red walls, blinds at the window, and dominated by the grand piano, it had a cloistered atmosphere. Outside, rain clattered through the leaves, and down the windowpane.

'I always shut out the world when I enter this room.' Weiss drew down the blind, and put on the lamp. 'And you are the first of my students ever to be invited in. You will play through your pieces today, to get the feel of the piano.'

Werner swallowed. He felt the force of his heartbeat in his chest and throat. It was a kind of agitation he'd never known, his body taut with a mixture of anxiety and elation.

'Sit down.' Weiss gestured to the piano stool. Werner sat rigid, his hands on his knee. 'Now, before we start, I wanted you to come here today as I have a plan. You may know that there's much talk amongst the authorities about the future of music, the development of an appropriate music for the age. A music symposium has been scheduled for next summer. It will be an important event, one that will set the tone for the next generation, indeed for the generation beyond the next. I'm one of a small number of composers to be asked to perform. I hope to present three pieces, and as my star pupil, I'd like you to play one of them.'

'Me? But I'm not good enough yet,' Werner stammered.

'I wouldn't ask you if I didn't think you could do it.'

'I'm not sure my father will give me permission.'

'Your father won't stand in your way. I've already spoken to him. He was delighted. It seems as if you're putting unnecessary blocks in the way, Werner. Are you trying to tell me that you don't want to do it?'

'No. I'm very honoured. I just can't take it in, sir.'

Weiss laughed. When Werner dared to look up at him, he thought he read tenderness in his face.

'You look terrified as a trapped rabbit. I thought I was giving you good news.'

'It's more than I could imagine.'

'Well you have a good long time to perfect it. Here's the score. I don't want to work on it today. We'll go through it movement by movement next time we meet. Take it away and study it.'

Werner took the score, opened it reverentially.

'It looks beautiful on the page. The way you've written it, so tiny and neat,' Werner said. 'I've never seen a handwritten score before.' He was aware of his hands shaking.

'The first you'll see of many. There is no title as yet. I don't always like to title my work, but I suppose it would be advantageous to do so. Cathedral of the Gods, Music for the Magnificent.'

Werner looked at him, puzzled by the thought of such odd titles. Weiss sneered.

'You didn't think I was serious, did you? I play the game, but I wouldn't take it that far. After all, they are the guardians of my work, the means to an end, if you like.'

Werner sat outside the church and let the rain soak into his clothes, run down his hair into his eyes. He clutched Weiss' score to his chest, under his coat, and tried to think about the Reich Music Symposium, but it all seemed remote and improbable. He couldn't see himself playing in a huge concert hall in front of a vast audience of Nazi officials. The thought of it made him sick. But how could he refuse?

Lately Herr Weiss was so changeable. In one breath he seemed to respect their occupiers, in another to dismiss them as ludicrous. He was inconsistent too in his manner towards Werner. Today he had been tender, almost fatherly in a way that Werner longed for his own father to be. Other times he was arrogant, distant, and unbearably harsh in his criticisms.

Once only, he had suddenly knelt at Werner's feet and taken his hands.

'You'll never again be as beautiful as you are now.' He spoke his name so tenderly. 'Dear Werner, my dear boy. Don't ever let anyone hurt you.'

It had never been like that again. The following week he'd been cold and pernickety about Werner's style. Recently Werner had felt a torment of uncertainty before every lesson. Perhaps this would change as they worked on the pieces, if he could find the courage to face the idea of performing at such a prestigious event.

He stared into space. He wanted oblivion, a field of clear white snow, but his eyes focussed through the trees to the posters plastered against the wall of the church. 'NSB A New Netherlands in a New Europe,' and an image of fists holding a German flag, rippling in the wind – above it 'Waffen SS With Hitler In A New Europe.'

He shivered. He hadn't realised how cold and damp it was. A crowded tram rattled by, heading for the station. He wished he could get on, take the first train away from the city, anywhere. He wanted to be a boy again, off for a day out with a friend. There would be other men like him in the army. There would be comrades.

Katje was coming downstairs when he let himself into the house.

'Oh God, Werner you look like a drowned rat,' she said. 'Wherever have you been? I'll fetch a towel.'

He stood blankly in the hall waiting until she'd returned.

'You'll catch cold if you're not careful.' He let her rub his head vigorously. She laughed. 'Now you look a bit more presentable, if a bit like a hedgehog. Go and get changed and I'll make you a cup of tea.'

Hair

'What's the most noticeable thing about me, Hedda?' Kai asked, as they lay together late in the evening.

She sat up on her elbow, tracing his brow and cheeks with her fingertips – his sun-browned skin, the fall of curls on his neck – beautiful, like an English Romantic poet, like a Pre-Raphaelite painting – no, more Spanish than that. So beautiful that I wonder why all the women in Amsterdam don't thirst to be his lover?

'That's easy to answer. The way you move, your straight spine, the way you hold your head. I remember the first time I ever saw you, thinking you must be a dancer.'

'Only you would see that though. What about other people?'

'How should I know? Your hair, I suppose. It's the first thing people usually notice about others, along with height and fatness. Why do you ask?'

'Things are difficult. I need to be able to disappear in a crowd. I don't think I do with hair like mine. Elise keeps telling me too. People have always described me as the boy with the curls.'

She lay down, her arm over his chest, pattering her fingers along the smooth ridge of his ribs.

'Sometimes, when I'm alone I'm so afraid for you. I don't know if it's safe for you staying here with me – I'm too obvious, an anti-Nazi German. They must be watching me.' Her voice was quiet, fearful. 'Then I get anxious even of Katje and that poor brother of hers, in case they inadvertently say something. I wish you hadn't shown her the roof space.'

He kissed the top of her head.

'Remember, I'm a survivor. A cat with nine lives, and I haven't lost one of them yet.'

She tried to smile, but tears clouded her eyes. With a Spanish father and a mother who looked Jewish, he'd always stand out.

'But I'll have a better chance of surviving without my hair. Will you cut it for me?'

'Oh darling. I haven't even got proper scissors, and I'm no barber.'

'I don't want anyone else to do it.'

'I remember my sister, Gitta, as a little girl, cutting a great chunk of her hair with the kitchen scissors. Mama was so cross, but Papa just said, it will grow again, don't fuss so.'

'He was right. It will grow again,' Kai said. 'When the Nazis are defeated.'

'Sometimes you're such a boy.'

'But they will be defeated. Believe it, Hedda.'

When he was in this mood, her love felt maternal, fiercely protective.

'It feels so odd after all this time,' Kai said the next morning, as Hedda snipped and his curls fell away. 'How have I got away with having long hair all my life? Let me look.'

He jumped up and went to the mirror in the bathroom. Hedda heard him laughing.

'Oh I don't recognise myself. I'm a stranger. Now I must go and face the world before I lose courage.'

He left to teach a violin lesson, with promises he'd be back later. Hedda went to the window and watched him. He doesn't look Dutch – and with those good looks too. My poor boy – he has no idea. The resistance must be full of naïve passionate young people. He looked back to her window and waved, even though she knew he was too far away to see her, then he too disappeared beyond the trees.

She turned back to the empty room, his hair scattered over the wooden floor, the scissors still open on the table. It is a small thing, these days, it's nothing really – the loss of beautiful curls. But she felt so sad. She still sensed the touch of his hands cupping her face before he left, his lips on her forehead and mouth.

She gathered his hair into a pile, scooped it up – soft enough to line a bird's nest. She kept one curl, and put it in an envelope, then opened the window and let the rest fall into the garden. Next spring the birds would find strands lying amongst the dead leaves. By then the war might have turned, the end might be in sight. Oh my love, I have to believe such a simple thing as a haircut will make you invisible, keep you safe.

Resistance

Katje sat on her bed with a pillow across her knees for a desk. Her fingers ached she wrote so fast, filling pages of her notebook, tearing them out and dropping them in a pile on the floor, pausing only briefly to rest.

All of you who read this, your help is needed. Don't turn away as if nothing is happening. You have to imagine what it's like to be forced to leave your house, to leave behind your pet dog you had since a puppy and your family photographs. Have you seen the number 8 tram, the only tram Jews are allowed on, going up to Central Station? Where are they being taken? What will happen to them? Do you ask yourself that question? Or do you just go off shopping so you don't have to see?

I am fifteen and still at school. I said goodbye to a friend one Friday and I haven't seen her since. Nobody talks about her any longer. My favourite teacher, who taught geography and made us all love it so much, disappeared last winter. I hate to go to school now.

The Hollandsche Schouwburg is closed. Jews are taken from their homes and sent there before going to concentration camps. We went to visit Mrs Goldstein, but she'd already gone. We saw soldiers and police pushing and shouting and beating people into the darkness of the theatre. Old people who could hardly walk, people carrying all their possessions in little bundles, mothers with tiny babies, and children crying because they'd lost their parents.

They tell us things that even the stupidest people know aren't true. What's happening? Where are they being taken? Why? If you search into your heart, your deepest thoughts, can you answer? The most wonderful future world can't justify it.

But there will be no wonderful world. They will all turn against each other and make an eternal Hell.

You must stand up and let your voice be heard, and say NO.

Katje de Jong

Katje stopped. Her finger was sore, she'd written so much. She looked at the clock, slithered off the bed, gathered up the pages and put them in her bag. She put on her coat, ran downstairs, quietly so nobody would hear her leaving, and out into the street.

September

Kai and Hedda cycled side by side along the river path, through sunlight and shade. Brown leaves and seeds twirled round them with each flurry of breeze. Hedda sang. Kai smiled, and they reached for each other's hands, slowed down a little to steady their wobbling bicycles.

They stopped beyond the outskirts of the city at a little café by the water's edge, and leaned the bicycles by the door. The river was bordered with rushes and willow, and beyond the houseboats, on the distant bank, the fields stretched far into the distance where the plane of land met sky in a dark flat line. They sat at a table close to the river where a rowing boat was moored. The waiter came. They ordered beer.

'What are you thinking?' Kai asked when they were alone. She was smiling as she gazed into the distance.

'I was remembering that time in Paris when The Green Table won the choreography competition. We celebrated, we really did that night. Nobody had any sleep. We danced along the streets back to the hotel like wild things, laughing and singing, and that was before we'd had much to drink. How strange – you'd have been little more than a child then.'

'I'd have been seventeen. By then I'd lost my father, moved to Amsterdam, gained another father and two sisters,' he responded with mock indignation.

She laughed.

'A child with experience.'

'I wonder where I was that night.'

'I used to stand in the wings and watch the Old Woman's solo. It's beautiful, so beautiful. Sometimes when I can't sleep, when you're not with me, I hear the music in my head, and I dance her part instead of the Partisan Girl. It always calms me.' She lifted her face up to the sky, then blinked, momentarily blinded by the sun. 'I miss my work,

214

my real work. I listen to you playing and I sit there, feeling so powerless. It's as if the less I'm able to dance, the more my mind is agitated. When we're free again, when all this is over...oh, I don't know. Sometimes I despair.'

'You'll make a brave new dance company, and I'll be your musical director.'

'No, you'll perform, Kai, you won't be my musical director. You're such a wonderful musician you'd be wasted in bureaucracy. And I'll have my musicians on stage with the dancers. That's how I see it. Not hidden away in an orchestra pit.'

The waiter came out with their beer. They watched him disappear into the café, then they raised their glasses and drank to the future, looking into each other's eyes, until Hedda had to turn away, so intense was his tender, questioning look. They fell silent. The light danced over the surface of the river, and beneath, tiny fish darted in shoals. Sometimes Hedda could scarcely believe their love, his fearless passion for her.

'When Gitta and I were little we used to pile up the dry leaves every autumn and try to build walls from them. Once we planned to make a whole palace. I knew it was impossible, but because Gitta was so sure, I thought it might just turn out in the end.' If you want something enough you can make it happen, she'd thought, as they crossed the lawn with their arms full of leaves. She imagined herself now, looking out of the window of their rustling palace.

'Our work, our life together,' she said softly, and could not bear to look at him. 'Look a fish, no lots of them, can you see?' She squatted to trail her hand in the water. 'Look. How brave they are, swarming towards this strange white hand. Or are they just curious, impetuous? They're like you, Kai.'

She knew he wanted her full attention, that he could be jealous even of the fish. She had the odd notion that if they

215

kept still they could stop time – delay forever the inevitable moment of separation. It seemed that fear made her love glance off him, made her distant where she longed to be intimate. She drew her hand out of the water, and turned back to him, met his gaze.

'What is it you want to say?' she asked.

He picked up a pebble and skimmed it across the river. He sighed.

'What is it, darling?'

'I've been advised to leave Amsterdam.'

In her panic it seemed that everything tightened around them, the river darkened, the sky gathered, too intensely blue.

'Is it your work with the organisation?' Her voice caught in her throat.

'No, thank God – less serious – though serious enough. No, I was involved with a group when I was teaching at the university. We refused to comply with certain restrictions, and sign their stupid documents. We campaigned to keep our Jewish members of staff. They're searching for members of that group now. We're wanted for questioning. I'm just afraid that will lead to worse.'

'This is why you cut your hair?'

'Partly. I need to stop appearing in concerts, and give up most of my teaching. I'm too easy to find if I'm performing. Papa has given me money. We've agreed I'll pay him back when I can. I can live on very little. But I can't risk living either in Leiden or with my parents. Both addresses are known.'

'So will you follow this advice?'

'I don't know. I'd go mad hiding out in the country. In Amsterdam I can at least continue to work for the organisation, and see my friends and you.'

She looked down at her hands. Shock had made her light-headed.

'I want you to be safe. You mustn't put yourself in unnecessary danger.'

'I don't want to go.' He was very still, gripping his elbows.

She didn't trust herself to speak without betraying her fear.

'Sometimes you're so remote,' he said, startling her with his anger. 'It's as if you cut yourself off from me. Don't you see? I don't want to leave you. Then I'm afraid I put you in danger too by staying with you, and I don't know what you think at all.'

'Oh Kai, if I seem cut off it's only because I'm afraid for you. We've talked about it before. I want you to stay with me, and at the same time I know it's unsafe. It's the price I pay for my outspokenness in the past.'

'I take the risk. You're at risk too. We can part now if we choose.'

'Is that what you choose?' she said, after a moment. She feared his answer, her heart so full she could hear it beating. Anticipating his reply she continued.

'You're young. One day this will be over and you'll want a wife and children, a life separate from me.'

'Why do you keep going on about our age?' he snapped. 'I'm old enough to know my mind. I want to stay with you. I want us to get married. You can be so stupid at times, Hedda. Fair enough if you don't love me…'

'Oh I do love you, Kai, never doubt that.' Her eyes filled with tears. She took his hand and they knotted their fingers together, held tight. 'It's not a world I feel safe or at home in any longer. I have no family but yours and I'm lost without my work.'

'Well then. Shall we get married? One day. I know we'll have to wait.'

A flock of crows rose into the air with a wild lonely cry that seemed to come from one body. At the same time she felt something release in her — a sense of restraint, so familiar she was only aware of it now it had given.

'If that's what you want, I want it too, with all my heart.'

'So there's no argument. Is there?'

They smiled at each other.

'There's every argument, and no argument.'

She leant her head against his shoulder, felt the warmth of his skin and the sunlight beyond her closed eyelids.

Part Five
1943

February

Waiting for Kai to return from wherever he goes these days – cold February eve, I've given up trying to light the stove.

On the British radio this morning – the German army has fallen at Stalingrad, defeated by the Russians. It's turned at last. There's no hope for Germany. God bless the Russians.

When Hitler is defeated Kai and I will get married. I'll start a new school, and he'll be able to teach in Leiden again – a new studio, a new dance company. Benjamin is strong. He'll return – with so many of our old friends.

I will go back to Germany and visit my father's grave, and see Gitta, and the children. I will write to Kurt. I will go with Kai to England to meet him.

Notes for a new ballet – a joyful, exhilarating work. Diagonal sequences of leaps, runs, turns, spins – fast flow of movement crossing the whole stage, start low level, to up-lifted, developing lifts, dancers carried high.

The girls in brilliantly-coloured, full-skirted gowns, swirling, running with lengths of rainbow coloured silk.

Yesterday, Katje standing against the light of the window, her arms stretching up, the grey winter sky behind her, extending her leg high, rising on to her toes, and balancing for longer than she'd ever managed. So funny, the look of incredulity on her face.

May

'I'm so sick of hearing that music,' Katje said. 'What is it?'

Werner had just finished his piano practice, and they were both in the hall preparing to go out.

'Herr Weiss' composition. The first movement.'

'I don't know how you can keep on playing it all these weeks.'

'I don't either,' he said quietly, as he put on his coat. 'But I haven't a lot of choice.'

Katje bent to fasten her shoes.

'Just tell him. Just say, Herr Weiss, I'm very sorry but I'm not up to this. Then leave and find a new teacher.'

Already Werner had gone without waiting for her. By the time she was ready he'd have reached the end of the street.

She'd discuss it with him later, and try not to argue, just tell him very gently that he didn't have to go through with the performance. It was not a matter of honour. Nazi symposium aside, it was clear his wretched Herr Weiss couldn't compose anything but rot.

She banged the door closed and set off for Hedda's, running, as she always did, so there'd be as much time as possible to dance.

Hedda was tired and distracted. She'd expected Kai home hours ago. He'd been away for two days.

'So many men and boys have been sent for forced labour in Germany this last month. I saw a group picked up only yesterday. You must warn Werner.'

'I would, if only he'd listen.'

'My darling Kai wouldn't last two weeks in a German munitions factory. I daresay Werner wouldn't either.'

Hedda was so irritable and anxious, she didn't know what to do to cheer her up. She went into the kitchen, boiled the kettle and took two cups from the hooks. She looked around but there was nothing to eat. When she took the teapot to the table she found Hedda resting her head in her hands.

'Oh I'm sorry. I feel old and used up,' she said. 'I've got a headache and I'm tired with the war, tired and dull with everyone's suffering, and my own petty suffering too. Kai comes and goes, and always I am sick with fear until he's home. The truth is there's no place of safety with me either – an outspoken anti-Nazi German!'

'Shall I dance? Will that help?'

'No. Today I have no feeling for dance. There's nothing left in me.'

'But I'll dance anyway, with my eyes closed.'

'Why with your eyes closed?' Hedda smiled for the first time.

'It feels so different. Be my eyes and tell me if I'm going to crash into the wall.'

Katje put on her ballet shoes, and pushed her chair back. She moved cautiously through the light and shadow in the room, feeling her way with her feet. Growing in confidence she forgot the edges of the room. She felt weightless – turning twisting floating through infinite white space, and so calm. It was a lovely feeling. When she opened her eyes, Hedda was watching her, hands pressed against her cheeks.

'And this endures. Despite everything,' she said.

Katje sat on a cushion on the floor, her back against Hedda's chair. She didn't want to ask what Hedda meant, or to break the quietness. She breathed in the scent of the room, old books, the fragrance of flowers or perfume.

'You've worked hard. One day we'll have a studio again,' Hedda said.

Briefly she laid her hand on Katje's head, and twisted a strand of her hair through her fingers.

'Did you hear the door just then?'

She went to the window facing the street.

'Erik Weiss. He was hanging around earlier. What's the matter with him? It's like being haunted. If he wants to see me why doesn't he ring the bell like any normal person?'

'I've seen him round here too. It's horrible. I'm scared he's watching for my brother.'

'I disagreed with him once,' Hedda interrupted. 'I should have been more cautious. I never realised quite how unbalanced he is. But I shouldn't be telling you such things.'

'You should. We're friends, united against the enemy.'

She stood next to Hedda looking down into the street.

'There's Kai now.'

In the distance they saw him crossing the bridge.

'Oh thank God.'

They watched Kai turn into the street, but seeing Weiss, he retraced his steps.

'Kai won't come now until he's sure Weiss had gone, in case he's seen.' Hedda stared blankly from the window.

'Perhaps I shouldn't visit any more either,' Katje said in a small voice. 'Herr Weiss might think you're dancing still if he sees me.'

'Oh don't worry, he won't be interested in my work now. I'm hardly staging an illicit opera, am I?'

'No, but do you remember, I told you about Werner playing Herr Weiss' music for a symposium?'

To her amazement Hedda laughed.

'Good God, well at least somebody likes his music. Poor Werner. How's he coping with that? When's the big event?'

'Soon I think. I should have talked to you weeks ago, but you always hate him being mentioned. Herr Weiss will be talking to all those Nazi Party members. If he thinks you're dancing, I don't trust him not to tell someone.'

'But I'm not dancing, not even teaching properly. And Kai's a member of the Kultuurkamer anyway, so he can play whatever he likes as long as it isn't Jewish music, or swing dance, or anything else they've decided to ban. Oh God, I wish he would come soon.'

She paced to the other window, opened it wide, leant out to look, then closed it again.

'Has Weiss gone?'

Katje looked out.

'Yes. He went towards Marnixstraat.'

'Katje, I think you should leave now he's off patrol. I'm sorry, I'm no company today, and I need to see Kai alone.'

With a hollow feeling, Katje picked up her bag.

'What shall I do?' she said. 'Shall I wait to hear from you?'

'I don't know. I can't think straight. Oh don't look so tragic.' She spoke impatiently, then relented and kissed Katje on the forehead. 'Of course we'll see each other soon and we'll dance. It's just that today – I'm all out of sorts.' She forced a smile. 'Everything will be fine. Don't worry.'

She opened the door, and Katje was dismissed down the stairs and out into the street, where she would have seen Hedda watching her from the window if she'd turned to look.

Kai returned, exhausted and hungry, bringing a small hard loaf of bread with him.

'I went into the bakery when I knew Weiss was on the prowl.' He took off his boots and collapsed on the sofa. He looked defeated, too tired to speak.

'I'm so glad you're back. We'll eat, then you can tell me.'

Hedda warmed vegetable soup and they ate, dipping pieces of bread.

'I've got to lie low for a while,' Kai said, when he'd scraped the bowl.

Hedda knelt on the sofa beside him.

'There's a man working with us – I never trusted him. The sort who thinks we're not doing enough, you know the type, full of big ideas, shouts a lot, never listens. We had so many discussions about how careful we must be, not jumping the gun. We thought he'd understood.'

'What happened?'

'He got picked up, followed all the way to the place where we meet, so that was raided too – documents and everything gone. We don't trust him not to talk.' He rubbed his hand over his eyes, then turned to lie with his head in Hedda's lap. 'I wish we could sleep and forget about it all. With Weiss hanging around, it makes me jumpy.'

Hedda rested her hand on his chest. The rise and fall of his breath was soothing.

'Katje was here. She thinks he's hanging round her brother. She told me Werner is playing Weiss' work in some big music symposium at the Concert Hall.'

'You're joking! I've seen the programme for that ghastly event and I'd be sure to remember if I'd seen Weiss' name on it. Poor kid. Weiss must have strung him along.'

She thought, as long as Weiss is occupied with his wild fantasies at least he won't be concerned with me. If he were going to betray me for some obscure reason, surely he'd have done it months ago? But poor Werner. There's nothing I can do to break the news to him without involving Katje. I suppose it will come out sooner or later then hopefully it will all be over.

'But what's Weiss doing on the corner of Egelantiersgracht if he's spying on Werner?' Kai said, breaking her train of thought. 'Unless he's watching out for all of us. He's completely mad. He should be arrested.'

Her body felt leaden. It didn't seem possible that through the window life went on as normal – voices of her neighbours in the courtyard. She sighed, longing for simplicity, for everyday things.

'It's not safe for you here any longer, is it?' she said at last. 'That's what you're trying to tell me?'

He didn't answer. He took her hand, gently pressed his thumb in her palm, and smoothed it down the length of her fingers.

'I've got a new student,' she continued. 'A Dutch official, big in the NSB, Speer. He's like a lizard. He seems to have taken to me. I suppose it's good – that he likes me...Where will you go, darling? Where will you hide? Are you able to tell me?' Her voice was very low.

'It will only be for a while. I'm hoping for somewhere we can both go, in the country. I have contacts. Until then I'll be in a room near Café Welling. Thank God Viktor's never been directly involved in the organisation.'

Stay here, she wanted to say, but couldn't speak.

'I can't stay with you, Hedda,' he said, as if hearing her thought. 'If I'm found here – you know what they'll do to you. With Weiss hanging round it's even more of a risk.'

'I'd rather be arrested with you.' She wept, with weariness and sadness. 'I'm not afraid for myself. How can I keep going without you, and without my work? I've forgotten the reason why I stay alive.'

'It won't be long. We've just got to hang on. Remember, I'm a survivor – the cat of nine lives. I know where to hide and how to run, and when to be cautious. And now I want to lie beside you. We'll give each other strength. And then we'll sleep.'

Meeting

Hedda left the apartment in the early morning. She looked up and down the street. Weiss wasn't to be seen. She hadn't seen him since Kai had left.

She passed the bakery where Kai had once, miraculously, bought cakes for her, and the loaf of bread the night he left. A little tabby cat sprawled in the window, and she thought of Benjamin's cat, now living with the Hoffmans. We'll have a cat of our own when we're married, she decided, as she walked on quickly, past the grocers, where queues were already forming. It was a hot day. She hadn't eaten breakfast. She had little more than an hour before she was expected to teach.

She reached Viktor's café in a quiet street behind the Concert Hall. Viktor greeted her as if she was a stranger. There were two other men inside, preoccupied with reading. She ordered coffee went to sit at a table on the street. Viktor brought her coffee and slipped the key into her hand.

'Stay as long as you like,' he said.

'Ah, if only I could. I'm teaching very soon. I would go sick...'

'Only that may cause more difficulties,' he said, reading her thoughts.

'Yes. Thank you, Viktor, for all your help.'

He looked sideways to avoid her eye.

'I do what I can.'

She found Kai sleeping on a mattress in the attic room two doors away from the café. She knelt by him looking down at his face, untroubled in sleep, like a child. She lowered her head, breathed the warmth of his skin, let her lips rest on his neck. He opened his eyes.

'I was dreaming about you, and now you're here.' He pulled her towards him, kissed her again and again. 'It's good, the best medicine, to see you.'

228

He slipped his hand under the bodice of her cotton dress that hung loosely from her.

'You've got thinner. You must keep strong.'

'I miss your cooking. It's tiresome to eat alone.'

She spoke lightly, touching his lips with her fingertips. She mustn't cry. In just a little time, only a matter of weeks, it would be over, one way or another. He'd have made his escape. She would find a way to join him. She thought of fields, trees, a cloudless sky and the distant sound of sea.

He unbuttoned her dress, pulled it down over her shoulders.

'Darling, I have so little time. A wretched lesson with The Lizard.'

'Damn him, he can wait, just once.'

She couldn't say that then he would question her, keep her longer so all the other lessons fell out of time. As if even that mattered. It didn't. If this was the last time she saw Kai nothing would matter.

'I've found somewhere for us,' Kai said, later. 'It's remote enough, a farm, and there are outbuildings where we can sleep, and we can help on the land.'

It all seemed distant and improbable. She thought of Gitta and the palace of dry leaves – if you want something enough, if you give it all your strength and love. She had done that when she'd trained to dance. Anything was possible.

'And we can find other work once we've settled.'

'Yes,' she said. 'It will be autumn. Maybe it won't be long. Maybe it's nearly over.'

'It is,' he said. 'A bed in the barn, with the swallows coming through.'

Hedda looked around at the dusty space filled with crates, a few broken chairs.

'It's bleak here. It must feel as if you're a prisoner, locked up day after day.'

'Viktor is good. He's no jailor, more my guardian. And I come and go as I please. Don't worry, I'm always careful. I can play the violin when it's noisy out in the street, or in the day when the house is empty. I'm quiet so nobody will hear.' He reached across her for his violin and bow that lay on a chair. 'I composed this last night for you, Hedda.'

He played, quietly, once, then again. He put the violin down, and lay in her arms.

'The sweetest music I've ever heard you play,' she said. She ran her fingers through his hair that had grown longer again.

Softly she sang the melody back to him.

Later, when Hedda returned from teaching, she lay down on the sofa without taking off her coat, and fell asleep in the afternoon sun. Half waking she heard rain falling. She was conscious of the street outside her open window, even as she was trapped by the illusion of her dream.

The corridors of the hospital were white; the atmosphere had a bleached quality as if drained of all life. She walked between beds of folded grey blankets, skidding on broken glass under her feet. Her mouth had been forced open and rammed with rubber tubing that pressed upon her teeth. Broken dolls were piled on the floor – parchment skin over brittle bone.

She had to dance. She tried to dance but her limbs wouldn't move. Terrified, with all her strength she flung out her arms, was jolted awake as if from deep water, drowning, gasping for air.

She sat, listening to the rain. She wanted Kai, his affectionate, reassuring presence, the quiet padding of his feet as he moved around the apartment, the sound of him tuning his violin. I need to be stronger. Why am I so weak?

With heaviness of heart, she remembered her lesson with the Lizard in the redbrick police building on Marnixstraat – Speer, with his heavy jowls and thick neck, slumped in his office chair. He had a slow lazy way of speaking – his eyes flickered over her. His German was good enough. She didn't know why her services were required. He wanted to perfect his grammar, he said. She had been perfunctory, refusing to be drawn into conversation about herself. She had managed to avoid twice weekly classes, by saying she was over-engaged. It was good, perhaps, that he liked her.

It would be beautiful now in the garden of her childhood home, with its huge trees, a canopy of copper leaves patterned under summer sun.

She took off her coat and went into the kitchen to boil the kettle. Waiting for it to boil, she gazed out at the sky – a slab grey sky, drenched with rain.

She imagined infinite blue space, cornflower blue, sea blue. She imagined moving slowly out into the blue, deeper, deeper into nothingness.

Child

One June evening, Hedda sat down in the little courtyard after her German class. She twisted round to rest her arm and head on the back of the bench. She put her trembling exhaustion down to the stress of waiting for news from Kai, the weekly lesson with Speer she dreaded. Even Katje's visit hadn't given her energy.

The air was too sweet with the fragrant roses that overhung the tree, and through an open window a waft of fried food sickened her. Is it possible I'm pregnant, she wondered? As soon as the thought entered her mind, she understood the subtle change she'd noticed in her body and spirit over the last weeks. Now it made sense. I can't be sure, she told herself, and yet she was sure and felt such joy that for a moment she lost all sense of everything. If only I could tell Kai. She got up, sat down again, put her hand to her belly and began to cry.

After a wearying morning teaching German to a group of Dutch students, she went to see Marten Hoffman in his surgery. He was sitting with his packet of sandwiches by the open window. His face broke into a smile of pleasure.

'How good to see you.' He moved a chair from behind the desk, and pushed his lunch to one side.

'And you, Marten. Please don't let me disturb you.'

'I'm delighted to be disturbed. Sit down, would you like a drink?'

'Just water, thank you. It's so warm and close out there, not a breath of wind.'

He left the room and came back with two glasses and a jug of water. As he set a glass beside her, Hedda noticed how strained he looked.

'Your visit is timely,' he said, as he sat down. 'I'm afraid things aren't good.'

'Oh no, Julia, the girls, are they well?'

'They're as fine as can be in the circumstances. We haven't heard from Kai for weeks, but these days no news is reassuring and we assume everything takes time.'

'Kai is like a moth, he comes out only at night.'

'Have you seen him? Julia would love to hear.'

'We daren't meet too often. I last saw him two weeks ago. I have notes from him regularly, thank God.'

'Ah, Hedda, that's hard for you, for all of us, but you especially.'

Sadness welled in her throat.

'It's the waiting that's hardest. He wanted me to tell you if I saw you before he was able to – he'll be leaving Amsterdam as soon as things are sorted out with his documents.'

'We know that much. Is anything more definite?'

'The plan is he'll stay on a farm in the south – people who have sympathies with the organisation, but know little enough to give Kai a measure of security. He can help with the farm work, and once he's settled, we'll find a way I can move out too.'

It seemed so vague, now she voiced it, so much a wild hope in the dark. She and Kai in a small room in the country, newly married, a child on the way. She thought she saw doubt in Marten's expression, or was it just a reflection of her own insecurity? So much relied upon the goodwill and courage of other people, strangers, she now realised. How can I put myself in their hands? It seems so much to ask. This is how Benjamin must have felt, why he didn't go into hiding. I couldn't do it for myself alone, but for our baby. Our baby – the thought was like sunlight filling a dark room – intense joy, incredulity.

She tried to focus on Marten, smiled absently. She hadn't intended to tell him, not before she told Kai, but then it seemed imperative and she said, 'I'm pregnant.'

He was asking her if she was sure, had she been to her doctor, how did she feel? She tried to answer coherently.

He was delighted, and Julia would be beside herself with joy.

'It's funny. I'm very fortunate – you must be the only parents in Amsterdam who would greet such news with pleasure, given our circumstances.'

'A new baby is always to be celebrated.'

'Yes. I never thought of myself as a mother, and now...' her throat tightened. She looked at Marten and he at her, with such warmth. Her eyes filled with tears. He gave her his handkerchief.

'I must pull myself together.' She smiled. 'But what were you going to tell me, Marten?'

'I hesitate after such wonderful news.'

'But you must. We've always shared these things. Is it to do with the Artsenkamer?'

'Yes. Of course, you of all people will understand.' He sighed. 'I never joined up, you know that. I feel the same as you did about the wretched Kultuurkamer. The difference being there were many more medics of like-mind.'

'Of course – there would be – your decision safeguards the security of your patients. For me, at the end of the day, it was mostly a thing of principle.'

'Nevertheless we all admired you for it. No, I thought, as there were many of us, there'd be safety in numbers. Yesterday I learned that two hundred doctors have been arrested. Somehow I was over-looked. You see Hedda, I would ask you to come to stay with us, but everything has changed. We're still in shock, but Julia and I need to talk. We're not sure yet what to do. I have my patients to think of.'

'But your own safety too, and your family,' Hedda burst out. 'I hate it, I would kill them, they deserve to hang,' she sobbed. 'I'm sorry, Marten. I shouldn't lose control. I should think of you. I am thinking of you.'

'I'm sorry, so sorry I had to tell you.'

She knew, in that moment, that she had told Marten of the baby in case she never had a chance to tell Kai. Was that just foolish paranoia? She put her head down on her arms and cried for the way sweet simple life was brutally swept away for some crazy empty ideology.

'Hedda, I'm so sorry.'

She cried for Marten and Julia, and Kai and herself, with tears she had held back too long. And Marten's arm round her shoulders, though reassuring, was not Kai's.

July 2ⁿᵈ 1943

Darling Kai, if only I could speak to you, hear your voice. I won't ever send you this letter, too harsh it will be, too full of my own sorrows and fears. I'll write another, of joy. But now I feel as if I'm speaking to you and that eases me. Why do I have such a sense of foreboding? I write quickly, hoping one day – if you survive – if I don't - you'll find my letter. This is how it has been since I saw you last.

I can hardly breathe when Speer comes close to me. He has this gross way of coming close and smiling. He has no respect for the distance there should be between people. Last week he told me he has 'researched my background.' Why had I stopped dancing, he asked, why had I closed my dancing school. I said an old spinal injury made it too painful. 'There is nothing wrong with your spine,' he said. I looked him straight in the eye and said that the pain, when I danced, was excruciating. I had to stop and for this reason I must teach German instead. He laughed and ran his hand down my back.

Later that day Katje visited, and for an afternoon life was good again. She brought yellow roses from her garden. They smell so sweet but they made me nauseous. I can't manage anything strongly scented any longer. We pushed the furniture back and she danced and I forgot all my anxiety. You should see her now, Kai. She practises often, in her own room at home, and she's become so strong, so free.

Today Speer told me that he knows everything about my background now. He knows I danced in Germany before the dance company escaped, and that I refused to join the Kultuurkamer. He knows I am far from being a Nazi. He looked me in the eye and told me he has grown fond of me and will not betray me. Then he laughed that hideous laugh, looking at me with his lascivious expression. He tried to touch me and I backed away, but he came close, breathing cigar and coffee in my face.

If only I could hear your footsteps on the stairs again, if you were to walk through the door, and I could hear your voice calling me, the sound of your violin, your Spanish dances.

We're going to have a baby, Kai. We have to survive for her. Brave little soul, as small as a nut kernel, floating in the sea of my belly.

She was aware of the silence and emptiness of her rooms. She put down the pen and went to the window. There was nothing unsettling – a brown dog tied to the railing of the house opposite, the canal, green like olives, Westertoren through the trees, against a white sky. But everything was coloured with anxiety for Kai, for herself, for the child. She thought of her mother, her grandmother she'd known but distantly. She saw the women of her family, a line of noble profiles stretching back through time, their hands clasped in prayer. Why did they pray? Was it for her, for Kai? For the baby?

She strained to hear his footsteps in the courtyard – nothing. In her mind she saw him running down an alley between tall buildings, nowhere to hide, crashing against a wall. Her heart contracted to a hard burning knot of pain, and then at the point when she could bear it no longer, it seemed to explode.

Afterwards – whiteness, peace, her window – leaves moving in cool air – the sound of rain falling on water.

The Cards

'I'd like to hear you play the Beethoven we looked at last week, first movement only. The score is there on the piano. Begin when you're ready.'

Werner glanced over the music. He'd practised, though not with as much attention as he'd given to Weiss' composition. Weiss listened without interrupting.

'That was adequate, accurate enough.'

He stood with his back to the blind, his face in shadow. Werner couldn't read his expression. Lately he'd become perfunctory in his teaching, as if it was a task to be endured. Doesn't he care, Werner thought? Is it that I'm no longer worth bothering with? The thought of playing in front of a hall of people woke him in the night, and he lay in a feverish panic. He was torn by his need to please Weiss, and a hope that he might never reach an adequate standard to perform in front of such important men.

'Der Führer is fond of Beethoven,' Weiss said suddenly. 'I have never cared for him very much, I'm sorry to say. There are composers who are out of favour with Der Führer. Do you know who they are, Werner?'

'No sir.'

'It would serve you well to find out. Mistakes mustn't be made.'

'But surely good music speaks for itself?'

Weiss laughed.

'So it does. We know that, both of us.' He sat down on a stool beside Werner. 'The Nazification of music, that doesn't interest me, although I see why certain composers must be eliminated. If you have a vision then everything must serve to realise that vision. Everything must be focussed on that one glorious goal, with no deviation through sentimentality. It's necessary that some people will sink, others must be annihilated. I play the game Werner. You must learn to play the game too. When a government is building a new society it's vital that elements don't get in the way. Do you understand that?'

Werner nodded. He wished Weiss wouldn't spend so much time talking about the government and his vision. It made him anxious when there was so much work to do for the symposium.

'Shall I play through your piece now? I've worked on the first movement all week.'

'Good. I'll hear it then.'

Weiss got up and stood by the window. Werner began to play. He stopped after the first few bars, aware he'd made several mistakes.

'Sorry.'

Herr Weiss made no comment. He'd pulled the blind back a fraction and was peering out, humming under his breath.

'Shall I start again?'

'If you like.'

'I need to know if I'm interpreting it as you wish,' he said nervously.

Herr Weiss didn't seem to understand how much encouragement and rehearsal he needed to get through this performance.

'To be truthful I'm not entirely happy with it. I'm thinking of reworking the first section.'

'But we don't have much time left.'

'We don't have much time left,' Weiss imitated in an exaggerated whine. 'Don't be so feeble. Play it again. I'm listening.'

Blind with hurt, Werner played. He had no need of the music. His hands moved automatically. For hours he'd attempted to make sense of Herr Weiss' sonata, to see the shape, to hear what he believed he was meant to hear. In an instant he knew that the struggle was over. He had cared so much, but now there was nothing left. He was exhausted.

'Forgive me for mentioning it, but I saw your sister leaving Frau Brandt's apartment yesterday,' Weiss said, when he'd finished. 'Are you aware that she visits?'

'I don't know, sir. The dancing school closed a long time ago.'

'Your sister is an ignorant and silly girl. She adores Brandt. She'd follow her to the end of the world. I'm telling you, in case your parents don't know, I'm certain Brandt is teaching dancing lessons from her rooms. This is absolutely forbidden by the authorities. She's not to be trusted.'

'I liked her,' Werner said quietly. 'She seemed very kind, when I met her. She was good to my sister.'

'Brandt can do as she likes, be a shopkeeper, a janitor, a whore, but not a dancer. She gave that up when she failed to comply with the authorities. She refused to be warned. Not only that, she's inciting her students to deliver anti-government tracts. She should be stopped.'

'I'm sure that she's not.'

'Believe what you like. I've seen the pages, scattered around bars. I have the evidence.'

Werner felt Herr Weiss' damp breath on his face. He could smell alcohol. He had a sensation of falling – of panic, followed by the shock and pain of impact. For a moment he stopped breathing. Weiss was very close. He could see the broken veins in the whites of his eyes.

'You're trembling. Do I frighten you?' Weiss asked.

'No,' Werner said. He drew back a little.

'You'll never again be as pure and perfect as you are this moment. Let me look at you.'

Werner lowered his eyes. Neither of them moved. The room was stifling.

'It's over,' Weiss said, so quietly Werner scarcely made out the words. He stood up. 'We will walk. I need a breath of air and a drink. The rain has stopped. Leave your music.'

Obediently Werner left the piano and followed Weiss out of the apartment.

They walked in silence. It was a beautiful evening, warm in the sun. On Rembrandtsplein they passed groups of people sitting at café tables under the plane trees. The Theater Tuschinski was adorned with Nazi flags moving slowly in the breeze. Werner didn't know where they were going. Since they'd left the music room, it was as if all sense of autonomy had gone. As he trailed beside Herr Weiss, it was a relief to feel nothing.

In the bar Weiss ordered his usual bottle of red wine.

'I never could stand the sun,' he said, leading Werner into a dark corner.

Werner hadn't eaten all morning. The wine affected him immediately. Three men wearing NSB badges on their lapels, came in, and their voices and laughter unsettled him. Herr Weiss sat opposite him, his expression blank as he stared into space, his features, the colour of his skin becoming more vivid as Werner drank. They finished the bottle and Weiss fetched another. Suddenly animated, he filled their glasses, and took a pack of cards from his jacket pocket. He shuffled them and spread them face down on the table.

'Card games are for fools and failures. My father used to play for money. I would never demean myself that way.' He laid his hand protectively over the cards. 'Before they were ever used for games or trickery, the cards were used to tell the future. I want you to pick one. Think of your life, your future, and take the first one your eyes light on.'

'I'd rather not, sir.' Werner said, disturbed by Weiss' change of mood.

'But it would please me if you would.' Weiss' eyes flickered away from the table to meet Werner's. 'The cards we choose will guide us.' His voice wavered. 'I beg you to choose a card.'

'Are you all right, are you well?' Werner asked. 'Maybe it would be best to go home.'

'I'm in great need of guidance,' he said, with such an air of portent, that rather than giving weight to his suffering, made him seem ludicrous.

There was no harm in humouring him. Werner took a card. It was the seven of hearts. He laid it face up and watched as Weiss did the same.

'The nine of spades.' Weiss drained his glass. He glanced round the bar. Two young men had just come in and were sitting by the window. 'Not good.' He made an odd chewing motion with his mouth, swept the cards into a pile and put them back in his pocket. He shook his head.

Werner searched for words to reassure him. They were only cards after all – the seven of hearts and the nine of spades.

'I'm sure the cards only have meaning if you want them to.' Cautiously he reached to touch Herr Weiss' arm.

Weiss grasped his hand for a moment, and then let go.

'It's bad. I have a sense of foreboding. I wanted the card to tell me of good fortune, believe me. I wouldn't have picked a card at all if I'd known it would be that one.'

'Was mine bad too?' Werner couldn't help asking.

Weiss stared down at the table and didn't answer.

Werner looked round the bar. He was aware of the men by the window watching. He waited. Weiss didn't seem inclined to speak. It was seven in the evening. His parents were going out. He was supposed to be home with Katje. Not that Katje needed his care, but he had reassured his father.

'I think I should go,' he said, standing up. 'I'll be expected at home.' He hadn't seen home as somewhere to retreat to for a long time, but now he could hardly wait for the peace of his bedroom. He would sleep and tomorrow he would speak to his father. Everything would become clear.

'Please don't go.'

The bar was hot and oppressive, unbearable. Werner sat down again.

'But I must leave soon.'

'The seven of hearts – the lovesick card. The nine of spades – it foretells ill fortune. It's one of the darkest cards.'

Lovesick – I've been sick with love for too long, Werner thought, and now it's over. Something that held me has broken. It seemed like a miracle. He felt a remote pity and tenderness, a sense of responsibility. More powerful was the need to get out of the bar, to escape the heavy atmosphere of dread incited by Weiss.

'Come with me, sir. I'll walk you back. I think you should go home and rest.'

He put out his hand as if to a child.

The walk home was long and slow. Weiss said they were being followed, and insisted on taking a circuitous route down side streets, oblivious to Werner's reassurance. With enormous relief he left Weiss at his door, but his relief was short-lived. By the time he reached home he felt sick and his head pounded.

He was glad to find the house empty. His parents had gone, taking Katje with them it seemed. It was eight in the evening. He fell onto his bed and slept, waking only half an hour later overcome with nausea. He staggered down to the bathroom and was sick again and again, retching black bile until it seemed his stomach was turned inside out. Trembling and wretched he groaned aloud, and lay on the tile floor. When he came to, Katje was kneeling beside him, holding a wet flannel to his head.

'I'm so glad the parents are away,' she said. 'You're supposed to be minding me and here you are passing out on the floor, drunk.'

'You were out,' he mumbled.

'I've been in all the time. I must have been in the garden when you got back. Where were you?'

He rolled over and lay on his back staring up at the light on the ceiling. His teeth chattered with cold.

'Piano lesson.'

She dropped the flannel and stood up.

'I've absolutely had enough. I'm going to tell Papa about Weiss getting you drunk and what an evil man he is. I don't care about the stupid symposium. I don't care if you never speak to me again. I don't want you dead. And now you can look after yourself.'

Hedda

Hedda gazed through the open window of Speer's office at the mass of trees, shimmering silver and green. She had never heard so clearly before the rustling and soughing of wind through the leaves, the depth and texture of sound, and beyond, the infinite space and silence.

A sense of calm had stayed with her all night, and now she turned to look at Speer as if from the great distance of another continent. What is it you want, she wondered? What do you want from me? She felt an odd sort of pity for this man with the heavy thighs and pasty face. All fear of him had gone. His face seemed to disintegrate into fragments of skin, and then reorganise again. She realised he was saying something.

'You know Erik Weiss.' It was a statement more than a question.

'I knew him well for a little while.'

'He was taken in for interrogation.' His mouth twisted in disgust. 'Homosexual activity. Corruption.'

'Poor Erik,' she said, quietly, understanding for the first time.

'Don't waste your time feeling sorry for him. He had no pity for you.' He watched her with his hooded eyes. 'He'll be released after more interrogation but he'll never play the piano again. They smashed his fingers.'

How would Erik live without his music? What could warrant such cruelty?

'Of course, Miss Brandt, it's easy to make people talk, and he gave away a great deal of information about you. Nothing much that I wasn't aware of already. Loyalty is skin deep. Why did you never join the Party?'

What was it motivated this man to torment her? Why didn't he say what he wanted to say? She felt invincible in a way she'd never known before. He couldn't harm her.

'Why would I want to join?'

'Duty to Germany.'

'If you look at it from my perspective – Germany killed my father, forced Kurt Jooss into exile – I have no loyalty to that country. Would you if you were in my position?'

'You know I could have you arrested any time?'

She turned to look out at the trees again. It was nearly over. It would be so good to be walking in the park, to meet Katje and sit in the little café by the pond, to drink real coffee with big slices of apple and cinnamon cake and cream. She was so hungry. She hadn't realised until now.

'Why do you smile?'

'I was thinking of food.' She turned to look at him. 'We should begin the lesson.'

'I don't think you heard what I said.'

'I heard, but I can't stop you doing anything you choose to do to me. My work has been taken away, my freedom to live as I choose. Tell me how a woman in my position should act? Do you expect me to go down on my knees, to plead? I refuse to be humiliated.'

'You are a remarkable woman. I've grown fond of you.' He eased his ponderous bulk out of the chair, perched on the edge of his desk and looked down at her. 'What do you think I should do? I have enough information on file to sentence you to long imprisonment at the very least. What would you do in my position?'

'Since I can't imagine what it's like to be in your position, I can't answer.'

He laughed abruptly.

'I wouldn't want you to come to any harm.'

Dancing is always moral. Kurt had said that long ago. It came back to her now she was faced with this gross man, who she knew wanted to take her hand and shove it down under the belt of his trousers, and press her hard to his cock. She smelt the stale cigar of his breath, the heat of his skin.

246

'Don't touch me.' The force of her voice made him back away. 'Don't come near me. You should be ashamed of yourself.'

There was a look of silly surprise on his face, and then embarrassment.

'Shall we begin the lesson?' she said.

Letters

Dear Herr Weiss,

I can't play in the symposium. I know everyone will say I'm unprofessional and I'm letting you down, but I can't. There are four reasons. One: I can't make sense of the music, and believe me, I've worked as hard as I can. Two: I can't play in front of all those people. I would freeze and it would be impossible. Three: I know now that I'm not destined to be a great pianist. Four: You will perform your own work better than I ever could, and do it justice. You will see now that I would let you down by trying to perform, not by refusing.

Dearest Kai – it will only be a matter of days until we're safe together. These last few days before I sleep I find myself praying. I haven't prayed since I was a child with my grandmother sitting beside me. After those nights when everything was so desperate, something in me broke. It happened in a moment, like an explosion in my head or my heart. There was only sweetness left. How extraordinary that seems, and at the same time quite natural. Now there is a deep comfort in my whispered prayers.

I feel compassion for them all, Speer, Erik with his broken hands, his madness, and poor lost Werner.

How delighted you were when I told you of the baby. I can see you, holding my hands, laughing with sheer joy, dancing around that miserable little yard in the twilight, and now, before I sleep, I imagine us in a few years – our little girl will be trotting around, clapping her hands, dancing in that delightful way tiny children have, finely balanced on her short legs.

I like to say your name, my generous, funny Kai, my sweet clown. I sing the music you played last time. How engrossed we

*were in our work, those days when we were free. Heaven is the life
we once had, the life we will have again.*

*There's blue light, I walk out into blue, infinite blue. If you
survive and I don't – if you find this letter – remember that it's
our love for each other and our work that matter. In some way,
whatever we must endure, this love is stronger. My darling Kai.*

Katje

The sun was too harsh, the movement of light over the water disturbing. Katje ran down the steps of her house into the street. You've got to tell Miss Brandt immediately, Werner had said. And I'll tell Father. He was talking about the stories she'd written and left lying on tables in the nearby cafés. He'd looked so frightened when he'd discovered. It was a long time ago, she said, it was last year. He'd shouted at her, how stupid she was and she'd burst into tears. Herr Weiss thinks Miss Brandt is encouraging her old students to commit treason. I never took any notice of him but now there's evidence. They'll see it as evidence. He'd cried too.

She ran towards Hedda's house and looked up to the blank window. Nobody answered the door, so she let herself in to wait until Hedda returned. Feeling faint, she grabbed at the doorframe, and stumbled to the sofa. Kai's voice swam towards her.

'What the hell are you doing bursting in? Hedda's not in.'

'I'm sorry. I didn't know you were here. I wouldn't have done if I'd known.'

He stood glaring at her. His hair had grown again and he was unshaven. She shook her head.

'You look done in,' he said, relenting. 'I'll fetch a drink.'

She heard him in the kitchen, the tap running. He came back and put the glass of water into her limp hand.

After a moment she pulled herself up and took a sip. Kai was at the piano, restlessly playing a run of notes.

'I'm sorry,' he said. 'You scared me. But it's good to see you. I miss friends.'

'There's bad news, Kai.'

He rubbed his hand over his face.

'What bad news? Look I shouldn't be here. I've taken a risk just so I can see Hedda – things aren't good. I need a cigarette. I don't suppose you have any?'

She shook her head.

'I didn't think so. I don't need more bad news.' Arms folded, he stared at the floor, his knee twitching. 'Well – you'd better not spare me any longer. Is it my family? I'll kill anyone who so much as touches any of my family.'

She swallowed, her mouth dry.

'Herr Weiss thinks Hedda's working against the government, and that she's recruited people like me, all her old students to help. Werner told me. He was scared for Hedda, in case Herr Weiss says something.'

'When did Werner tell you this?'

'This morning. I came as soon as I could.'

'What exactly did he say?'

'He said Herr Weiss has seen me and Elise visiting Hedda, and that Hedda betrayed him and she's not to be trusted with young impressionable minds.'

'God I hate the man. I did from the moment I met him.'

'Me too.'

For a second their eyes met.

'What else did your brother say?

'That Hedda encouraged us to commit treason.'

'Well there's no evidence, so I think we can all relax. There are worse things to get worked up about. The man's completely insane.'

'But I did something stupid.'

'What are you talking about?'

Wiping her eyes with her sleeve, she told him about the letters she'd left in bars.

'Herr Weiss must have found one of the letters, or seen me, or why would he think these things about Hedda?'

'Oh God. Stop crying, Katje.' He sat beside her, his arm across her shoulders. 'There's no use crying or blaming yourself for anything. What's done is done. You're not the first schoolgirl to make a mess of meaning well. Elise always said you were naïve.'

'But it was Elise who had the idea about writing stories in the first place,' she protested.

'And did she ask you to carry it through?'

'No. Later she wouldn't talk about it.'

'She was right. Leave that to people who know what they're doing. Weiss has been against Hedda since she refused to work with his music, if she'd but seen it. I don't suppose your efforts amount to much. What's done is done.'

He took his arm from her shoulders. She heard the soft fluttering of a butterfly against the top window pane.

'Hedda must leave, mustn't she? Find a safe place to hide?' she said in a small voice.

'Oh yes, easy as that.'

'You could hide in our beach house. I'm sure I could get the key.'

'The coast is impossible. People are taken there to be shot.'

He got up, reached for the butterfly, cupping his hands around it. 'Open the back window.'

She did as he asked, and he released it into the sunlight. They watched it flying to rest on a rose by the seat, then away out of sight.

'I thought I'd found us a place, but it's fallen apart since the latest strike. That's how it is. People are scared. My father could admit Hedda to hospital, but that's only a temporary solution.'

He crossed the room to the canal side window, and stood watching, where he couldn't be seen from the street. When he turned back she blinked under his scrutiny.

'We've always got on, haven't we, you and me? I liked you despite your awful father. You always seemed more at home with us than your own family.'

She nodded.

252

'I know you just think I'm a child, but I'll do anything I can to help. I can be trusted, absolutely,' she said. 'I understand better now I'm older.'

'I'm not going to leave Hedda again. Whatever happens we stay together. We've got to survive, and it's not safe here. You can do something to help.'

'I'll do anything.'

'I want you to take a message to a café behind the Concert Hall. Café Welling. There's a man who works there. He'll be there this afternoon. Can you do that?'

'Who do I look out for?'

'A small man, grey hair, moustache, kind face, in his fifties, you won't miss him because the others working there are all very much younger.'

He went to Hedda's desk and found a pad of paper, tore a page and sat down, writing hurriedly. 'His name is Viktor. You're sensible enough to check you have the right man. Give him this.'

He put the note into an envelope, sealed it, and picked up a book from the shelf. 'It's between the pages of this, so you must pretend you're reading until you're sure nobody is watching. In fact wait until nobody is around at all. Tell him it's from Jaap Schuyler. Then wait. He may have a reply. If he does it will be just a word or two. If there's no reply then don't come back here, best not to risk that unnecessarily.'

She nodded.

'Don't look so sad, Katje. I can't stand it.'

'I'm afraid for you staying here.'

'I can hide up on the roof if anyone comes. I've shown you before.'

'There's a pain always here in my heart, these days. I'm scared for you and Hedda.'

She was crying again, and she felt ashamed, but he took her hand and squeezed it.

'It will all be over one day,' he said. 'Think of Elise's next birthday... music, plenty of good food and wine. I often think of you both dancing that night of the performance, what a great night that was.'

'The best night of my life.'

They fell silent for a moment.

'I love Hedda more than I've ever loved anyone, even my family.' He spoke as much to himself as to her. 'If anything happens to me, tell her that. She matters more to me than the world.' He laughed suddenly. 'My mother would never believe I said that.'

He placed his palm gently on the side of her face.

'You're a brave girl. I've always thought that, and open. That's what Hedda loves about you. Now go and deliver the message, and be safe until we meet again. And when you see my family, tell them I'll be back as soon as I can.'

They both stood up.

'Goodbye Katje.'

She embraced him. He held her close, then turned abruptly and walked away towards the window. She put the book into her bag, and ran downstairs without looking back.

The Concert Hall was hung with black and red drapes. 'With Adolf Hitler in a New Europe' was printed on a banner stretching from gable to gable of the grand building. There had been a huge open-air meeting in the museum square. Katje slowed down as a sea of people wearing NSB uniform and carrying Nazi flags surged towards her.

She found the café on the corner of Jan Willen Brouwersstraat. Tables and chairs spilled out onto the pavement, every table taken by Dutch Nazis. Sick with anxiety she hung back. Why would Kai send her to a bar frequented by these people? What if Viktor wasn't there? If anything happens, look after Hedda for me, Kai had said. Sparrows flittered in the creeper that hung over the entrance. She opened the door.

The interior was panelled in wood but plastered in posters of singers and musicians. A brass lantern hung on a chain from the ceiling, and sunlight glinted gold, silver, and green over the bottles and the mirror behind.

There were two young men who looked like brothers serving. She felt cold sweat breaking over her as she scanned the bar looking for Viktor. He wasn't there. She slunk back behind a taller man, and back again until she stood well away from the bar, amongst the tables. She sank down on an old velvet sofa in the shade of lace blinds at the window. She took the book from her bag.

It was a book about anatomy. How unlikely she should be reading such a book. She opened it, gripping the cover to stop her hands shaking. She kept glancing up until she saw the man who must be Viktor clearing and wiping the tables. She waited as he came nearer, and then checked that nobody was watching.

'Viktor,' she said in a low voice, as he bent over the table next to her. He turned and looked at her blankly.

'A message,' she said quickly.

'How are you?' he asked, his back shielding her from the door. 'Haven't seen you in a while.' He smiled.

'No, I've been busy looking after my mother, she's been ill. Jaap Schuyler sends his greetings.' She slid the note into his hand. He put it into the pocket of his trousers.

'Can you stay a while? You want a coffee?'

'Thanks.'

She went back to her book but the letters danced and nothing made any sense.

Two young men came up with their beers.

'Mind if we share your table?'

Why would they share her table when there were other tables free?

'I'm waiting for a friend,' she lied.

'Well we'll move on when he comes.'

They drew the chairs back and slumped down. They'd already drunk a fair bit and wanted to talk.

'Been to the rally?' The bigger one asked, flicking his hair off his sunburned face.

'Nah, she's not that sort of girl,' the other joked. 'You can see. She's waiting for her boyfriend. She's not been at any rally.'

She pretended to continue reading.

'She doesn't want to talk to us. She's engrossed! What're you reading sweetheart?'

She showed them the cover of the book.

'Means nothing to me.'

Nor me at this moment, she thought to herself, praying they would leave before Viktor returned with her coffee and a message.

'Bodies, bones, organs, you a doctor then?'

She shook my head.

'Oh leave her alone, she doesn't want to talk to us,' the other said, winking.

'No, I don't much want to talk to anyone,' she said, and closed the book, jumped up and left the cafe.

She sat down on the only free chair outside, too anxious to think clearly, her heart beating so hard it must be obvious to anyone who looked.

Viktor came out with the coffee on a tray.

'They came to talk to me, I couldn't stop them,' she said.

'It's all right. I'll sort them out. They're mourning the loss of you this very moment.' He handed her the coffee. 'No need to pay.'

She looked at him. There seemed to be no message for Jaap Schuyler.

'Is it good news then?' she couldn't help asking.

He didn't answer.

'I'll see you around. Call in again.' He smiled.

She gulped her coffee. It was still early afternoon. Overcome with the need to see Hedda, she stood up. It was possible she could meet her from her class if she walked to Marnixstraat and waited. She must be finished by mid-afternoon.

'Katje, what are you doing here?'

Hedda had become so thin that her summer dress hung off her. She hadn't seen Katje until she'd almost fallen over her.

'I hoped I'd meet you. I thought it was just possible you'd walk back this way.'

Hedda took Katje's arm.

'Well you've never done that before. How did you know where I was?' She saw Katje's expression and her tone changed. 'What's the matter?'

Without another word they both walked to a bench by the canal, and sat down.

'Now tell me what's wrong.'

Katje told her everything she'd told Kai, and how the safe place Kai had found them had fallen through. Sunlight fell dappled over the tiny blue flowers on Hedda's dress, her small bony hands. She seemed unmoved.

'You understand. I think Viktor will find a safe place for you and Kai. I think that's what no message meant. As long as you get away in time, you should be safe.'

'Oh I understand all right. But I think it's too late anyway.'

'No. It can't be. You could leave tonight, or tomorrow at the latest – I'm sure that's what Viktor intended.'

Hedda shook her head. 'I can't.'

Katje began to cry. Hedda took her hand.

'I'm so sorry you ever got involved in all this Katje. You're too young.'

'You know I'm not. Even tiny babies aren't spared.'

She cried quietly and Hedda held her hand.

'The last months have been awful. My old friends, they've gone, one by one, either into hiding, or away. It's terrible when you cannot even save the people you love. Walk home with me. Kai's there, you say. So I'll see him again. Dry your eyes. You must be strong. You have a life to live, a good one.' She smiled. 'Let us talk of something else, and try to be cheerful.' She stood up. 'Well, will you come with me, at least some of the way?'

They walked in silence. Everything is coming to an end. I may never see her again, never dance with her, Katje thought, but her mind couldn't absorb such finality. Hedda was peaceful, looking around with interest as she walked, as if they were taking a Sunday stroll.

'There's that lovely tabby cat. She's always sitting there.' She pointed to a cat curled on a window ledge in the sun. 'One day I'll have a cat again. I had one when I was a little girl. Look at the window of that bakery. How sad it is now. Do you remember the cakes they used to sell? The best coffee cake in the land. I always had cake on Saturday morning after the little ones' class.'

She fell into silence again. They reached the end of the street where they should say goodbye, and stopped by the bridge.

'Look after your brother. Whatever Erik Weiss was like, he was a good teacher. Your brother will need you.'

They faced each other, neither wanting to move. A momentary breeze ruffled the water, and a leaf twirled down like a little boat floating towards them.

'I so wish it was all over. I want to dance again. I want to be back with Kurt Jooss. I'd go anywhere, England, America, just to dance. Anywhere except Germany. I will never go back to my country. But wishing will not change anything.'

She took Katje's hand and squeezed it.

'You're a good friend, and the best student. Let's say goodbye here. I must go home to Kai.'

Her face was fleetingly brilliant with joy.

Rooms

Werner reached Weiss' apartment for his scheduled lesson. Letter unsent, he didn't know what he would say to Weiss. For two days he'd been wretched with anxiety for Katje, and remorse that he hadn't taken more seriously all Weiss' fabrications about Miss Brandt. The symposium hardly seemed significant any longer, except that he must go ahead with it. If he didn't, Weiss might turn against him and report Katje to the Gestapo. He had to keep going, more lessons, rehearsals, the sick dread of that performance. Conflicting voices scrambled his thinking. He should speak to his father. He didn't know how to begin. He wanted Katje's help, to go to him together, and explain, but she'd returned silent, crying all day and refusing to speak to anyone.

He rang the doorbell and waited, fingering the key he'd been given. Weiss always took time to answer. After a while, he unlocked the door and went up to the first floor. It seemed so much longer ago than three days since the last time. He found the door to the apartment already open, as if somebody had broken in.

He went into the music room. How odd it seemed, so quiet, everything was as they had left it days before – the blind almost down, the lamp still on, Weiss' score sitting on top of the piano in the exact position they'd left it. Weiss must have been back? Where else would he have gone? And if he'd been back, he'd surely have been in the music room?

'Herr Weiss,' he called. Nervously he opened the door into the room he'd never seen. Since the first time Weiss had invited him to the apartment, he had tried to imagine that room, and Weiss' life within it.

It was the light that struck him first. Sunlight poured through huge windows over the marble floor, and the glass chandelier cast brilliant rainbows over the white walls. It was magnificent, as he had always known it would be. He blinked and looked around.

One piece of furniture dominated the room. It must have been beautiful with its panels of inlaid flowers and drawers, but the front of it was shattered and splintered as if it had been scoured over and over with a knife. The little drawers had been thrown over the floor. The red silk interior was ripped to shreds.

A young woman saw him stumbling out into the street. She lived in the apartment next door. She was smoking a cigarette on the step.

'You're one of Herr Weiss' boys, aren't you? I wouldn't hang around here. It's not safe for the likes of you to be seen.'

The window was open onto the courtyard. The yellow print curtain had flapped out over the sill in the wind. Now it was drenched with rain that had fallen in sheets all morning. Kai's coat lay over the back of the sofa and Hedda's worn out canvas teaching shoes on the rug, as if she'd just slipped them off, her stockings in a little heap next to them. The violin, half removed from its case, was covered with Hedda's red shawl, and pushed not far enough under the sofa to be completely hidden. On the table were two blue cups, one half filled with coffee, the other almost empty. The coffee had gone cold. A faint scum had formed on the side of the cups.

In the kitchen a knife lay on the chopping board next to a bowl of chopped cabbage and another of sliced carrots. The tap dripped into a pan of water that overflowed into the sink. A bunch of sunflowers wilted, still wrapped in newspaper, on the kitchen table.

In the little bedroom behind the velvet curtain, the bed was unmade, the pillows still held the shape of sleep, the top blanket pulled back. A green silk dress hung on the mirror. Hairpins were scattered on the dressing table over a film of face powder. A faint scent of rose water lingered in the air.

There was the quiet, desolate sound of rain on roof and window and a single bird singing down in the courtyard.

Holding Hedda's notes under her coat, to keep them dry, Katje sat under the cherry tree. Her hair and face streamed with rain and tears.

They came for Erik Weiss for the second time just before dawn broke. He'd only been back in his apartment a few hours. There were two of them. He heard their feet on the stairs and cowered in his room, shivering with fever. He moaned and cried out as they kicked his face, beat him, shoved him out into the street to the edge of the canal. They tied his broken hands behind him with a piece of rope, and rolled him into the water.

Oranjehotel

Katje telephoned the Hoffmans' and held her breath, willing someone to answer. She telephoned every hour. She went to the house the next day, and when nobody came to the door, she rang the bell of the other apartment, once and then again. After a long time, a woman she'd never met unlocked the door and peered out, her face expressionless.

'Do you know what happened to the Hoffmans?'

The woman looked her up and down.

'I don't know anything. I'm sorry.'

She closed the door.

Katje leant against the wall staring up at the pale sky beyond the towers of Vondelkerk. A cat balanced along the railings towards her. It wasn't one of Elise's cats. That was a good sign. Wherever they'd gone, they'd surely take the animals with them. She stroked her, picked her up, putting her forehead to her warm herb-scented fur.

'If only you would tell me everything you know. If you know anything at all.'

The cat struggled and jumped down, slipping through the gate into the shrubbery.

She didn't know why she hadn't thought of going to see Viktor earlier, but now she turned through the park gates and down the path alongside Elise's garden, to the water, across the wooden bridge and past the Tea House. It began to spit with rain. She reached the gates to Van Eeghenlaan, round the corner over the tramlines to the streets behind the Concert Hall. Outside the café, she stopped, afraid, her heart thudding – it was still possible to go home. Hope was possible as long as she knew nothing.

She opened the door. The atmosphere was thick with the smell of warm bodies and smoke, the murmur of voices. Viktor stood behind the bar with a younger man. Looking up, he nodded, almost imperceptibly. She glanced around. Nobody else had looked in her direction, as far as she could tell. Everything made her jumpy now.

She sat at the only free table by the window. She was trembling and her hands were cold. She stood up and went through the tiny lobby where coats hung, to the ladies' room, washed her hands and face. Viktor was standing by the door when she came out.

'I'll meet you in the park by the Tea House as soon as I can get away,' he said. 'You'd better stay for a drink now you're here.'

They took a table on the terrace under the trees. The rain had stopped but it was damp and only a few couples sat outside. People passed by on bicycles. A squirrel bounced over the grass and up the trunk of a tree. They didn't speak until their tea was brought.

'How much do you know?' Viktor asked.

'Only that I went to Hedda's apartment and could see she must have been arrested. I don't know if Kai was with her.'

'It's not good news,' he said. 'I'm sorry. They were both taken to the Oranjehotel sometime in the night last week.' He paused. They met each other's eyes. 'I see the name means nothing to you.'

She shook her head. She tried to swallow away the lump in her throat. She put her hands around her cup for warmth.

'I need to know,' she said.

'It's the name we give the prison where they're taken – our people. You understand? We don't know the outcome yet.'

'What are the possible outcomes?'

She had a feeling of disconnection from her own body, as if watching the scene, a young girl and an older man, from a distance. A robin hopped onto the table.

'They'll be released, sent to a concentration camp, or executed.' He cleared his throat. 'I'm afraid very few are released.'

She froze. It was all right as long as she didn't move, as long as she remained distant.

'I don't know where the Hoffmans have gone,' he said. 'But I knew they were leaving. They had to. They were afraid for Elise, for her involvement.'

'Elise's involvement?'

'I thought you knew.'

'Yes,' she said.

Now it made sense. Of course Elise would be involved. How could she not have realised.

There wasn't much more to say. Afterwards they walked, round the lake, back through the trees. The sun went down. It helped to walk.

The Dunes

All night the prisoners in the cells nearest the sea heard the pounding of waves, and nearer still, the rods of rain clattering on the thin roof. At dawn the sky cleared and later the sun rose and the long stretch of sand turned from blue-grey to golden.

With sunrise the birds broke into song, and the sound of the sea was drowned with multitudinous chattering from trees and shrubs and rooftops.

Rain still swirled in the gutters. At seven in the morning, before the café owners drew up the blinds, and lined the street with tables and chairs, five people, three men and two women, were led by guards through a door in the prison wall, onto Van Alkemadelaan. A woman, up early, sweeping dust from the streets, glanced up, saw them. Two of the men were scarcely out of boyhood, their faces pale and unshaven. Only one man gazed directly at her until she turned away. The others looked down at their feet.

The track led through a copse of pine trees, to open ground, sandy hills of gorse, myrtle and sea thyme. A rabbit, disturbed, darted up the track and under cover ahead of them.

They walked for fifteen minutes to a hollow in the dunes. A light breeze blew in from the sea. Lined up, their hands tied together, they waited. One of the guards took a cigarette from his pocket, lit up, glanced at the other guards, and offered a cigarette to the nearest prisoner whose one hand was free. The young man, refusing, kept his gaze focused on the horizon.

Winter

Late in the summer, Werner fell ill. The fever came quickly and by the end of the day his temperature soared and he couldn't stand up. He burned and then shivered with cold. In his mind he was compelled to keep walking across a beach to the sea, but with each step the water receded. Exhausted he tried to sink down on the sand; relentlessly he was dragged back to his feet until he lost consciousness.

He thought he heard Katje crying, but the sound was drowned by a choir singing. Voices and lights came in waves of intensity. He tried to open his eyes, to move his hands and feet, but his body no longer responded to his will. He was aware of being carried from the house, of sunlight and shadow over his eyes, of waking briefly in a strange room.

Winter came, empty white and hollow. Werner lay looking out through a high window at the falling snow. When he tried to sit up his loose-ragged body crumpled and slipped sideways off the pillow. Nurses whispered when they came near. He thought he was dying, and didn't care very much. They propped him up to sip tepid water.

He was trying to remember something, but it was fractured as a dream. A young man had come late at night to stand beside his bed. 'Tell your sister Hedda Brandt was released,' he said. 'Be sure to tell her. Hedda Brandt is free.' Then he'd gone. In the morning Werner couldn't remember what the young man looked like or if he'd ever been there at all.

He woke and Katje was sitting on the chair beside his bed. She wore a blue coat and was sewing something white. He'd never seen her sewing before. When she looked up her eyes were red as if she'd been crying. He wanted to comfort her, but his hand was too heavy to lift and he was too exhausted to speak.

Part Six
1945

May 5th

'The Germans have capitulated. The war is over.' Werner stood in the doorway of the kitchen. 'The war is over!'

Katje let the knife she was using to cut the carrots slip and slice into her thumb. The blood rose into the wound and she buried it in her palm. Water splashed from the tap onto the floor, but nobody turned it off. Katje dropped the knife and ran out of the kitchen.

Up in her room she tore the blackout paper from the windows. Her thumb smeared blood over the paper as she crumpled it onto the floor. She threw up the sash window and breathed in the new air. Is this it? Are we free at last? Is it really over? In the garden the shrubbery was bright with new green leaf. She went out into the landing and opened the window to the canal. The breeze moved through the house.

'Are you sure?' she shouted down to Werner. 'Are you quite certain?'

He stood in the hall looking up at her.

'Yes.'

She sat down on the landing floor in a daze. Werner made tea and went to sit with her, neither of them able to say anything.

Katje scattered her treasures over the bed; a photograph of Elise standing on the veranda with the cat in her arms, another of Kai and Hedda looking at each other, laughing, the programme from Hedda's performance with its smell of ink, and Hedda's white handkerchief edged with lace. She unfolded the handkerchief. Hedda had handed it to her to dry her eyes that day, but it had been too beautiful to spoil with tears. She had taken it inadvertently, and then decided to keep it. It was a kind of stealing, she supposed, but she'd wanted something to remember Hedda by, as if she'd known even then. She held it to her cheek, and breathed in the faint scent of rosewater.

It's good to question, Hedda had once said, it's good not to sit down and accept everything you're told. She could still hear the clear, defined tone of her voice.

Kai, you will never know that it's over at last. I've cried so many hours for you.

A shadow crossed the window. She looked up hearing the beating of wings. The pigeons, forbidden for so long, had been released. I would like to be free, she thought. I want to dance again. She stood up on her thin legs and rose onto her toes, reaching her arms up, as if she could reach back to her younger self, back to the time when they were all innocent – in rehearsal for Hedda's ballet. When Hedda Brandt, raged at them, terrified them, inspired them – when for that one night they 'danced like angels.'

Doors opened, the neighbours poured out onto the street, shouting, waving, and embracing. There wasn't a German soldier in sight.

The Canadian Army rolled through the city in their tanks and everyone cheered and sang. Out on the corner of the street people lit a bonfire, dragging anything they had left to burn. The canal was golden with light from the flames. Somewhere somebody played a violin. Not Kai. She'd never see Kai again. A little girl danced, waving the Dutch flag in her fist, and a young man caught her and spun her round so her skirts flew out and she giggled. Katje turned away from the warmth of the fire and walked slowly along the edge of the canal. The whole city was celebrating. She looked up through the network of branches. The sky beyond was dusky blue. She searched for the first stars of twilight; the three stars that Kai once said marked the beginning of a new day. One, two, three, they were glimmering there, beyond the spire of Westertoren.

For the first time in many months she took the familiar route over the bridge along Egelantiersgracht, stopping at the corner where Hedda used to wave from her window. How could Hedda return to the place where she'd been arrested with Kai that beautiful summer evening? But she still hoped, looking up at the empty window. Soon I'll hear, surely there'll be news. She sat on the wall of the canal, gathered a few little stones around her and let them plop into the water one at a time, watching them break the surface in concentric circles.

I want to be a dancer, she said. The realisation took her by surprise and she said it again. Of course I want to be a dancer. That's what I've always wanted. She felt something like a bubble burst in her heart, and then warmth, as if the sun had come out after winter's cold. She scrambled up, and buzzing with ideas of how to restart training, she made her way back to the house.

Werner was standing on the step outside the door. He waved when he saw her, and called out – Werner looking excited and happy. She ran towards him.

'Elise is here,' he said, before she'd reached the steps.

'Elise! Where?'

'In the front parlour.'

She pushed past him and ran up the steps, but before she reached the parlour, she stopped, her impulse to burst in restrained by unfamiliar reserve. The door was ajar and she could see Elise sitting on the sofa, her hair drawn back from a face in repose that was so much older than the last time she'd seen her. She smiled as she turned to Katje.

'Hello Katje.'

'You're back.' Katje's voice broke; she put her hand to her throat and swallowed. 'I didn't know if I'd ever see you again.'

There was a moment when everything was suspended and she was aware of the clock ticking, the sound of

Werner's footsteps along the hall, her own breath held. Then Elise stood. She had no crutches. She stepped towards Katje, and Katje to her, and they held each other without speaking. They sat down on the sofa, still gripping each other's hands.

'You look so different,' Katje said, 'and yet the same. Thank goodness the same.'

'You too.'

'After you left I used to play games with fate,' she said. 'Things like if I could hold my breath for as long as it took to cross the road, then you'd be safe. But then the challenges got harder and harder, and I knew I had to stop. That nothing was in my power anyway.'

'I know. It was the same for me. I was so afraid for you last winter.'

'We were fortunate,' Katje said. 'Mother stored tins and dried food for months. It was as if she knew it was going to happen, and my father – well he had contacts. You know what he's like? It was very hard, but we had more food than many others.'

She fell silent, thinking of the endless winter with no light, no warmth, and the continual pain of hunger. People had dropped dead in the streets. Others scurried by, rigidly determined to live, intent on long exhausting journeys into the country to find food. Then she turned to look at Elise.

'You survived too somehow.'

'We were living in the east, so we weren't cut off from supplies. Katje I'm so sorry, I couldn't write or telephone, you see. They were looking for me too. We tried to get a message to you through a friend, but it wasn't safe after Kai was taken, and I couldn't let you know where I was... we had to be so careful.'

Katje looked down at Elise's small delicate hand, still holding hers.

'Viktor told me everything he knew,' she said when she could speak again. 'Until he was taken too.'

'I know. We heard only days ago.'

'And your parents?'

'They're as well as they can be. They refuse to be broken, Mama especially. I think her rage kept her going this last year.'

The door opened and Werner came in bringing tea. They turned to watch him, glad for the distraction. He put the tray down on the table.

'I'll leave you alone to talk,' he said.

'He's much changed,' Elise said, when he'd left. 'I could see as soon as he came to the door.'

'Yes. He was very ill after you left. He was in hospital with glandular fever then pneumonia. We thought he was going to die.' She leant forward and poured the tea. 'But he pulled through, and in the end it was his illness and hospital that saved him. He was called up to fight for Germany last summer, but he was far too weak to go. I don't think he'd have survived that.'

'Does he still play the piano?'

'Oh yes. For a long time he didn't touch it, and I didn't dance either. Then it seemed as if we'd let them win if we just gave up everything we loved. So we encouraged each other to start again. It was so hard at first, in every way. Hard work practising, but also everything seemed even more empty and lonely, remembering how it was. But we had each other.' She stopped. She couldn't talk about dancing without thinking of Hedda, afraid because Elise hadn't mentioned her, that the news was bad. 'I know it seems strange thinking about dancing and music when we were so cold, and hungry, but it helped. In the end it helped us survive, I'm sure of that.' She drew breath, and then rushed on. 'Viktor never knew anything except that Hedda was released from prison. He never heard what happened to her or where she went. Do you know anything?'

'Oh Katje, didn't you ever get that message either, the only message I risked sending. I suppose the news can't have reached Viktor either before he was taken. Hedda's with us. We're staying in an apartment in Amstelveen near the woods – what little remain of them. Papa went to fetch her as soon as we heard she'd been reprieved. She needed looking after until the baby was born.'

'Baby?'

'Yes, she was about two months pregnant when they were arrested. Kai knew and she'd told Pa too. She was released in time – there was a death sentence but she thinks it was a Dutch police officer she taught who appealed for her. She was very weak when she came to us. Nobody thought she'd make it, but she did.'

'Did the baby die?'

Elise's face lit up.

'Oh no, little Dora. She's very much alive, she's enchanting. She's nearly one and a half. She's walking around and trying to talk all the time. She gives us everything to live for.'

The Small Dance

Hedda woke early and lay listening to the tiny sounds of her daughter stirring and snuffling in her sleep. She lay still. Daylight whitened the room and the birds began to sing. It was a fine morning, and in a little while Dora would wake, throwing off her cover and scrambling onto her legs. The day would begin.

Quietly she got out of bed and put on her dressing gown. She pulled a brush through her hair and went down to make tea, leaving the door open so she could hear as soon as Dora called for her. The rest of the household still slept.

She opened the window onto the square of garden with its willow tree and the swing. There was that early morning haze, dew on grass, and a pearly sky. Opposite there was a row of houses edging the woods. She didn't know her neighbours. She preferred to keep to herself, not to have to talk to anyone, to answer questions. Sometimes it seemed as if she was biding time, as if Kai might return, as if miracles were possible, and she waited.

She heard Dora's singsong voice, and swallowing down her tea, she went up to her room, determined to be there before anyone got up to help her. They were all so caring, helping her with Dora, not letting her tire, but she needed to get stronger, to live her own life again.

She'd laid Dora's clothes out on the dressing table the night before, a red and white checked dress and red shoes, still quietly marvelling at the tiny things and the notion they had anything to do with her. Dora beamed and lifted her arms, kicking her legs as she was lifted out of the cot.

'Shall we go and have a wash?'

But Dora was already busy with her pull-along train. Hedda sat on the floor beside her. There was time enough to wash and get dressed and eat breakfast.

Later, when the sun was full and the others had eaten, and Dora had played the piano with Marianne whilst Hedda got dressed, she packed Dora's milk and biscuits, and a pad of paper and crayons. Holding her hand, they wandered across the road and down a track in the long grass to the pools. Dora was a good walker if they went slowly, stopping to peer at insects, to watch a bee buzzing in the throat of a flower or inspect the droppings of a rabbit.

Here the trees had survived the winter – so many had been taken for firewood, but the forest would recover one day. She laid a rug down in the shade, took the drawing things from her bag and knelt down beside Dora to look at a caterpillar on the underside of a leaf.

'Shall we draw the caterpillar?'

Dora was always eager to draw. She spilled the crayons from their box onto the grass, and picked a red one. They both sat intent over their work. Later they'd return with pages of Dora's scribbles to show the family, and Hedda's sketches of Dora, that she kept to herself.

Dora was singing. Hedda recognised the fragment of Kai's music. She must have been humming it herself earlier. Looking down at her dark curls, she felt a great rush of love.

'Katje is coming today,' she said. She smiled. 'Shall we dance for Katje?'

Dora clapped her hands and laughed. She often danced with Aunt Elise.

'You're my treasure, my great treasure trove of loveliness.'

She forgot the time, even forgot Katje's visit. In the woods, in the sunlight, it was possible, briefly, to forget everything. The family were used to Hedda and Dora disappearing for hours, returning to the house only when Dora was hungry.

When at last they wandered home, the fragrant warmth of coffee filled the house. Delicious coffee with all the memories it evoked. Six drained cups were left on the table and a coat that must belong to Katje, over the back of a chair. Fresh flowers were in the vase on the table.

Someone was playing the piano in the drawing room. It didn't sound like Julia or Marianne – a Bach Prelude, beautiful. She listened as she poured a beaker of milk for Dora, and investigated the coffee pot, pouring the dregs into her cup, delaying the moment of meeting. She picked up Dora, buried her face in the little girl's dress, the sweet milky smell of her.

Nobody heard her open the door. It must be Werner sitting at the piano, but he looked so different, a young man, not a boy – so much more confident than she'd seen him last, bone thin, but still that quiet beauty she remembered. Where was Katje? Elise turned, saw her and smiled, her finger to her lips. Katje was going to dance for them. She was behind the piano, just out of sight. Hedda moved round to watch.

She was wearing a green, sleeveless dress. The sunlight lit the side of her face, her light hair. As she turned her hand, her fingers reaching, her body stretching upwards from the floor, Hedda remembered The Small Dance. She put Dora down on Julia's lap and stepped back to sit beside Elise on the sofa. She had never imagined Katje dancing to Bach, this tall graceful girl, she'd last seen so desperately unhappy that terrible afternoon. Hedda watched, her body alert and responsive, as if she danced herself. When Katje turned, she saw her, but danced on to the end of the piece, and balanced, perfectly, for a moment before coming to rest. She looked at Hedda. Hedda held out her hands.

Leaving

Katje and Werner walked home from Leidseplein where they'd got off the bus, as the setting sun filtered through the trees in the square. They passed a florist open late.

'Wait for me.'

Werner came out a moment later with a white rose.

'To mark the day,' he said and gave it to his sister.

'It's like the rose Hedda gave me the night of the performance. Oh it was a good meeting today, wasn't it?'

'It was.'

'And Dora is so enchanting.'

They walked on quietly. How changed Hedda was, she thought. It had been a shock to see her looking old, but the biggest change was her quietness. Hedda who had raged at her students as she taught, who always had so much to say about anything, had sat watching, listening, and smiling – hardly saying anything. But in the end they had danced. That was the extraordinary thing. Hedda stood up as Julia played the piano, and with their arms around each other, their heads touching, Hedda's tiny body in her arms, they had danced.

As they reached the Westerkerk, Werner said, 'Hedda thinks you should consider going to England.'

Katje stopped.

'When did she say that?'

'You were playing with Dora. We talked.'

They hadn't mentioned Weiss. They had looked at each other and a feeling of unspoken sympathy had drawn them together – he liked her so much. What was there to say? Weiss was gone, wherever he had gone, if he were even alive. They had talked instead about Katje.

'Oh Werner, how could that be possible?'

'She said you should find her old friend, Kurt Jooss, and train with him.'

A parcel arrived for Katje. She tore away the paper. Inside was the costume Hedda had worn as the Partisan Girl, the red dress, and the long white scarf. Gathering them up she ran up to her parents' dressing room, undressed and pulled the dress over her head, wriggling into the long sleeves, smoothing it over her hips. She scrutinised herself in the long mirror, a tall, willowy girl with pale skin and fine pale hair. She supposed she looked more like a dancer than she ever had.

She reached for the folded scarf, and as the white silk unravelled there was her aunt's ruby brooch and an envelope with her name on it. Trembling she sat down and took out the letter and began to read.

Dearest Katje – It's possible to write when I'm at a loss for words to speak.

Those afternoons when we danced together in my rooms gave colour to everything that was grey. Your dancing delighted, and sometimes frustrated me, but I loved teaching you from the moment you walked into my studio.

I see you dancing into a future I'll never know. I think you should consider going to England to train with Kurt Jooss, or if you can one day, to New York. There are great dancers and teachers.

Here's your Aunt's brooch. I managed, despite everything, to keep it safe for you, and my costume for the Partisan Girl. I have no need for it now.

Watching you dance yesterday I felt hope in the future – that I might one day teach again. Our friendship and work are strong and have endured.

With my love, Hedda

Epilogue

On a September evening Katje stood on deck watching the flat line of bleak Dutch coastline slip away into the distance. Fine rain dampened her cheeks.

Werner and Elise had taken the tram with her to the station, and Werner had bought her cakes in a cardboard box from the bakery. As they stood together on the platform, Elise gave her a notebook bound in dark red leather.

'It's so you can write your adventures. Oh I wish I could come too,' she said. 'Dance for me. Don't forget me.'

'As if I could forget you. Anyway, you'll visit me. Please. I'll be so lonely without you.'

'As soon as we can.'

'One day I'll choreograph a piece for you.'

Elise laughed.

'I will. A beautiful dance dedicated to my friend, Elise. Remember the night we first danced in your bedroom?'

'You held me and I balanced, for the first time.'

'You were my inspiration.'

'Katje, you always say such funny things.'

Werner carried her cases onto the train, and hugged her.

'You'll be all right?'

'You know I will. And you?'

'Yes.'

He bent to kiss her. The whistle blew, and he jumped from the carriage. The train began to move, almost imperceptibly at first.

'Goodbye darling, goodbye,' Elise called. Briefly they tried to run alongside the carriage.

Katje leant from the window and waved, watching them slip away, further and further, until the curve of the track cut them off from view. I'm completely alone, she said, as she settled in her seat, and she felt strange, and somehow new, unburdened.

Now she stood on the deck looking out to sea. The night was falling, the deep blue gloom of evening. She saw the dark shape of a bird blown momentarily off course by the wind. She shivered and a sense of stillness fell over her. Nobody else was out on deck.

Hedda would be putting Dora to bed. Werner was taking Elise out for dinner. They'd be in the restaurant by now. Her parents would have finished their meal and would be sitting with the radio. Kai, where was he? Where did the dead go – the unfathomable void? His death had seemed impossible to bear, but they'd all gone on living, day at a time, and life without him moved on.

Tomorrow morning the train will pull into Liverpool St Station and I'll begin my new life. What an adventure. All the people I've yet to meet, and my new room, and the street where I'll live. They'll all become familiar in just a few hours, but just now I can't even imagine. Everything I know is behind me, floating further and further away.

She walked slowly to the front of the ship and there was only water, air, night, and emptiness.

'Yes, she shouted into the waves. 'Yes.'

She hugged herself with anticipation.